I0651791

Crucible for Silver and Furnace for Gold

Moraa Gitaa

Nsemia
PUBLISHERS

First Edition September, 2008

Edited by Carol A. Pitt, Barbados

Published by Nsemia Inc.
www.nsemia.com

Cover Design: Carol Pitt
Cover Photograph: Gabriel Robledo

Note for Librarians:
A cataloguing record for this book is available
from Library and Archives Canada

ISBN: 978-0-9810362-2-9   paperback

From an author clearly proud of her heritage and the beauty of her country comes a romantic tale set in Kenya. Featuring a jaw-achingly handsome Italian man and a beautiful, talented, but troubled local girl, the romance unfolds in a light teasing manner until the twist in the tale turns out to be a moral dilemma that would test the strength of any relationship.

A remarkable tale of love that keeps you turning the pages deep into the night. As you close the last page, you are, without choice, left with the burning question: How do I live my life?

ABOUT THE AUTHOR

Moraa Gitaa was born, bred and raised in the port city of Mombasa, Kenya's second largest city. She has lived and worked in the coastal beach town all her life and only recently moved to Nairobi where she is a full-time writer and is working on plans to initiate an organization that provides books for disadvantaged children residing in informal settlements and those challenged by dyslexia, a condition that had challenged her daughter.

She attended the Aga Khan group of schools in Mombasa and studied Administration and IT at the Coast College of Commerce.

This is her debut novel. She has a finished teen novella which is yet to be published, and is currently working on her second novel entitled *The Devil is in the Detail* and a memoir provisionally titled *To Serenity via Perdition: A Midnight Memoir*, of which a chapter excerpt titled 'From Shifting Sands to Deeper Dimensions' has won the NBDC(K) National Book Development Council of Kenya, Literary Awards Book Week 1st Prize Adult Fiction Category at the 11th Nairobi International Book Fair September 2008.

Until most recently she was the Kenya staff writer for G21 and also writes for the American publications *Mshale* and *African Magazine*. She has penned a couple of book reviews for the Kenyan newspaper The Sunday Nation.

She has several short stories published in various anthologies including G21's *Africa Fresh!–New voices from the first continent (2007)* and Author-Me's *Author Africa–2008 Anthology*, some of which were submitted for the Caine Prize for African writing. In 2005-2006 with 11 other screen-writers they co-authored and created a concept in the form of a new TV crime detective series titled *CID Nairobi* but are yet to get funding for the 13 series shoot.

She cites her greatest inspiration as her thirteen year-old daughter Tracy and the Kenyan-African woman who struggles daily to ensure she provides for her family.

ACKNOWLEDGEMENTS

My uncle Dr. Matunda Nyanchama for helping me realize my dream by believing in my writing and financing the publication of this debut novel.

Hon. Sergio Lieman (Honorary Spanish Consular, Mombasa, Kenya) for all the financial help in the pursuit of the same and believing in investing in the talent of various young Kenyan artistes.

All my sisters in the writing world, including Professor Emilia Ilieava for an email (and a letter!) she sent eight years ago (which she probably doesn't remember) that re-kindled the passion for writing and set me along the right path.

Khadija (George) Sessay for sowing the right seed in my heart many years back about our writing as women being about what most affects us.

Muthoni Garland of 'Story Moja' for all the encouragement and her persistence in dragging young Kenyans from the underground to write!

Not forgetting my brother in writing Rod Amis of G21 for your belief in African writers from the continent and for publishing my first articles and stories online.

Bruce Cook of 'Author-Me' for giving space and voices to African authors.

All the contributors who critiqued Kenyan writing in the defunct Standard Newspaper's 'Literary Forum' (Writing is a talent, but they were unknowingly - maybe albeit unwittingly - my teachers, as I couldn't afford to go to school to learn the finer details of writing) and currently the same Kenyan newspaper's 'Literary Discourse'.

Ross Smith, my former Sector Head at the Aga Khan Foundation (Kenya) Coastal Rural Support Programme now with UNICEF - New York, for imparting to me crucial research, monitoring & evaluation skills which have made me more meticulous and detail-oriented in my writing, and for those moments he made me laugh when he would say he had never met an African writer who keeps at her writing despite the odds of a day job and writing at night.

Many thanks to Carol Pitt, Director of Caribbean Chapters Publishing, for the meticulous and thorough editorial services.

The reviewers and readers for pointing out oversights and offering their insight, and for the kind reviews.

Thanks to Professor Ken Kamoche, I call him our globe-trotting Kenyan academic, for taking time off his busy schedule to read this novel and pen the enlightening foreword. And for being a good teacher, mentor and friend. I look forward to another plate of Ethiopian Ijara and next time we shall throw in the salsa dancing!

FOREWORD

I have known Moraa Gitaa ever since the time, some years ago, when we both wrote for www.G21.net, an e-magazine edited by that great supporter of aspiring writers, Rod Amis. Moraa's writing always struck me as insightful, honest, prepared to tackle head-on the burning issues of the day. I was privileged to share space with her in a G21 anthology entitled:- *'Africa Fresh! New Voices from the First Continent'*.

Moraa's story was a sobering and moving account of her struggles against an unscrupulous employer and the police. Her writing, which I have always enjoyed, made you want to meet this writer who wrote with such passion, honesty and a keen ear for the challenges of the new generation of Kenyans.

As a fellow Kenyan I felt I could identify with many of these struggles, dreams and aspirations, but I looked forward to hearing her convey them face to face. I wanted to know what inspired her, what drove her to keep writing even when the odds seemed so impossibly stacked up against her.

I first met Moraa when I was promoting my debut anthology, *A Fragile Hope*, in Nairobi. It was a fantastic meeting. In person, she comes through with the same enthusiasm, the same passion and warmth that I have come to expect from her written word.

It is not every day that I meet Kenyan writers, and I have to say that talking to her helped put into perspective the continuing struggles of aspiring writers on the continent, the frustrations and disappointments that I myself have endured in the past at the hands of local publishers who look at your work of fiction and ask if you've ever considered writing a text book. 'Why?' you ask. 'Because that is where the money is.'

Moraa has endured these frustrations and more, even as she fought her own personal battles, dealing with employers who did not hesitate to destroy her manuscripts, raising a child, being driven to jettison her work, and yet she fought on, and lived to tell the tale. And part of that tale is this story you are just about to read, a story that is as moving in its portrayal of characters who leap out at you as it is unflinching in its treatment of taboo topics.

Moraa is a writer of great promise, and I am already looking forward to her next novel.

Professor Ken N Kamoche
Nottingham Trent University - Nottingham Business School

Ken Kamoche's *A Fragile Hope* was longlisted for the Frank O'Connor Prize and shortlisted for the Commonwealth Writers First Book Award. *A Glimpse of Life*, a story in the collection, won second place in the Olaudah Equiano Prize for African Fiction.

Dedicated to my dear departed friends:
Rosemary, Anita, Myra, Faith and Lorna. God Speed.

Dedicated to my parents Mr. Ishmael Gitaa and
Mrs. Billiah Gitaa for inculcating a reading culture in me at
a tender age, and to my siblings for always being there for me
through what they sometimes termed as dreaming whenever I
engaged in my writing, especially my frequent flights of fantasy
and persistence from the age of ten that I was going to pen a
novel one day, never mind that it has taken twenty years!

Dedicated to my daughter Tracy for constantly
pushing me to the edge to finish this novel, and to write
a teen novella that she can understand!

"I am a female. I understand better what a woman is, because I have grown up being a woman. I don't know much about men so I can't write as much about them as I could with women."

Dr. Margaret Ogola, Kenyan author of 'The River and the Source", winner of the Jomo Kenyatta prize for literature (Kenya, 1995) and the Commonwealth Writer's prize for Africa region, best first book, 1995).

Chapter 1

Malindi, Coastal Northern Beach Resort town of Kenya.

Wearing nothing but the briefest of bikini bottoms, Lavina stretched her hands leisurely above her head. She rarely bothered with the bikini top. It was very private here—no prying and peeping eyes. She lifted her heavy, jet black hair off her brown shoulders, anchoring it with a coconut shell hair clip at the crown of her head. Her hair never ceased to amaze most people she met, for it was long and fell way past her shoulders, and that was saying something about the hair of a pure African.

Secure in the knowledge that she was totally alone, and revelling in the cool northerly breeze whispering over her body, she kicked off her plastic sandals and ran down the clean beach to the water.

It was late afternoon and it was low tide. The only sounds were the crash and hiss of the waves breaking on the hard, wet but clean sand, and the plaintive cries of the seagulls perched on the trees of the Arabuko Sokoke forest[1], a gazetted tourist attraction at one extreme end of the stretch of silvery beach, and on the other end, the towering coconut trees in between the tall mangrove stalks.

The coastal archipelago was famous for its flora and fauna. The peace and solitude were bliss for her aching heart, and a soothing balm for her hurting soul, and she saw the sea as a way of escape from her desperate dilemma. The villagers of Watamu and Malindi would only whisper sadly and call it an unfortunate accident. The tourists who were visiting these historic resort towns on the coastal strip of Kenya would shake their heads and wonder why she had ventured to the deep sea if she couldn't swim. As for her hosts, the mayor of Malindi and his lovely family, she didn't want to dwell on them. They would be so devastated.

She felt haunted by her predicament, which was turning out to be as oppressive as the humid coastal heat. She felt so desperately lonely, which was why she had to escape from the town of Mombasa. She needed to get away from all those knowing glances being cast her way.

She waded into the water and plunged into the waves. Striking out forcefully, she headed seaward.

The cool water rippled like velvet over her already smooth skin. As she swam she deliberately blanked her mind and concentrated solely on pushing her body to its limits, hoping that in punishing, physical effort, she would find respite from a problem to which there seemed to be no escape apart from death. She was going to swim until the tide and current overtook her, and by then she was going to be so tired that she could not make it to the beach.

She could just imagine the headlines in the local dailies:

'BEACH TRAGEDY AS LADY DROWNS AT SEA ...'

Taking deep breaths, Lavina dove beneath the swell. With powerful kicks, she drove through the translucent water. She swam for a long time, enjoying the weightlessness and freedom of moving in several dimensions at once.

She finally resurfaced, gasping. She blinked the salty water out of her stinging eyes and wiped her face with hands that trembled from exertion. She tried to tread water and gauge where she was. She was deep into the sea. She could not even get a glimpse of the white stretch of beach. Her heartbeat hammered in her ears and her breathing rasped. She lay on her back, floating, just wishing for the to tide carry her, to overwhelm her and take her life with it. And then, suddenly, she wanted to live.

Is this what victims of circumstance who want to commit suicide feel at the last minute of life? This urge of wanting to live yet they were too far gone? Lavina now desperately valued life as she thought of her family back at Kericho, the lush and evergreen highland tea-growing zone of Kenya—her mum, her dad though she was not on talking terms with him, her sister, brother and three beautiful nieces. She wondered if she were to die at sea and her body lost never to be recovered, whether her father would follow their culture and bury a banana stem to signify her body.

Tears started falling down her face, mingling with the salty water. The thought of how transient life is flashed through her mind as she struck out forcefully for the direction of the beach, now fighting for survival, the muscles in her right leg fluttering and tightening in an ominous warning. Every bone in her body was tight with fatigue. She had burned up more energy than she thought. Every stroke was an effort.

With speed and style she had taken to the water at the tender age of two, as she was born in the coastal beach city of Mombasa. This fact, which was usually a source of modest pride, was now forgotten. All that mattered was reaching the shore. How much further? She didn't dare look. Anyway, how could she see anything when her head kept slipping beneath the water due to fatigue? She was so tired—oh, so very, very tired…

Suddenly, as though from a red-hot knife, pain plunged into her right calf.

"Oh my God, no! Not a muscle-pull, when I want so very much to live." groaned Lavina silently in pain. She rolled over, swallowed mouthfuls of salty water and splashed to the surface, choking and spluttering as she fought for breath. Her nose was running and tears poured down her contorted face. From the back of her knee to her ankle, the muscle felt as though it was being gripped in a vice. Drawing her leg up, she clutched at her calf, and in the process swallowed more salty water. Her eyes, nose and throat stung and burned as waves slapped into her face.

She fought the urge to shout. This was a private beach plot. With no one to hear her, it would be a dangerous waste of energy to try to shout, and anyway her voice would be carried away to sea by the wind.

She tried to remember her life-saving drills in first-aid lessons for medals in the President's Award Scheme[2] so long ago, but the pain was like a thick, dark blanket, smothering her ability to think. Her usually alert mental faculties seemed to be turning topsy-turvy. Her strength was ebbing out fast; surely she was going to drown. Even though she had wanted to die, it seemed cruel. She could not envision such a death now.

Suddenly a swift, dark shadow passed beneath her. She thought it was a shark. But seconds later knew it wasn't when a muscular arm slid diagonally over her right shoulder and across her bare breasts, holding her firmly under the left armpit.

A split second later her chin was held fast in the palm of a large, strong hand, and beneath her shoulders she felt the hair-roughened warmth of a man's chest.

All this registered in a few moments of paralysing shock before her basic survival instinct took over and she screamed, choking on a mouthful of sea water and almost swallowing slimy seaweeds. Galvanised by sheer terror, she lashed out with her feet, fists and elbows. The pain in her calf was excruciating.

Above the frenzied splashing and her own gasps she heard him shout as some of her blows connected, but she was too panic-stricken to make out the words. Though her chin was freed, the arm around her body did not relax. Instead it tightened hard, so that she could not breathe. Powerful legs with muscles like iron encircled her hips and slid down to close tight about her thighs. Imprisoned and unable to move, Lavina was plunged beneath the surface. At first her struggles weakened, becoming aimless as the desperate urge to breathe cancelled every other thought.

Her lungs were about to explode and there was a red mist in front of her eyes. She saw stars darting in slivers round her head. For once she understood what people meant when they said that they had seen stars, especially after knocking their heads on a hard surface. She couldn't hold out any longer. They both shot to the surface.

Never, never had air tasted so sweet. Lavina breathed it into her tortured lungs in great heaving gasps, then she started struggling again.

"Stop it! Be still, woman, or we'll both drown, I'm trying to help you!" A deep, male voice roared in her ear.

"Get away from me!" Lavina's voice was a half-shriek, half-croak from the combined effects of fright and the seawater she had swallowed.

"Keep still or I'll take you under water again. I mean it!" he warned as she continued to wriggle and squirm in an effort to break free.

His legs tightened around her once more, and, realising he had every intention of carrying out his threat, Lavina stopped fighting him.

He was treading water, keeping both of them afloat. While she was thrashing about in the water, he shifted his grip and now held her clamped against his chest with one arm around her rib cage, his other hand across the front of her shoulders. He held both of her hands and prevented her from hitting him again. His right arm half-covered her left breast. Either he was unaware, or simply didn't care, but for Lavina, the brutal intimacy was a frightening illustration of her helplessness.

She vowed that if she ever got out of this alive, she would never again go swimming topless, or even in the nude as she was wont to do sometimes. The sea that was so cool and refreshing at the beginning was now numbingly cold. Except for the white-hot throbbing pain in her calf, she was chilled to the bone. She clenched her teeth to stop the chattering and to hold back whimpers of pain. She had no strength left to fight. She just wanted the oblivion of unconsciousness.

She could feel that they were swimming, but knew it was a solo effort by her rescuer, as she was hardly putting any effort into it.

Moments later he slackened his fireman's grip on her, then a stinging slap on her cheek jerked her back to consciousness.

"Don't sleep! Come on, we're nearly there. You should be able to stand now. Put your feet down you're quite safe. I won't let you sink. Come on, stand up. Up!"

Lavina was distantly aware of a strong arm encircling her waist, half-carrying her. Is that really sand under my feet? She swayed and staggered drunkenly, her right leg useless, the muscles knotted and set.

"Walk! Make the muscles work. It's the only way to free them."

She winced, blinking away tears. "It hurts."

"The sooner you loosen up, the sooner the pain will stop." came the brisk reply.

"Oh, shut up!" she cried, hiding her face against his shoulder as pain stabbed and gnawed at her calf. "What do you know?"

"Stop being so lazy. Make an effort."

"Lazy?" The barb went deep.

"How dare you?" She rasped as his patronizing tone pricked at her. She was brought up short. The shock sizzled through her nerves. She had not looked at him all through their struggle, but now she was seeing a white man. That explained the strange inflection in his voice that had been registering in her subconscious all along. Maybe she should say 'male caucasian' —she was used to such terms after being in the medical profession for a few years.

All the while, she'd been thinking that it was one of the local fishermen or a watersports lover who had strayed to the private beach, seen her in trouble, and come to her rescue.

Seawater dripped from his dark curly hair and ran in rivulets down the hard planes of his face. Narrowed and squinting against the now encroaching darkness, his sky-blue eyes gleamed with a condescending look.

That body! That physique! What skimpy, almost all-revealing swimming trunks! Had the Greeks been thinking of such bodies when they named the god of the seas Neptune? Or the lord of wine Bacchus? The thoughts raced through her mind.

"You have no right to call me lazy." Lavina hurled her indignation at him. "You don't know anything about me."

"That's more like it." He said, sounding pleased. "The madder you get, the better. A shot of adrenalin in your system to boost your heart rate and speed up your circulation is just what you need."

"What?" Lavina's frown mirrored her confusion. "Why?"

"I can think of several reasons," he answered dryly. "But in this particular instance, the idea is to get rid of that cramp."

Clinging to him, she put more weight on her right leg, testing it gingerly. It felt badly bruised and throbbed with pain like an abscessed tooth. They had reached the shallow water's edge near the beach.

As Lavina limped slowly ashore, her petite frame racked by spasms of shivering. All she could think of was her bed. She felt so exhausted.

"So tired," she muttered, "I can't." Closing her eyes, she slid from his grasp and stretched out on the sand.

From far away in her fuzzy brain, she heard him drop to his knees beside her and felt him lift her leg, then his strong fingers began to knead and massage her knotted calf. She whimpered and bit her lip, but after a few seconds the muscle began to relax. The knifing pain began to ebb away, and with it the tension that had gripped her whole body. As her calf returned to its normal suppleness, relief and gratitude overwhelmed her.

The combination of the tropical evening coolness and his soothing hands sent a delicious languor sliding over her. Then she felt it. The first twinges of unease. Where his hands touched, millions of nerve-ends exploded at the contact, sending back messages to her brain which was becoming deeply disquieted and disturbed.

Something inside her was stirring. It had been so long since she had felt such sensations. It should not be happening. Not now, not like this. Not with him, a total stranger. He had no right to be here in the first place. He was an intruder on private property, she herself was a guest here. And now his touch had gone beyond simple first-aid, and was an invasion into her very private space. She was even conveniently forgetting that he had saved her life!

She didn't open her eyes, terrified that he might see in them what she was suppressing, the feelings she was fighting, but she couldn't simply lie there.

She silently wished him to go away. Why isn't he leaving? What am I going to do? She let her hands fall to her sides and dig into the soft grains of sand lest they betray her by straying towards his head. He tapped her leg slightly.

"You're tensing up again. Come on."

He took her hand.

"On your feet! I think you'll find that's cured it."

Hating him for making her feel strange things she didn't want to cope with in her current predicament, and also hating herself for responding to him in this way, Lavina stood up.

"Okay now?"

She nodded, giving him a quick, suspicious glance. Ironic amusement hovered at the corners of his mouth. She looked away quickly, then her breath caught in her throat. In her agony and pain, she had forgotten she was semi-naked!

To her horror and total dismay she felt her breasts tighten, the nipples standing out proud and taut, not from the cold this time, but from her involuntary reaction to the sheer sexual magnetism of the man beside her. Her embarrassment was so great that she just stared at her toes.

"I – I - my clothes," she gulped, stammering and pointing up the beach.

He did not release her hand, and neither did the pressure of his grip alter. In fact, he betrayed not the slightest reaction, but he stood staring at her, mesmerised and transfixed by the sight before him.

She shivered, keeping her head down, pulled her hand away and started up the beach.

All that remained of the crippling muscle-pull was a faint soreness. He had been staring at her hauntingly beautiful black eyes before she looked away. He felt like he was drowning in their pools. There was something there, an underlying sadness, an emotion he couldn't pinpoint. He followed her slowly.

"Desperate situations, require desperate measures," his voice was more gentle, trying to make light of the situation. "It was touch and go for a while out there. You were lucky I was around. You aren't the easiest person to rescue. I was beginning to wonder if I would have to knock you out. But tell me something, why were you trying to kill yourself?"

There was a deep silence. Lavina swallowed hard. He wanted an explanation. She pretended to be peering at her waterproof Gucci watch.

"You're mistaken, I wasn't trying to kill myself, I just got a muscle-pull!" she blazed at him.

He raised the hand holding hers to reveal livid welts and scratches down the inside of his white, but sun-browned arm. Some of the scratches stippled with blood.

"You were trying to kill yourself," was his quick rejoinder. "Before you got the spasm, you went way out to sea and then you seemed to change your mind and started struggling to come back to land, that's when the cramp hit you."

"Well," she said. "You had no business being here at all. This is a private beach."

Her voice shook with anger she couldn't explain, as it was directed partly to him, and partly to herself and to the treacherous reaction of her own body. How could a total stranger have provoked these urgent melting sensations?

"You are mistaken. I had every right to be here. Anyway why are you also here?"

Before she could offer an explanation, he enquired silkily:

"However, that aside, what do you suppose would have happened to you if I hadn't been here?"

Lavina bit her lower lip, unable to meet his eyes. They both knew it was very unlikely that she would have survived. He had saved her life. She ought to be grateful, and yet she was only grudgingly thankful.

They reached her clothes. Her leso[3], top and sandals were lying in a small, untidy heap. It seemed like eons ago since she had dropped them there.

Breaking away from him, Lavina bent down and snatched up her top, but clumsy in her embarrassment, she dropped it. Before she could move, he had picked it up and was holding it out for her to put her arms through. As he helped her, his fingers brushed her spine and lingered fractionally on her shoulders. Flinching, Lavina leaped away as if she had been stung. She whirled around to face him, clutching the billowing gypsy-style blouse tightly across her breasts.

"Who are you anyway?" she cried, "And what were you doing out her- ?" The words died in her throat as she looked at him properly for the first time.

Lavina felt as if she had been transported to the silver screen and was watching a re-enactment in the flesh of Johnny Depp starring as a buccaneer Captain, or a cross between Captain Jack Sparrow and Captain Barbossa in prequels and sequels of Pirates Of The Caribbean—all the episodes rolled into one from The Curse of The Black Pearl, Dead Man's Chest to At World's End.

Thick, dark hair was plastered in spiky curls onto a deep forehead. High cheekbones and an aquiline nose gave his features a chiselled and almost aristocratic appearance, only softened by the ironic smile lifting one corner of his wide mouth. Rugged, but definitely Italian. She had seen quite a number of Italian investors and tourists in Malindi and Watamu to be able to point them out. She'd never really given them a second thought, but this one was definitely handsome! But it was his eyes that had reduced her to tongue-tied silence. They were azure-blue, and now in the fading light they seemed a deep, deep, purple/indigo. They danced with amusement, and with something more directed to her, a challenge she didn't quite understand.

Apprehension quivered in the pit of her stomach. So this is how people feel when they talk about having butterflies in their tummies. He took a step forward, his eyes holding hers. She was transfixed, rooted to the spot, and even when he brought his head slowly down as if giving her the chance to avert her head, she was incapable of moving. His lips touched hers.

"*Dio Santo*! (My God!) You're beautiful! An African mermaid, I've just rescued!"

His mouth moved on hers, at first gentle, coaxing, but growing hungry and more demanding. Lavina made a soft, wordless sound. Helpless, hating herself, hating him, yet unable to resist, she felt herself respond. But then she slowly came back to her senses. Pushing him away, she stumbled backwards. His dark brows rose, mocking her wide-eyed stare. In spite of the warmth he had ignited deep in the centre of her body, a chill feathered over her skin. He shrugged and let go of her hand, the movement drawing her eyes to his tanned and heavily muscled shoulders.

His gaze travelled slowly over her, and she realised with a sense of foreboding that she was still wearing next to nothing. She shuddered, glancing uneasily in the direction of the forest, wondering if the Kaya[4] of the Mijikenda[5] had anything to do with what was happening to her. She quickly fastened the buttons on her blouse with unsteady fingers and she shuddered again, wondering if the distant chanting and Kayamba[6] sounds and Ngoma[7] beats were figments of her imagination, as she imagined the locals dancing and singing, clad in their Mahandos[8] and Kikois[9] around the shrines now, and appeasing the gods as they often did in times of fortune and misfortune.

She wrapped her khanga over her hips, secured it tightly in a knot at her waist, slipped her feet into her sandals and took to her heels fast. She actually ran up the beach, her hair flying behind her, and up the ancient winding stony steps hewn out of the coral, all the time thinking of how late she was going to be for the Munges' dinner party.

I'm going to find you Princess… I'm going to find you my African mermaid, were the thoughts going round and round Giorgio's head as he watched the fleeing figure looking like an African goddess in the setting dusk. She may be African but she was not just one of the local inhabitants. He had noted the latest pure gold waterproof Gucci timepiece, the lingering scent of designer perfume he was so sure was Chanel's new fragrance 'Allure', the excellent English. He stood there staring absentmindedly into the African sunset.

When he finally cast his pensive eyes downwards he caught sight of something strange lying near his feet. He picked it up and swore softly.

"*Si deve passare sul mio cadavere!* (Over my dead body!)"

It was an anklet or armlet of sorts. Strange. Teeth—actual incisors of a certain animal stringed through a strip of dried hide of a cow or some similiar animal. He was sure the artifact had something to do with his fleeing African princess because the strip was broken.

Chapter 2

The pale light of evening filtered through the partings of the batiked curtains in African print. Her eyelids felt like the soapstone paper weights she had been working on for a client the previous day. She couldn't open her eyes. Somewhere someone was calling her name urgently.

"Lavy, sweetheart are you up yet?"

Her brain was swimming around her head. Was she still at the beach? Then she remembered. She was in bed at the Munges' and they were having a dinner party. And here she was thinking it was morning!

The voice called again.

"Lavy!"

It was Lynne's voice, accompanied by frenzied, loud knocking on the door. Her eyes flew open. It was almost eight p.m. She had slept for more than an hour, and yet when she came running in from the beach she promised Lynne that she was only having a nap 'for half an hour or so'! No wonder Lynne was frantic with worry – the party must be underway! She tossed back the bed covers.

"I'm up," she said through the closed door to Lynne, who by now should be mingling with her guests and not up here, worrying and baby-sitting her. Lynne must have had enough of baby-sittting this evening when she settled her babies for the night.

"All right dear." Lynne replied, her steps receding down the stairs.

Lavina switched on the overhead light and looked at herself in the mirror. Her eyes were heavy with sleep and her hair was a mess. She would have to pull herself together somehow or she would not be a civilised addition to Tim and Lynne's party.

She put on her shower cap and went into the bathroom. She sluiced water over her face and eyes with her hands cupped to the spray, letting the chill wash the sleep away. She left the shower on cold and scrubbed her body thoroughly to remove the saltiness.

On reaching to scrub her upper left arm, she realised with disquiet that her lion-teeth armlet was missing. She always had it on, no matter what dress code the occasion called for. Some people who saw her wearing it always thought that she was being fashion-conscious and trendy, following the latest fad of ethnic jewellery, but that was not the case. Her heart skipped a beat. She'd had it for years, ever since her grandfather passed away and bequeathed it to her. She had never removed it since.

She must have lost it at sea or the beach earlier in the day. I'll try and look for it tomorrow, she decided, that is if the high tide doesn't wash it out to sea, she thought wryly.

She forced her mind to stop drifting away, removed the shower cap and turned the tap of the shower to warm.She did not want the cold water to get into her hair, otherwise it would be even more tangled than when she'd come in from the beach. She shampooed her hair quickly, washing away the salty sea water, rinsed it, and got out of the shower. She wrapped herself in a fluffy towel and stepped out of the bathroom.

She went into the bedroom. Her search through the many compartments of the dressing unit unearthed a hand-held blow dryer and an electric tonger *cum* flat iron – perfect. She plugged in the tongs and blow-dryer and got to work.

She brushed her hair and thoroughly dried it using the blow dryer. She then added liberal amounts of her favourite Soft n' Free hair-revitalising crème, a must-have in her purse. Next, she flattened her hair with the flat iron and curled the edges using the tongs into a simple but bouncy bob brushing her shoulders.

She sat on the edge of the bed musing over what to wear. Then she remembered her black number. That should be suitable for tonight. It was a black silk dress cut like a slip with spaghetti straps, narrow waist and a hem that fell to slightly below the knees. The creases would fall out of it the minute she put it on. It seemed like a safe choice, and she was running out of time.

It was good that she had quite a few of her outfits here, otherwise in such situations she would have been forced to go trudging back to her cottage to change. She applied her favourite Johnson's Baby Lotion all over her body and then put on her delicate G-string panties. No bra, the low cut of the bust-line would not allow it.

She slid the silk garment over her head and adjusted the straps on her shoulders. Back at the mirror she dabbed a little base foundation to her face and carefully touched up her lashes with a mascara wand. At last satisfied that she had accentuated the long, full length of her lashes, she applied silver-gray eyeshadow to her eyelids to bring out the black brilliance of her eyes. She rarely applied makeup, but she needed it tonight so that her complexion wouldn't look so washed out after her harrowing experience at the beach today.

She applied Nikki lip gloss and hesitated between 'Beyond Paradise' and 'Pleasures' both scents by Estee Lauder. Unable to decide between the two, she finally chose Calvin Klein's new scent 'Euphoria', also an all-time absolute favorite beside Chanel's current competition 'Allure Sensuelle' because of its mildness. She hurriedly dabbed a little behind her ears and wrists and she was ready.

She stood back and looked in the full-length mirror at the reflection of her black dress against her creamy chocolate-brown skin. No shiny jewellery for her as usual, only accessories she'd crafted herself—batiked cow horn earrings, Malakoti[10] wood bracelet, a teardrop shaped soapstone pendant with tiny motifs engraved on it, and ebony black hair. Her complexion was dramatic and she had dressed to make the most of it. A pair of low black Esperit Italian evening sandals completed her outfit.

Her huge black eyes and black hair against a backdrop of brown skin was what usually caught people's eyes.

Tim and Lynne wanted her to meet a very important guest and friend of theirs. They had told her that he seemed very much interested in her wood carvings and soapstone sculptures that he'd seen around their home so far. Lynne always talked of him as a genius. They also told her that he was an engineer and that Tim had met him on one of his many duties as the mayor of Malindi. What was he like, this irascible old man who bordered on genius?

She turned from the mirror. There was only one way to find out. She descended the stairs, her heart pounding against her ribs. Her mouth felt dry as if she was stepping out for an audition or selection of sorts.

She stood on the last step at the bottom of the stairs and took a deep breath, letting it out slowly. Then she arranged her mouth into a smile and stepped into the living room. She knew the value of an entrance, but she did not particularly want to pose that way tonight. She looked around, searching for her hosts.

She finally saw Tim standing next to Lynne, one arm around his wife's waist, the other holding a glass he had raised to drive home and punctuate a point made to the man who was standing across from him.

As Lavina turned slightly she could see the backs of the heads of the three people sitting on the coach in front of the wall unit cum mantelpiece. An Asian woman in purple velvet was in profile, laughing at something the white man seated next to her had said.

Lavina took another step further into the room. At that same instant, the white man lifted his head. In the mirror that covered the wall from mantle to ceiling, Lavina found herself looking into male eyes that glittered like blue diamonds in the overhead light shining from the chandelier suspended from the ceiling high above. A couple of hours had not been enough for her to forget those eyes! And certainly there could not be another pair like that in the entire globe!

Shock sizzled through her entire body! Oh God, no! It was the man from her earlier beach encounter, and with one short, sharp stab of feminine intuition she knew that this was it. This was the man Tim and Lynne wanted her to meet!

Irascible he might be, but certainly not old! Was he going to be her nemesis?

Thinking of her late grandfather, she lifted her right hand to lightly caress the armlet on her bare left arm as she normally did in times of turmoil, only to remember she had lost it.

Chapter 3

"Lavina!"

Tim's voice boomed out to her, stopping all the conversation that was going on mid-stream. In the deadly quiet, she said,

"Hello Tim."

"Come in, come in," he continued, "we've been waiting for you."

She subconsciously dug into the poise she had developed during years of exposure to various personalities and dignitaries, and crossed the room with her graceful walk to stop at his side. She had not seen him since the previous day.

Steadying herself on his arm, she reached up to give him a peck. His cheek was warm against her mouth, his arm iron-hard under her hand. At around forty-five he adhered to a strict routine of exercise, including a daily jog up and down the beach that gave him the physique of a far much younger man. His navy blue suit was impeccable. Tim Munge smiled, a movement of his lips that lit up his eyes.

"You look beautiful, come let us introduce you around."

"Thank you, Tim."

Lynne took over. She looked stunning in a lavender evening number. She nodded towards the tall dark man who had been talking with her husband a while back.

"Lavy, I gather you know Tony Kamunde?"

Lavina held out her hand.

"Yes, of course. We met a couple of times in Mombasa."

Met. Now that was an understatement if there ever was one. Bad blood, like a river, flowed between them.

"How are you Tony?"

"Nice to see you again, Lavina. You're growing more and more beautiful by the day." His tone was certainly not very complimentary.

Lavina was distracted because Lynne was explaining to her about Tony being there with the engineer they wanted her to meet. She felt an uneasy prickling sensation along her backbone, as if the visual heat from probing male eyes was burning into the part of her back that wasn't covered by her dress. She could not have said what the rest of the conversation was about if you were to ask her. She was only aware of its inevitable end, and Lynne touching her arm and saying,

"Come, meet the others before we go in."

She was led by Lynne to the coach and introduced to a young architect and his lawyer wife who was obviously expecting, and looked like she might go into labour at any moment. Lavina felt a twinge of envy and remorse as she shook their hands. She loved children so much. She had always wished she would have children one day. She wanted a child so very much, but that was now out of the question with the situation she was in.

The flicker of remorse and regret vanished. Every cell in her body tingled with awareness as the other man, the European, rose from the coach and now leaned against the wall unit, his lean body taut in an expensively cut gray suit. It looked suspiciously like an Armani. She could almost smell the designer labels on him. His tie was definitely Givenchy, his shirt a Stephano Ritchie and his twelve-eyelid laced shoes looked like Pierre Cardin. His hair was as dark as the night outside.

In the end, of course, she had to face him. She met those blue eyes and something primitive and wild beat in her veins. Is this what people call love at first sight? Or was it lust? She had never felt such intense emotions before.

He looked as virile and attractive as he had earlier in the cool evening of the beach; perhaps more so. Somehow, surrounded by a civilised setting, there was an elemental vibrance about him, almost primitive, that made her nerves tighten in response.

Lynne said brightly,

"Lavina, this is Giorgio Santini, the engineer we've been talking about. Aero-engineer actually. He's gone gaga over your sculptures and carvings. He's completely crazy about them. He's really been looking forward to meeting you, because he doesn't believe that a friend of mine has actually done them. You know, he only gets to see them in the busy market place or already in the curio shops on sale for the tourists."

Lynne came to a breathless stop. "And Giorgio, please meet Lavina Kante."

Lavina tried to turn her brittle look into a light casual smile, but a backlash of excitement clawed at her throat. She could not trust her voice. She extended her hand to him wordlessly, and felt the hard warmth of his on the icy coldness of hers. A hard smile lifted the harsh curve of his lips. To anyone else, she was sure, he looked casually polite.

"*Buona sera Signorina Kante*," he said in Italian, nodding.

Her voice, when she found it, surprised her by sounding normal.

"Signora Santini." She acknowledged his evening greetings.

His eyes flickered over her and then he smiled slowly as if he was remembering her struggles with him in the deep sea.

"You reached home safely I see."

She withdrew her hand from his grasp.

"I'm normally a very careful swimmer Mr. Santini, but I – I – am sorry about what happened earlier at the bea…"

Lynne looked from Lavina to Giorgio and her brows drew together in a puzzled frown.

"Then you've already met Giorgio. I mean when did you two meet?"

"Well, not exactly. That is, we have met, but I didn't know he was…" she faltered, knowing that he would think she was apologizing because she now knew that he was a friend of the Mayor, and she also knew that

Lynne would be wondering why she hadn't told her of her earlier beach escapade.

For a moment his name didn't connect. Then an image flashed before Lavina's eyes, a distinctive logo she had seen embossed in gold on expensive stationery, and some advertisements featuring real estate on adverts before prime time news and the larger-than-life Monier, Eagle, Magnate and Alliance media billboards all over the country registered in her brain. Santini Developments… God, it can't be!

Feeling as though she had actually turned into very fine Kitengela[11] glass and that one more shock would shatter her into a thousand fragments, Lavina stared at him, her face a frozen mask. Lynne, sensing and feeling the tense undercurrents hovering in the atmosphere like static and wanting to make good her escape, looked at them, puzzled. She noticed that lavina was not backing down, neither was she letting Giorgio outstare her. Her eyes did not even waver. Lynne wondered how the two had met earlier on. And why the clash of wills?

As the African tropical night smell of the beach wafted into the room, mingling with the different whiffs of perfumes of colognes and sprays, the handsome and suave Italian gentleman, his leonine stance reminded Lynne of the big cats of the Maasai Mara[12] – and the beautiful and captivating African lady, her grace, reminding Lynne of the wary gazelles sprinting off Into the vast savannah plains of the Tsavo[13]. How different they were as they sized each other up. Talk about the clash of the titans! They blended in perfectly with the murals of African landscapes on one wall of the dining room. Lynne eventually cast a meaningful glance at Lavina and drifted away towards the kitchen, leaving the two alone.

Only time will tell, Lavina thought as she came back to earth from memories she was trying to suppress which had been triggered off by a Swahili proverb… *yaliyopita si ndwele, ganga yajayo*[14]. Was she ready to let bygones be bygones and lead a normal life?

Giorgio, on the other hand, was thinking to himself that he had never seen such strong will in someone's eyes, he had to tread carefully here. He discreetly put his hand into his jacket pocket and touched the strange armlet. It reassured him. It was like a talisman to him now. Seeing her here tonight had just proved to him that he had been right all along. She was no ordinary beach girl.

On the other hand, Lavina's brain turned into an uncooperative lump, her throat dry. She simply couldn't talk to him, not after what had transpired at the beach earlier on. She had not even heard what he just said, and was surprised that she held a glass of white wine in her hand. She didn't know how it got there.

"The Munges' are quite something," Giorgio Santini repeated, staring at Lavina as if he expected that to be an opening or a cue for her.

"Yes, they are a wonderful couple." Lavina agreed, unsure of why the intentness of his words made her uneasy. She lifted her glass and lubricated her parched throat.

At that moment Lynne returned to the room and went to talk to her husband, who then announced dinner. To Lavina's utmost relief, Lynne stepped to Giorgio's side and took his arm, leading him into the dining room. Vaguely, she placed her empty glass on a passing waiter's tray.

All through dinner she smiled and laughed and gave a reasonable appearance of normality, but inside her stomach churned. She was disturbed and upset at the feelings Giorgio Santini was arousing deep within her, and it seemed as if she was going to have to spend considerable time close to him. She tried to concentrate on her surroundings, which were elegant to say the least. She had always admired the Munges' residence.

A new chandelier, brilliant with crystal pendants, hung over the oval table. Light gleamed off the polished silver in use on the table. There was a bowl of pink roses in a soapstone vase in the middle of the table. She reminisced about the time when she gave the vase to Tim and Lynne because of their special care and concern for her well being.

She ate slowly, trying to savour and not analyze the chicken rice pilaf before her, as she was also an excellent cook. She tried to focus her attention on the topic of the expectant lawyer who was seated to her immediate left. She was discussing the elements of a rare case which seemed to have the undivided attention of the members of the LSK[15] and the general public countrywide. In her own opinion the judgement was going to set a precedent whichever way it was decided. She tried to keep her eyes away from Giorgio Santini. He was seated next to Lynne on the other side of the table, diagonally across from her so he was not directly in her line of vision, but her gaze seemed to drift to him on its own. There was a subtle fascination about him, in the way the light danced across the planes of his face. One moment the bones were harsh against the skin, in the next instant there were crinkling lines of amusement along his mouth and eyes as he laughed at something his neighbour said.

Suddenly, as if telepathically sensing her eyes on him, he turned his head and looked at her. The knowing curve of his mouth told her that he was also very much aware of her. She found herself really hoping that after tonight she would not see him again. Yet, again and again, she kept glancing at him from the periphery.

When the meal was finally over and Lynne had invited the guests to go into the living room for some more chatting, Giorgio fell behind the others and grasped Lavina by the elbow. She was too startled to pull away.

"Lynne, the dinner was superb," he said smoothly. "You won't mind if I borrow Lavina for a few minutes, will you? I have something I want to discuss with her." Lynne smiled at him courteously.

"No, of course not G. I thought perhaps you'd want some time to talk with our Lavy alone."

There was a soft, intent undertone in his voice as he said: "Yes."

When Lynne had gone, they were alone in the empty dining room. Aware of his masculine attraction with every fibre of her being, Lavina tugged at her arm.

"I think we've said all we have to say to each other."

"No, I don't think so," was his smooth rejoinder, ignoring her crisp tone and guiding her towards the dining table. Lavina watched out of the corner of her eye as he reached sideways to pick up the soapstone flower vase, his expression suddenly intent.

"Is this one of yours? You know I am incredibly fascinated by you. Tim told me that you are a medical graduate and you are also an expert sculptor."

"Yes."

She glanced up warily. In fact, making soapstone vases was her favourite theme. She had been experimenting with different glazes, and this one had proved to be a major breakthrough.

She had turned the basic cream colour of the soapstone into flame, and towards the top it was an effervescent pearly silver. It was an effect she was trying to repeat, this time with a colour base of aquamarine and turquoise.

"It's beautiful," he said in awe.

Lavina could not suppress a smile.

"You sound surprised. Wait till you see my animals, chess boards and other pieces."

What on earth was she saying? Barely a few minutes ago, she'd been fervently praying that they don't meet again, and yet here she was inviting him to see her other works.

"I am surprised, but not in the sense that you mean," he replied. "You see when I met you today, it was like destiny's hand at play, though I don't believe in that jargon. I didn't just chance upon you, I had been watching you on the beach from a distance, before you even ventured into the water. I was drawn to you. Something fascinated me about you, my mermaid. I knew then that you were no ordinary native girl on the private beach. When I heard you talk for the first time after I'd rescued you, your voice, it was so cultured, and lilting in that soothing way…"

Though the more than four foot thick walls kept the room comfortably cool even in the hottest of weather, perspiration glazed her forehead. Never in her life had she been so aware of a man.

"How long does it take to make one?"

His uncanny ability of shifting moods and changing topics threw Lavina off-balance once again. She shrugged.

"A few days. It's just a hobby really." He shook his head.

"You shouldn't be wasting your time – "

Lavina was vexed. "Actually," she interrupted defensively and proudly, "I've managed to sell quite a good number, I have a unique touch."

"You didn't let me finish," he chided. "I was about to say you shouldn't be wasting your time doing anything else when you have talent that can produce work like this. How much do you charge for them?"

"Two hundred shillings for the small ones and five hundred for the big ones. I know it sounds expensive," she added hurriedly, "But it's mainly to cover the cost of materials, and I also need the money, as I'm not working currently."

"My dear mermaid," he frowned, "These are a collectors' items. They are worth at least twenty times that amount, with the correct marketing strategy, especially abroad."

Lavina gasped at him stunned. He pulled out one of the dining chairs for her and took another one for himself. His statement had quite literally taken her breath away.

"You're joking! Right?" she managed at last, a disbelieving smile trembling on her lips.

"I never joke about money, that's why I am where I am, an engineer of repute worldwide though I prefer architecture nowadays. And Lavina you know sometimes in Italy we say, '*rischiare tutto provare a fare con tutte le forze*', it means go for broke." Was his dry response.

'Would you allow me to take a few of your items? I understand you also undertake woodcarving. There's someone whose opinion I value and respect in Italy, I want him to see and evaluate these pieces. I'll be leaving for Milan in a few days time."

Totally bemused, staring at him as he straddled the chair like a motor bike and leaning his chin on the backrest, Lavina made a vague gesture of acquiescence.

"I understand that the Munges have given you a studio cum cottage on the grounds?' He asked.

"Yes," she replied.

"So when you're not sculpting, what do you do apart from your medical profession, that is?"

Lavina gestured helplessly. She was completely out of her comfort zone and she had a strong suspicion that not only was Giorgio Santini fully aware of this, but that he was making small talk in an effort to make her relax.

"I cook, I mean excellently," she blurted out and then slowed down, "I do strictly small time catering for exclusive private parties, I can cook the most delicious of our traditional dishes, and also gourmet and a la-carte food. You name it, I'll cook it."

He looked at her gently.

"You know something *Mia Cara*, I would like to know you more. I can see that you have no intention of believing me, at least not without some action. Anyway, I'm surprised that I've not met you these sides of Malindi before, as I've been in your enchanting country for the past couple of years, initially at the invitation of your government for consultations over the Dongo Kundu[16] project, and later on as an interested foreign investor in the EPZ[17] scheme."

Lavina, noting his twice-repeated use of the Italian endearment Mia Cara which means 'My Dear', edged in with a cagey reply,

"Well, I've only been in Malindi for the past few months, I'm usually in Mombasa[18]."

He turned abruptly to her, as if it was an afterthought,

"What are you doing tomorrow? It's Sunday." As if that explained a lot. "I'd like to make a suggestion. I know one is supposed to wait until asked, but by the look of things you might not offer, and I'm dying to look at some of your work." He paused for a few moments, and then continued, "I specialise in luxury developments for the top end of the market, you know, mansions and bungalows, and tomorrow I'm going on a tour of my projects. Why don't you come with me? I usually value other opinions, and then later you can invite me to your cottage to have a look at your art and have one of your excellent meals. Deal?"

And he had the audacity to stick out his right hand arrogantly, as if to shake on the deal.

God! The man was pompous and he had guts, or what the Jewish call chutzpah and the Britons gumption!

"Don't worry, I understand your cottage is on the grounds. We'll be suitably chaperoned by Tim and Lynne, if that's your worry." He concluded ironically.

What was he thinking? That she was in her teens, or something along those lines? Please! The man was insufferable! Lavina eyed him sceptically.

"Why should you care what I think of you, your money, or your projects?"

His gaze held hers steadily.

"I can't imagine." was his sardonic reply.

He got smoothly to his feet.

"I'm afraid I have to go, there's a call I'm expecting and I didn't carry my cellphone with me. May I go in and pick up the vase? I'll say bye to my hosts on the way out. I'll pick you up tomorrow at ten in the morning."

Why was he so sure of himself? Scrambling to her feet, Lavina faced him.

"I haven't said I'll come."

He glanced at her with his all-knowing smile.

"If you really want to know this man –" His wide sweeping arms making an encompassing gesture of his body, " – and if your eyes are anything to go by, how can you afford not to?" He stressed nonchalantly. "And isn't this yours?" He put his hand into his jacket pocket and dangled the armlet.

Lavina opened and closed her mouth like a fish out of water, but nodded and moved towards him with her right hand outstretched towards it. He moved it out of her reach.

"Well then, if you want it back you have to honour our date tomorrow so that you can also tell me the story behind this mysterious and intriguing charm."

Is it his second nature to always have the last word? Lavina thought bemusedly, as he sauntered away arrogantly. This is uncanny, now he seems to be able to read my mind as well!

Chapter 4

After Giorgio Santini had gone, the other guests also bid their goodbyes and left. Lavina pleaded a headache and said goodbye, leaving the housekeeper to help Lynne clear the table. She strolled to her cottage just a few metres away.

A cold shower helped to refresh her as she fervently wished his memory away. Why did she keep thinking of him?

She put on her shower cap, and as she tilted her head back, lifted her face to the needle-sharp spray. He was all she could see. Images of him were indelibly printed on the inside of her eyelids and no amount of will power was strong enough to remove them.

Half an hour later, dressed in her light cotton pyjamas, Lavina perched on the high wooden stool in her workroom, chewing on her small finger nail. Now that was a bad sign! It meant that her stress levels were building up.

She stared unseeingly at the uncompleted white clay-like figure of a Maasai moran amidst clutters of unfinished wood carvings… She felt different somehow, she was different, and it had something to do with Giorgio Santini, crashing into her life with the subtlety of the transit trucks from the Congo traversing the Kenyan landscape.

He had caused the changes which she sensed with a sinking heart were irrevocable. His hands on her skin, the knowing glances thrown her way intimating a thousand shared secrets and his amused ironic smile had catapulted her into a new and deeper dimension of awareness.

As far as her carving and sculpting were concerned, she'd told him the truth. The pleasure she got out of it was far more important to her than the monetary value attached, which was something most people never understood, unless you were really very close to her and knew that she picked up the art from her late grandfather, bless his soul. He had taught her all there was to learn. She reminisced about her excursions with him down stone quarries and up the cream soapstone cliffs of Tabaka[19] to harvest and chip away at the gigantic towering smoothness. What a beautiful country this was.

Not that the belittling attitude and comments of some people like, 'Messing about with clay and wood...,' bothered her unduly, because the appreciation of others for her efforts was a bonus; welcome, but not sought after. Yet she had soaked up Giorgio Santini's compliments as if they'd been cool water in a desert. Why? Why should she care two Kenyan cents what he thought? Who was he anyway? A foreigner, an engineer, a property developer, laughing all the way to the bank? Why did she always have the misfortune of getting entangled with tycoons of sorts all the time?

She thought of Rawal and all the opulence. Look at what it had gotten her into. She was certainly not part of the jetsetting crowd when she met Rawal, but he changed that. It began as one big lie after another, and then she had suddenly found herself in too deep to get out. It cut to the quick just to think of bygones, she should leave well enough alone.

Still, try as she did to hang on to her indignation, it trickled away like the fine beach sand. Listlessly, she relieved the powerful and disturbing sensations she had experienced in Giorgio's arms and that single, subtle but exquisite, gentle kiss on the beach.

Aloof and forbidding one moment, he could be lightly self-mocking the next. He seemed manipulative, magnetic and very, very dangerous. More so perhaps when you got to know him better.

Sitting here fretting and worrying was not going to change anything.

Sighing resignedly, she rose, went to the bathroom, brushed her teeth, and went to bed.

ക്ഷ

Watamu Village (Beach Resort Town, 5 Kilometres from Malindi)

Giorgio stared at his computer screen, but his mind was elsewhere. He was working on a paper about the Gede ruins[20]. He wanted to present it at an architects' symposium he had been invited to in Vienna. He was mesmerised by Kenya, actually enthralled, ever since he had set foot here more than five years ago after his friend, Bjorn, told him of his escapades here. The clincher had come after he'd stumbled upon 'THE ROUGH GUIDE TO KENYA' researched and written by Richard Trillo.

Just the opening paragraph of the introduction had gotten him hooked and obsessed with the idea of visiting Kenya. He remembered it as if it was yesterday... and even now picked up the now dog-eared, but treasured, book from his shelf to leaf through again.

"...lying on the equator, with the glaciated peaks of Mount Kenya, the second highest mountain in Africa, rising from a natural environment of exceptional beauty, Kenya is a hugely rewarding place to travel... the country's dramatically diverse Geography has resulted in a great range of natural habitats, while its History of migration and conquest has brought about a complex social panorama... but if the world-famous national parks, colourful ethnic mix and superb beaches lend an exotic image, the glossy hype of the tourism industry ignores Kenya's post-colonial poverty and deep political tensions...yet they inter-mingle with a ceaselessly active landscape of farms and fields, of streams and bush paths, of wooden and corrugated iron shacks, tea shops and lodging houses, of crammed buses and pick-up vans, of overloaded bicycles and *of streets wandered by goats, chicken and toddlers...off the more heavily trodden tourist routes, you'll find a rewarding degree of warmth, openness and curiosity in Kenya's towns and villages.... out in the wild there is an abundance of superb scenery – vistas of rolling savannah... Maasai and their herds... Kikuyu moorlands... dense forests bursting with bird song, insect noise and shimmering desert, all of which come into focus when experienced in the context of an economically beleaguered African nation four decades after independence.... Kenyan society consists of a huge, impoverished underclass, a small but growing middle class and a tiny rich elite whose successes often owe much to nepotism and graft..."*

More like political patronage, Giorgio had thought to himself, and been proved right on more than one occasion.

One snippet on the fact file never ceased to catch his eye time and again, '...corruption percolates every corner of the country and most official transactions....' In the few years he had been here, he sadly realized that the statement was very true. He stayed anyway and witnessed the spectacular annual wildebeest migration across the Mara to the Serengeti and back again. He knew come what may or wherever he ended up, he would never forget the sight of thousands of stampeding wildebeests. No wonder recently, an american ABC documentary had declared the phenomenon as one of the seventh wonders of the world.

He had been fascinated by Lamu; a 14th century Islamic town, a place of pristine beaches, a place you fly out to, or sail to in a boat, and ride on a donkey as there are no roads for vehicles! Only three vehicles available, the district commissioner's car, one tractor and a motor bike belonging to one of the rich German blokes. That leaves the rest of the populace to race around in donkeys and he finally understood where the saying that goes, as stubborn as a mule came from while trying to squeeze through a narrow alley at the same time with two laden, obstinate asses!

He had been hooked on two dhows and always crossed the channels above them. Mirfat meaning 'the star' and Al-Quamar which means 'The moon'. The only modern rest houses with pubs which serve alcohol are

Jannat house and Petley's Inn.

An ancient town where you get yesterday's dailies today. Or sometimes not at all and you get the Ethiopian paper first and listen to Eritrean Radio… He had been drawn there when he heard talk of Lamu's very own 'Socrates', one old man named Mohamed Abubakar Kijumwa. No wonder Lamu was inducted in 2001 into an exclusive UNESCO world heritage site.

He had been fascinated by the Lamu and Manda islands and the connecting Mokowe jetty all the way to Shela beach. He had been even more fascinated by the Siwa; a long beautifully curved, blown horn made of bronze. He actually bought one, and it cost him a fortune.

An actual splendour of heritage, the Maulidi festival commemorating the birth of prophet Muhammad, was still intact. It is a wonderful festival. Not forgetting the phenomenon that the annual Lamu Cultural Festival has become with the seafront packed throughout the days of the festival and the exhilarating fun with what has come to be known as the Four D's; the donkey race, the dhow races featuring the jahazi, which is the bigger dhow and the mashua the smaller ones, and the dances, especially the ancient Kirumbizi dance, a fast and furious mock dance performed by youth using bakora, a walking stick, before tossing themselves with glee into the open sea swimming gala, where the youths dive into the ocean with abandon to complete the fourth D.

To Giorgio this festival was only comparable to the festival of dhow countries held annually in Zanzibar. The Swahili women, always clad in bui bui, their black cloaks and veils, and the men in their flowing white kanzu dancing and moving to music which is a blend of Arab-AfroBerber and Hispanic beats, all borrowed from the colonial times and interactions with the Portuguese and other visitors centuries back, culminating into taarab and bango beats famous on the East African coast. The way they have preserved their culture fiercely, guarding their traditions from Western influence, reminded him of Timbuktu in West Africa and Kathmandu in Nepal. Lamu. A naked ancient postcard town that had grabbed world attention recently when the German Prince of Hanover gave one of the millionaire foreign residents of the town a thorough beating over a misunderstanding that had ended up in the Law courts amid name droppings and diplomatic immunity covers!

Giorgio chuckled as he remembered the incident. He had been held captive by coastal Kenya's Swahili interior décor with the mix of cosmopolitan and contemporary pieces, artifacts and furniture from yore. He was fascinated by the Lamu wooden door with its ornate carvings. He learnt that in ancient times all modern doors in Lamu had prominent, shining brass studs and the wooden doors were carved with the motifs of chains and ropes to chase away djinns and evil spirits. The belief was and still is that the main door being auspicious and the entrance to the main house, had to be protected from evil intruders.

It is believed that the compromise with the prominent brass studs will warn the djinns and evil spirit that they will be pierced and the ropes and chains will tie them up. The inhabitants believe that this is known to the evil spirits and that they get so scared that they immediately turn away knowing that this is a protected house. Though enhanced to fit the modern and contemporary era the twenty first century has become, the beliefs still remain intact and most clients will not hear of a Lamu door without the brass studs, chains and rope design carved into the wooden sides!

Sometimes he would get away to his favourite pub in Mombasa, the A. C. De Souza, popularly known as Kilindini (Swahili for Port) bar which had never closed its doors for the past one hundred years! Not even during the two world wars! The Pub featured a collection of wooden artefacts, a carryover from the nineteenth century. A maroon coach which survived the turbulent monsoon trade winds on a dhow from Scotland and to complete the history Ernest Hemingway is said to have luxuriated in its soft bottom! The Mau Mau came and went, and so did the Great Depression in America and Europe. All these tales he had heard from Grace De Souza. Grace was a third generation Asian whose grandfather A C De Souza had come to Kenya aboard a dhow from Goa in 1898 and started the historical enterprise.

He had hoped to finish his paper soon and have it developed into a feature documentary. But now an alluring African Princess had him firmly in her clutches.

All he could see was her face. She was bewitching.

He went back to his laptop and commenced his typing, which he interspersed with high resolution scanned photographs.

'THE GEDE RUINS NESTLE IN A 45-ACRE PRIMEVAL FOREST. DATED TOMB – 1399 AD. GEDE MEANS 'PRECIOUS'. THE GREAT MOSQUE, INITIALLY BUILT IN THE 15TH CENTURY. A WEST WING WITH UNDERGROUND ROOMS MEANT TO HAVE BEEN RECEPTION AREAS FOR WOMENFOLK. AT THE ENTRANCE IS AN EARTHENWARE POT, USED TO HOUSE A FIGO (CHARM) IN THE PAST. THOSE WHO LIVED IN THE PALACE BELIEVED A GUARDIAN SPIRIT OR JINNI COULD BE INDUCED TO TAKE UP RESIDENCE IN THE POT IF THE APPROPRIATE RITUAL WAS PERFORMED. THEY BELIEVED THAT IF ANYONE ENTERED THE PALACE WITH EVIL INTENTIONS, THE CHARM WOULD DRIVE THEM OUT AND THEY WOULD EVENTUALLY GO MAD. NEAR THE ENTRANCE TO THE PALACE'S AUDIENCE COURT, IS A GROUP OF TOMBS, INCLUDING A HEXAGONAL PILLAR TOMB THAT IS WELL PRESERVED.

THE RUINS INCLUDE: THE HOUSE OF COWRIES, HOUSE OF PORCELAIN BOWL, HOUSE OF CISTERN, HOUSE OF PANELLED WALLS, HOUSE OF IRON LAMP, HOUSE OF DOUBLE COURT, AND THE MOSQUE OF THREE AISLES…'

One page down he realised when he looked at the monitor that he was mixing up his pieces; how did Serena Beach Hotel (one of the five star beach hotels in Mombasa and one of only a few amongst the roll of honour of prestigious leading resorts of the world, done in Lamu architecture) get mixed up with his piece on Gede? He had promised his friend, Abdalla Ali the curator at Gede, that he would give him the piece to read after finishing it, and here he was messing up! He still had to start working on his other piece about Jumba La Mtwana[21]. The architecture that was Mtwana fascinated him.

At first he had not believed what he heard until he personally saw the ruins of the fourteenth century Mosque on the beach only comparable to the only other fourteenth century Mosque he's seen once in Timbuktu called Djingereiber and had for the first time understood and given meaning to the old adage, seeing is really believing.

He decided to give the typing a rest and stood up. He went to the bar and fixed himself a neat whiskey, which he tossed back, fixed another one, and paced about restlessly. Here he was, almost forty years old. He had not realised how lonely he was. He had everything, or so he thought, until he had looked into Lavina's black deep eyes. He knew he was hooked. Where was he headed?

He was a multi-millionaire. But of what use was the money if he did not have children to spend it on? A wife? A family to take on vacation? The minute he had looked into Lavina's eyes he had known what he wanted.

He thought of his mother back in Italy. What would she think if she knew that he was contemplating marrying a foreigner? For that matter an African? A Kenyan?

He mentally pictured his old madre's face as she ticked on her fingers asking in rapid Italian, "*Mia bravo bambino! Buona educazione? Buona condotta? Buon Cristiano? Buon carattere? Buon cittadino? Buona disposizione? Influsso positivo?*" ('My good child! Is she of good breeding? Good behavior? Good Christian? Good character? Good citizen? Good disposition? Positive influence on you?')

Though knowing that she had his best interests at heart, he would still be tempted to shout back, "*Madre! Ha sufficientemente buono mi!* ('Mother! She's good enough for me!')"

He had a feeling that in the end his mother would not mind. Love always won out in the end was her philosophy. She was a romantic through and through. He smiled as he pictured his doting mother's face in his mind. He strolled out to the verandah with a small balcony overlooking the beach.

He adjusted the telescope mounted on a tripod stand and looked out to sea, staring at the pillar in the distance, mounted out at sea by the Portuguese explorer Vasco Da Gama when he had come calling many centuries ago in 1498. It was now locally referred to as 'The beacon of

Malindi'.

He kept muttering under his breath… "*Mai in vita mia*! ('Never in my life!') Never did I think I will feel this way about one particular woman!"

Finally he went back into the house, raking his hands in a frustrated gesture through his dark springy hair, thinking of tomorrow.

Chapter 5

Lavina awoke with a start, her stomach heaving. She was not looking forward to the day ahead, but she had to go, she had no choice. She just didn't want to seem discourteous to a friend of the Munges.

The clock on the small hyacinth chest of drawers beside her bed read a quarter to eight. Lavina sat up quickly. She had better move, and fast. A quick shower would have to do.

It wasn't surprising that she woke up so late. Unable to switch her mind off Giorgio Santini and the complex emotions she thought she had long buried, now rekindling in her, she had not slept until around two in the morning.

At a quarter to nine she rushed into the tiny bathroom just off the kitchenette and frowned into the mirrored compartments of the medicine cabinet, as she made a final check on her appearance.

Wearing a close-fitting but comfortable pair of jeans, a navy blue and white stripped rugby shirt and canvas shoes, she kept her make-up to her usual bare minimum, a touch of wanja, a type of black kohl used as mascara by the coastal people to define and accentuate their lashes and eyebrows, also said to have a medicinal substance that soothes tired eyes, and soft peach lip-balm which added lustre to her mouth and enhanced her complexion which was today back to its usual glowing self.

Unwilling to waste time styling her hair, Lavina combed it quickly, and hunted in the drawers for her black pony-band. With the soft black hair held back off her brown oval face, and black eyes bright with challenge at the thought of the day ahead, the image gazing back at her was very different from the one she had recently been seeing normally in the mornings.

Never before had she looked so vibrantly alive. It was simply the prospect of a change from her mundane activity, Lavina told herself. It was a welcome break from the routine of being in her workroom or worrying about her situation, such a break itself was enough to make her feel as if she had champagne, instead of blood pumping through her veins. What adrenalin!

A quick dab of Estee Lauder's 'White Linen' behind her ears and she was all set. She preferred mild scents and one could never go wrong with Estee Lauder or Chanel, they were her absolute favorites.

Even though she was expecting it, the knock on the door made her jump. As she turned the key in the double-latch lock, her heart was hammering so hard that it made her feel slightly dizzy. He smiled, and as his gaze travelled over her. She felt as if her heart had jumped right out through her mouth and onto the floor!

Freshly shaved, his thick hair still damp and raked with comb marks, Giorgio Santini was also wearing jeans, which were definitely Italian, topped with a white polo shirt. Lavina breathed an inward sigh of relief. With no idea where they were going, she had not been sure if her choice of clothes was suitable, and he had not been specific. When he hinted at projects, it had been a clue and her instincts leaned towards the outdoors.

"What a lovely sight to greet a man on a Sunday morning, or any other morning for that matter."

Lavina's heart gave an extra beat. Though she could do nothing about the expressiveness of her eyes, she was careful to keep her own smile polite rather than warm.

"Tell me, Mr. Santini –"

"Whoa! Hold it." He raised his hands. "Couldn't we ease up on the formalities? You have a beautiful and unusual name. I'd like to have the pleasure of using it, but it will give me an unfair advantage. And that," he added dryly, "is something I'm sure both of us would prefer to avoid. So unless you want me to address you as Miss Kante for the rest of the day, you'll have to start calling me Giorgio or G for that matter, in fact I prefer G, that's what most of my friends call me."

Why not? She wasn't conceding anything, and it did indeed put them on a more equal footing, she didn't want him to have any extra edge over her. Lavina shrugged her petite shoulders with elaborate indifference.

"Alright." She said.

"Alright G." He intoned.

"Alright G." she repeated. He grinned.

"I like the way you manage to invest it with so many subtle inflections in that sing-song and lilting voice. Now," he went on, as she drew a breath to challenge him, "Why don't we go up the lane, so we can inform the Munges that I've taken you away for the day."

Her expression alternated between indecision and uncertainty.

"I'm just wondering if you are a mixture of Italian and something else, you are too damned domineering!"

For a moment he looked puzzled, then his mouth twitched.

"No. As a matter of fact my grandparents were the ultimate Italians. Whatever eloquence I possess comes from a total belief and confidence in what I'm saying. You look as fresh as a baby," he paused, his voice deepening, "I'd like to see you wake up."

To do that he would need to be with her while she slept. The implications made her stomach plummet and then contract in a tantalising blend of fear and excitement. His gaze held hers, and, dry-mouthed, Lavina bowed her head, fervently hoping he would interpret her tongue-tied silence as a sort of cool self-possession.

"Shall we go?" She suggested briskly, turning away to pick up her small rucksack. He stared at her long and hard as he said,

"I've been in Kenya long enough to be able to tell someone's ethnicity or rather tribal inclinations, but I am not able to pin-point yours, you don't seem to be Luo, Taita, Maasai, Kikuyu….."

He observed, ticking them off his fingers as they walked up the lane towards the Munges sprawling mansion. Taken aback by his knowledge of the more than forty Kenyan tribes, she stopped.

"I'm actually a cocktail of sorts." She giggled. "Kikuyu, Pokomo, and Maasai. In school, whenever someone asked me my tribe, I would say I'm a Kipoma, an acronym I made up for my lineage, and my paternal grandmother had Kisii blood, that's where I picked up the soapstone sculpting from, the wood carving I picked along the way. My maternal grandfather was Maasai. That's how I got my armlet. Long ago Maasai men had to kill a lion bare-handed for them to be initiated into adulthood. He skinned his lion and took the teeth. He gave me the armlet at his deathbed a few years back."

Giorgio whistled, staring at her in amazement. "That's a powerful concoction, no wonder you are so breathtaking."

And when he rested one hand on her shoulder while emphasising with the other, she remembered what a friend had once told her, that Italian men wouldn't be able to speak if they sat on their hands, because so much of their conversation is centred on expressive gestures and flamboyant hand-waving.

The friend had confided further that she knew through experience that, any man who expresses himself by spreading his hands, pressing his palms together, putting a finger to his lips, or a hand on your arm, to make a point, is showing that he's uninhibited and tactile and you can expect a lot of good things from him. Dare she?

"Listen," he continued. "I think there's something we should get straight. One of the reasons I'm taking you out today is to get to know you better or rather for us to get to know one another better. We have mutual friends in the Munges and I actually want to see what I can do about your so-called hobby."

"Yes," she consented reluctantly, avoiding his eyes, acutely aware of the warmth of his palm. He was indeed turning out to be a very tactile man.

The need to touch, to learn through texture and shape, was very much a part of her own life and the driving force behind her love of sculpture and carving, and also her other profession as a hospital laboratory technician. It seemed so far away now. She understood this need in others. Yet this was different. This was him.

Her heart kept going into over-drive and all her senses were on red alert. Not that he had been overly familiar in the physical sense, or tried in any way to take advantage. It was just that when he touched her, every cell in her body was charged with a mysterious energy, and she was drawn to him like steel to magnet.

In such circumstances it was extremely difficult to remain detached, aloof and objective.

Yet it was vital that she does exactly that, remain detached.

"So perhaps if you could relax just a little, and stop treating me like pariah as if I'm a re-incarnation of the devil himself, we might avoid any misunderstanding, …umm?"

Lavina recalled the beautifully tailored designer suit he had worn the previous night. Superimposed in the memory was a vivid mental picture of her struggles with him while near nude at the sea, and now this casual Giorgio. A shudder rippled down her spine, but nevertheless, to change the subject, she asked,

"Can I please have my armlet back? You know the story now."

"Sure. I repaired the broken fastener."

Sliding his hand down to grasp her arm very lightly above the elbow, he took the armlet from his jeans pocket and fastened it to her upper forearm where he could see the mark of where it had been before and then started up the path once more, drawing her into step with him. Soon she was ringing the bell at the Munges' front door.

"*Habari ya asubuhi?*"

She greeted the elderly house help in kiswahili language: ('How is the Morning')?

"*Mzuri sana,*" the old woman replied. ('It's fine.')

"*Mama yuko?*" Lavina asked her, referring to Lynne. ('Is mama in?')

"*Ndiyo, yuko. Karibu ndani. Subirini kidogo nimjulishe muko hapa.*" She replied, ushering them into the living room. ('Yes, she is. Come in.

Wait for a moment I will let her know you are here.')

After a couple of minutes Lynne came down the stairs with her six-month old son still suckling at her breast, and was delighted to see them. She explained that Tim had left early that morning to check on some official matters.

"Lavy?" Lynne's voice called out to her, "Are you going out?"

"Yes."

She came down the stairs and stood looking down at them. They could see the excitement in her eyes.

"You're going out with G? Oh. That's wonderful." She enthused.

Makena's figure hurtled out of the kitchen straight to Lavina's knees, hugging her tightly and almost knocking her over. Lavina bent down to hug the chubby girl. Makena was the Munges' vivacious six-year old daughter. Makena means the 'happy/smiling one'. And Makena was ever that, no wonder her father called her 'Daddy's black beauty.'

She now looked up smiling at Lavina.

"Aunt Lavina you promised me the beach today. Are we gonna go?" She asked, smiling expectantly and revealing the gap where she had recently lost one of her milk teeth. She looked very pretty in her colourful flowery sundress.

"Are we going? Not gonna, Makena." Lavina corrected automatically. Wanting a child, yet knowing deep down she couldn't risk it, she had slowly learnt to make herself impervious to verbal attacks and snide innuendos. She knelt down so that she could be nearer to the small girl's height. She patted her dark pigtails and whispered into her ear.

"I have to go somewhere with Mr. Santini, but tomorrow we'll go to the beach."

"Promith?" the child lisped.

"Promise."

Lavina looked up and caught Giorgio staring at them with a look on his face that bordered on yearning, but he quickly masked it. Lynne interrupted.

"Makena please go into the kitchen and finish your breakfast."

"But mom, I want to watch Tom and Jerr – " Makena pouted back, before her mother interjected again in a sterner voice.

"Now Makena! Later you'll watch the whole cartoon network."

"Yes mommy." Makena replied, skipping happily into the kitchen. Lynne peered into Lavina's eyes.

"You look as if you need an outing. And a change is as good as a rest."

Lavina stood silently, submitting to her perusal. Lynne lifted her chin slightly and looked at Giorgio.

"Will you take care of her for me? She's very precious to us."

He frowned seriously as if Lynne had asked him for an opinion analysis of a complex structural engineering equation, but he replied,

"*Capisco*. ('I understand'). Of course. We are just going on a sight-seeing tour of my projects."

Lynne smiled in a mischievous manner. "Please come to the kitchen with me. I'll put together a picnic hamper for you."

Lynne handed over the baby who was still tugging at her breast with his chubby hands to Lavina. The baby put his finger into Lavina's mouth cooing happily. Again Lavina caught the strange fleeting look on Giorgio's face and so did Lynne, who silently thought to herself: *Serves you right Giorgio! I hope your paternal instincts are awakening*, and proceeded into the kitchen while Giorgio followed behind.

Chapter 6

Moments later they were out of the house. They strolled up the tree-lined driveway to the electronic gates, while waving to Makena as Lynne shouted after them not to forget the Mayor's Ball the following day.

Leshampta, the Maasai guard in traditional regalia and red ochered hair, his skin glistening with oil, mockingly raised his club at Giorgio. Giorgio waved back.

"*Ero Sopa!*" he greeted him in Maa, the dialect of the Maasai people.

He remembered that Leshampta had told him that he treasured the wooden club because it had been handed down to him by his father at an initiation ceremony, together with a buffalo hide shield, as a rite of passage, instead of killing a lion barehanded. This had been outlawed and thus phased out because the rite endangered and threatened the big cats with extinction. Giorgio smiled wryly as the mental picture of Lavina's grandfather skinning a lion and removing its teeth flashed through his mind.

Unlocking the passenger door, he held it open for her as she got in with the picnic hamper, closed it and went round to the driver's side. Half-turning towards her to fasten his seat belt, he looked up with a grin that made her heart roll over.

"Ah. This is good, I enjoy your company."

Lavina gave him a frosty glance.

"Of course you do. We've known each other sooo… long, and we're suchhh…. good friends. Don't patronise me Mr. Santini." She stressed sarcastically. "I'm nothing like the women you're used to."

"There you go again generalizing. Sarcasm doesn't become you." He sighed with mock exasperation, "Stereotyping and jumping to conclusions about me. Though, as happens in this case, you're right. You are most definitely not like most of the women I've met here and even abroad. This is a new experience for me." His voice softened, "It's rather like trying to handle a fragile figurine of the most delicate China. There's something gentle about you, and its drawing me to you… I can't help it."

Lavina felt slightly disturbed as she recognised that his feelings were an almost exact replica of her own! He was describing what she herself was feeling. Dare she reciprocate and tell him? She turned her head away because she was sure the confusion she was feeling must be mirrored on her face.

She gazed out of the side window as they hit the highway. She could catch glimpses of the sea in the far distance, through the density of the Arabuko Sokoke forest.

He glanced at her and looked ahead again. She bit her lip thoughtfully. He could hardly blame her. He must know she was confused, but then she could also hardly blame him, until yesterday the name 'Santini Developments' had only signified a faceless corporation, but now it seemed to start besieging her thoughts. Her life was already in turmoil, as it were.

Yet there was something about him which, even in the face of her current predicament, attracted her to him, and while that didn't make the slightest difference to her decision not to get involved, it meant that the longer the time she spent in close proximity to him, the more confusing her feelings became. She just had to try and avoid spending a lot of time in his company!

As they headed in the direction of the airport, Giorgio glanced sideways at her.

"How was your night?"

She stared out through the windscreen. She didn't want to think about last night. Despite her being mentally and physically exhausted, sleep had eluded her except for brief spells of fitful, restless dreaming in which he had featured far too strongly. Every minute had dragged, but if he thought she was going to bare her soul to him, he was very much mistaken. She might have been sensitive in her current state, but she was not stupid. Honesty was one thing, but to give a man like Giorgio Santini ammunition of that calibre to use against her, was a different issue altogether.

"Lavina?" He prompted.

"It was just like any other night." She replied, "too short for enough sleep." She shrugged. "You know…." Irony tinged his half-smile and his eyes met hers briefly before returning to the road.

"And the Pope ain't German! Anyway, it sounds just like mine." He said with a tinge of sarcasm. He knew. Lavina turned her head, concentrating fiercely on the passing scenery as she read the billboards advertising several tourist attractions and beach hotels.

A monkey ran across their path instead of using the overhead rope ladders that had been tied high up across the tree branches to aid them in crossing the road, but she was not distracted from her thumping heart.

"*Asti, Prossima fermatta…* Oops! Lavina, you need to learn Italian Pronto! What I mean is that our destination is just round the corner."

They left the highway and turned down a side road, she knew this side road. She had used it often with Tim and Lynne when coming to the airport to fly somewhere or welcome a guest.

As Giorgio drove in through the entrance, Lavina stiffened in her seat, her startled gaze darted around the airport.

"What –?" her voice emerged a croak. Clearing her throat, she licked her dry lips and tried again. "Why have we come here?"

Giorgio glanced across at her.

"To pick up our transport."

"What!?"

"You seem surprised." He grinned, "Lavina, I'm not running some small back-street mediocre operation. My developments are spread all over the country, and right across the world for that matter."

Giorgio parked the car and opened his door.

"Don't forget our picnic hamper." He said, reaching into the backseat for his laptop which was encased in leather like an attaché case. He locked it in the trunk of the car. She picked up her rucksack and hamper and followed him towards the reception area.

He seemed well known, judging by the greetings he got, and no one seemed to bother him with the filling out of any formalities. They went to the office block near the control tower. She was very uncomfortable, she was hardly aware of the uniformed attendant talking to Giorgio.

Then she was ushered to the wide area of tarmac. To their right at one end of the runway, three small planes belonging to Air Kenya were lined up near the perimeter fence at the turning of the circle, bright and smart in their red and white colours, with their registered trade marks clearly visible on the fuselage.

Slipping his hand under her elbow, he propelled her forwards.

"Good morning Juma," he greeted the mechanic in overalls, climbing out of the nearest plane.

"Good morning Mr. Santini," he replied, wiping his greasy hands on an oily rag.

"I've parked yours on the other side." He jerked his head sideways in the opposite direction.

"*Grazie.*" Giorgio thanked him in Italian.

"But excuse me – how are we going to view the proje – ?" Lavina started, and then it registered! Yours. The mechanic had said Yours. Good Lord! What was she getting herself into?

Giorgio guided her past the half-open doors of the cavernous hangar. There at the farthest side of the small airstrip, on a circular pad of tarmac surrounded by close-cropped grass, sat a small helicopter. The top half was painted a sea blue, the underside and landing gear an off-white colour.

"In that." He gestured in answer to her half-uttered startled question. "Like any small light plane, Cessna's are great for a sightseeing flip up the coast, but you can't land just anywhere. So unless where you want to go happens to have an airfield right next to you, you've got problems. I usually prefer a chopper. They are far more convenient for such jaunts. I use this one nearly as much as I use my four-wheel drives."

"This is yours?"

He nodded.

"How the other half live. Status symbols for the financially savvy." Lavina murmured wryly under her breath.

She had thought the likes of Rawal had it all, now she knew better… His swift glance held surprise, quickly masked. He then shrugged.

"It's merely an aid to efficiency. I can keep an eye on several projects at once, and deal with any problems in the field immediately they arise." He opened the door for her. "Up you get."

She had been in planes many times before, but never in a chopper, and she realised the difference as he seated himself beside her after sliding the basket in behind the seats. She was suddenly aware of how much less room there seemed to be in this one compared to the other yet even smaller planes she had been in.

Though equally comfortable, the seats were narrower. The panels above their heads were covered with switches and indicator lights, and behind them headsets hung on yet another control panel. She was gazing warily around when, without warning, Giorgio leaned across her. She quickly disguised her swift intake of breath as a cough, but could do nothing about the heated rush of awareness that made her skin prickle and her shirt stick to her back.

His gaze flickered to her mouth.

"I have to make sure your safety harness is properly fastened." His voice was more a vibration than sound.

"Yes of course." She whispered.

He had moved even closer in order to accomplish the task, and her nostrils were now full of the faint fragrance of his soap. His head was so close she could see each separate hair; dry now, tousled by the breeze, it smelled of fresh air and the warm musky scent that was unmistakably and peculiarly his. Her fingers itched to smooth it back, to bury themselves in the thick springy waves. She clenched her fists in self-control before they betrayed her of their own volition.

He turned and their eyes met. Code Red! Code Red! Code Red! The warning bells started tolling in her head! She held her breath as a shaft of sensation swept through her, sharp, sweet and unfamiliar. She felt suddenly shaky. What was happening to her? She averted her gaze while putting her arms through the straps he held, looking anywhere but at him. In the confined space it was inevitable that arms and bodies would collide, the contact brief but electrifying.

"It may get a little bit bumpy, because of the heat." He sounded slightly hoarse.

"I don't want you rattling around like a rag doll, tiny as you are." He continued.

"No, of course not." She answered back automatically.

His fingers grazed the tops of her thighs and she bit her lip as he clipped the buckle across her hips and pulled the strap tight. Lifting one of the headsets with attached microphone from the hook, he placed it over her ears.

"Once I start the engines and the rotors begin to wind up, normal speech and conversation will be impossible." He explained. "We'll have to do all our talking through this, ok?"

She nodded, and as he turned away to strap himself in, she noticed that his forehead was shining with perspiration. So she wasn't the only one affected by their closeness after all… something incredible was happening between them…

For the next few minutes he was fully occupied, talking to the control tower and preparing for take-off. Lavina was more than content to simply watch and listen. Then suddenly the helicopter seemed to tilt forward slightly, and then they were airborne, banking around to the right as they climbed into the cloudless sky. After a while she relaxed, held firmly against the seat by the safety harness.

"Alright?" Giorgio's voice came clearly through the headset.

Lavina nodded, gazing in wonder at the panorama below. She had flown by plane many times before, but never by chopper, so she had never had the privilege of enjoying the view this way.

"Glad you came?"

The irony in his demand brought Lavina's head round quickly.

"I wouldn't have missed this for anything." She replied with total honesty. "I'm used to planes flying high up, you hardly see a thing."

"Then I'll have to make sure that the rest of the day lives up to it." He promised.

"That won't be easy." She warned, peering down as they flew over a traditional Giriama village[22].

His soft laughter raised goose bumps on her arms. "We'll see."

She could hear him humming under his breath as they flew on through the bright morning.

Chapter 7

"This was one of my early projects when I came to Kenya." Giorgio said, bringing the helicopter lower and banking around in a wide circle.

The development formed a shallow 'S' on the gently sloping shoreline. On either side of the road, clusters of properties nestled in large gardens bursting with colour and bordered by bushes and shrubs. Any fences or electric burglar systems were virtually invisible under splashes of pink, white, red and purple bougainvillea. There were rows upon rows of vivid red hibiscus iinterspersed with white yasmin. It was breathtaking and beautiful.

The stately mansions looked like palaces, and the bungalows resembling quaint cottages were made even more diverse by the variation in colour and finish on walls and paint-work.

"It doesn't look like an estate at all." Lavina said, startled. The corners of Giorgio's mouth twitched.

"Exactly. That's what I always strive to portray, homely cosiness."

In the far distance, they could see the famous stone ruins that are the Gede ruins.

"As it happens, I lead a very mobile life. It has its advantages, but I'm finding myself fascinated by this country, its people, history and culture.

I would like to settle here."

"Oh yes?" Lavina made no effort to hide her scepticism, "How do you grade it?"

"This is a beautiful country," he replied. "I get to see more of it than most people born and bred here. And I'm always meeting new people of diverse cultures and backgrounds."

"And just how many do you actually get to know?" she scoffed cynically. "Meeting new people isn't the same as being part of a community."

"What is so wonderful about belonging to a community?" his tone was acid. "*A mio credere* ('In my opinion'), if you happen to be in any way different, you are an immediate target for curiosity and gossip. Everyone has an opinion, and they don't allow ignorance of the facts to stop them from voicing it. If anything, they go full force with it. If you're a foreigner and rich," he stressed, "Then you're not honest. It's either you are a terrorist, a hitman or are dealing with illegal drugs, or some other dubious scam. I really get pissed off!" He paused. "Surely you must have seen this happening?"

Unwilling to admit the truth, but unable to deny it, Lavina shrugged.

"That's just human nature. It's not limited to countries or communities. People don't have to know you to be curious. Look at newspapers and magazines worldwide. When it's not politics or disasters, the tabloids and other rags hook on to gossip and scandals about the rich and celebrities to keep their circulation high."

"Umm... and do you find such curiosity intrusive?" he pressed.

Memories of what she had gone through last year in Mombasa bubbled to the surface of her mind; veiled taunts, even from friends, the way they would fall silent when she chanced upon them suddenly. At a very superficial level she had started to avoid them too.

With all the precision of a surgeon wielding a scalpel, he was laying bare the pain that she was trying to keep buried. She had slowly and painfully learnt that self-pity destroys and yet sympathy on the other hand simply enervates. Shaken, but determined not to show it, Lavina shifted on her seat.

"Are we almost through?"

"Not yet," he replied blandly. "I simply keep getting this feeling that you change the subject every time I get personal with you. What is it Lavina? I sense that you seem to have this idea that in outlook and attitude we are such total opposites."

"Of course we are!" She exploded. "There is no comparison! For a start I don't go around sightseeing over the coastal strip in a helicopter!" she stressed sarcastically.

His look of contained impatience made her feel like those times in boarding school when they were rebellious and would then be hauled up in front of their matron.

"Come now." He remonstrated. "I can see that you are used to money – and lots of it by the look of things."

She didn't think that such a remark dignified a reply. So she reserved her comments.

Lavina looked down. Below was another cluster of houses and bungalows built on rising land above the rocks where the tide could not reach, but she could see the sea winding like a blue silver ribbon in the distance. Though they appeared randomly placed, the properties followed the curve of the shore and land so that each gained maximum sunlight, yet was sheltered from the prevailing wind.

"Another of your projects?" she enquired.

He nodded, but gave her no chance to make any further comments.

"How about some lunch? I don't know about you, but I'm starving."

The morning's nervous tension had given Lavina a hollow feeling in the pit of her stomach which, during the past hour, had been growing steadily and becoming more and more gnawingly uncomfortable.

"I could do with a bite." She admitted.

"You'll have to come a little closer."

"What?"

"I can't reach you from here." He explained patiently.

Lavina glanced up at him. "Oh, very funny. So where are we going to eat?"

"Relax, I've got everything organised."

"You would have." She muttered.

"I've chosen somewhere with spectacular views," he announced. "The food is excellent and the service personal without being pushy."

"It sounds rather exclusive, don't you think?" Lavina's voice reflected her uncertainty as she glanced down at her jeans and rugby shirt.

"Oh, it is. It is." Giorgio agreed. "Don't worry," he added mockingly when he saw her glance down at herself. "We won't be turned away, in fact with any luck, we'll be the only ones there."

Disconcerted by his ability to pick up her thoughts, Lavina wondered how he could be so sure that they might actually be the only ones at the restaurant he was talking about. Ten minutes later, she knew! She had completely forgotten about the picnic hamper Lynne had packed for them!

Giorgio had set the helicopter down as lightly as a feather in the shadow of a cluster of coconut trees high up on a grassy hilltop. With the breeze cooling her, Lavina stood, hands in pockets, gazing spellbound across a panorama of fields, farms, small makuti[23] thatched villages in the sprawling town, and the sea beyond.

A little way behind her, Giorgio took out a small mkeka[24] and began unpacking the banana fibre hamper Lynne had given them.

"Lunch is served *Mia cara*," he said.

The Italian endearment startled her again. 'My dear'. She wondered if he used the term often to flatter his various conquests.

"You'd better get here on the double, or I won't be responsible for my actions if I don't eat soon." He called out. "There's some roast chicken here. I love my Chicken, avian bird flu threats notwithstanding!"

"I can't remember the last time I went on a picnic." Lavina said as she sat cross-legged opposite him. Giorgio glanced up.

"I wanted to make this day different. Something special. Lunch at one of your four or five star hotels would have been too much."

Startled, Lavina had to clamp down hard on her treacherous delight. She could not afford to forget that beneath all his efforts to win her over he might have a prime motive.

He indicated the array of hotpots neatly packed with food covered in silver foil. Lavina's empty stomach gurgled as she feasted her eyes on the mouth-watering dishes: roast chicken, ham sandwiches, fresh vegetable salad, fresh bread rolls, butter, fresh fruits… umm… He handed her a paper plate, serviette and plastic cutlery.

"Help yourself."

"This is certainly a different slant on personal service." Lavina quipped.

"I'm a great believer in efficiency and energy conservation." Was his bland rejoinder, "I've supplied it. You choose what and how much you want…" he continued.

Lavina forked some of the sliced meat onto her plate, while she dwelled on his definitely double-edged words. Her head came up briefly. As their eyes met, she read pointed irony in his gaze.

He stood up, strolled to the helicopter and came back holding a cooler, he opened it and took out a bottle of champagne. As she read the Heinkel Trocken label, Lavina's eyes grew round.

"That's quite expensive." She observed.

"Surely it's the quality and taste that counts? And didn't the Latinos say *en vino veritas*? The truth is in the wine?" he rebuked.

"Of course, I didn't mean –" she stammered, and jumped as the cork flew out with a loud pop and the clear liquid foamed into the crystal champagne flute he was holding.

Handing it to her, he filled another for himself. As he raised it in a mocking salute she saw thin red lines forming weals on the inside of his wrist and fore-arm. The healing scratches and the inflexion in his voice brought it all flooding back. Their semi-naked struggle in the water, her near-drowning and his implications that she had been trying to kill herself. With embarrassment, her lashes fluttering down, she inclined her head in tongue-tied silence and lifted the glass to her mouth.

Before she could taste the wine, the bubbles teasing her nostrils, he stopped her trembling hand.

"Wouldn't you like to propose a toast?"

As he stayed her wrist, though cool, his fingers burned like the branding irons they used back home on herds of cattle. *Let me be! Get out of my life and leave me in peace, that's my toast!* She cried silently, but if she were to give him even a hint of her thoughts, he would have an edge over her.

"I – er -," she moistened her lips with the tip of her tongue. "I can't think of one right now." His gaze held hers and then he stared at her lips.

"No? You're not usually lost for words my dear. Still perhaps I can suggest something suitable for my mermaid."

That lovely Italian accent which he rarely let slip, was now sliding its inflection into his speech. It was getting to her. It mesmerised her.

"To our continued friendship. Take note that I don't view you as an acquaintance."

As she raised her glass in acknowledgement, he continued.

"Why don't you start by telling me something about yourself? I only have the scant details I've managed to gather from Tim and Lynne."

"I've no doubt you're dying of curiosity!" She retorted sweetly. She raised her glass again mockingly. "Cheers."

The chilled drink slid down her parched throat, sharpening her appetite to the point where hunger overrode all reserve. Helping herself from each of the dishes, she began to eat.

"This is really a remarkable change." Giorgio observed.

Gazing around, Lavina nodded.

"Yes. Food is usually tastier outdoors, I don't know why."

"Actually, I meant eating with a woman who sees food as a pleasure, not an enemy." He corrected her. 'I really get tired of all the bulimic women around talking of diets and trying to lose weight in the name of fashion, not realising they're becoming anorexic."

He refilled her glass, and she was surprised to see that it was already empty. She gave a tinkling laugh, and her sudden cheerful attitude surprised her.

"You should see my friend Rachel's sister, she is a model, and picks at her food like a kuku[25] or rather kifaranga[26]." She came to an abrupt halt, when she realised she was going on and on.

"It's alright, don't stop. I want you to open up to me. I wish I could meet all your friends." Giorgio said, helping himself to more chicken.

"Maybe you will, one day soon." Lavina said, waving her fork expansively. "But most of my friends are scattered far and wide. When I take the occasional break, I go visiting." She pulled a wry face. "The trouble is, I can only take the breaks when I can least afford them," she giggled, "because that's when the business is very bad in the low season."

Giorgio was completely absorbed in her words. He turned the stem of his glass, still half full of the golden liquid, between his fingers, his eyes not leaving hers.

"Go on," he said as he topped her glass yet again.

"No. Stop it! That's enough." She covered her flute with her left palm. "Are you trying to get me tipsy? Anyway, well…" She shook her head. "No, I don't think I should continue blabbering… I've said more than enough about myself…"

"Lavina, look at me." Giorgio's voice was soft, but held a steely command she found impossible to disobey. "You can tell me anything. I'm an understanding man, you have my word."

His word? Yet she believed him. Was she mad? Maybe. She took another mouthful from her glass.

"You seem tired." Giorgio's eyes glittered like sunlight falling on ice-cubes, but his voice revealed only a mild interest. "Would you mind if we rest a while?"

A little while later, Lavina put down her fork, and after draining the last sparkling drops from her flute, lay back on the mkeka, stretching luxuriously.

"Oh, I've enjoyed that."

Filled with a glorious sense of well-being, she closed her eyes and filled her lungs with a deep sigh of satisfaction. The sun was hotter than ever. The breeze had died away completely, even the birds were silent. She soon slipped into a light nap.

A little while later she felt something brush her arm and with great effort, she opened her eyes. Giorgio was stretched out beside her. Lying on his stomach, he was propped up on his elbows rubbing a blade of grass between his fingers – so that was what had tickled her arm - as he gazed at the view.

As he wasn't looking at her, Lavina didn't feel threatened by his closeness. She studied his craggy profile for a moment. She'd met many European men before, but he really did have a marvellous bone structure. Even when he grew old, he would still be an extraordinarily good-looking man.

Slowly, almost lazily, he turned his head in a leonine sort of way, like she'd seen the lions out in the Mara do. Amusement was hovering at his lips.

"Well, well, what a compliment. Thank you for the vote of confidence."

She gazed at him, uncomprehending, then realisation dawned. She was mortified. She had actually spoken her thoughts aloud!

"Oh dear." She bit her lip, embarrassment fleeting momentarily across her smooth baby face. "You mustn't misunderstand me, I mean I wasn't being personal." She cautioned.

"No?" The amusement deepened, traces of Italian accent shading the single word.

"No. Definitely not." Lifting her head, she shook it vigorously to show how serious she was, but the action made her dizzy and she fell back on the mkeka.

"It was purely an... an... an objective observation." She tried to pronounce and articulate the words carefully, wondering why her tongue and brain were not coordinating as well as they usually did.

Giorgio stared at her. This African princess had him squarely in her clutches. Even a look, a word, mesmerised him... transported him to a different world altogether!

"You were speaking purely as an artist?" She nodded. Thank God he understood. He looked at her again and said,

"You know, myself as an architect and thinking of your carvings, when you chip away at the wood or soapstone, Lavina, with your delicate hands, I should think that sculpture is three-dimensional, not flat like a painting."

Rolling on his side, he grasped her wrist. Transfixed by his piercing gaze, Lavina was incapable of resisting as he lifted it to his face. He slid his hand over hers and pressed her palm against his cheek. She was acutely aware of the firm texture of his skin, at the faintest hint of stubbles of beard despite his morning shave.

"To look is not enough." He turned his head so his lips were against her palm as he spoke. "You cannot fully experience anything through sense alone."

As he followed her heart-line with the tip of his tongue, she caught her breath, shuddering violently as her eyelids fluttered shut.

Oh God, she prayed silently, don't let me feel this way about him, in my current situation, at this moment I have no right at all to feel this way about anybody... Raising her hand slightly, he grazed the soft flesh at the base of her thumb with his teeth.

"You have to touch..." With one fluid movement, he rolled over again, his body half covering hers, his warm weight pinning her to the traditional mat. "To smell..."

Panic ran through her body as he buried his face in the hollow between her neck and shoulder, inhaling deeply, as he lifted his head. His eyes, cloudy and heavy-lidded, were now turning an indigo hue from their normal blue. He stroked her hair back, as it had come loose from the restraining pony-band. A different kind of tension gathered like a swelling wave of the sea in the centre of Lavina's body. Code Red! Code Red! Code Red!

As earlier in the chopper, the warning bells started again in her head reminding her of the times she used to work at the hospital during emergencies. This was definitely a code red! Oh dear God! She had to stop her treacherous responses to him!

Oh God, she prayed again silently, Give me the strength and courage to tell him....

'To taste..." he whispered and lowered his head. "Only one *bacio profondo amore mio*" ('deep kiss, my love').

His mouth took possession of hers. Scalding heat flooded through her. With lips and tongue, he teased, coaxed, demanded a response and it was impossible to deny him. People usually read of such torrid emotions only in romantic novels, and here it was happening to her.

The same thoughts were going through Giorgio's mind. He had heard of these fairy tales, 'tourist tales' he called them, of visitors falling in love on golden African tropical beaches and here he was. Trust it to happen in Kenya! A re-enactment of Kuki Gallman's 'I Dreamt of Kenya.' He couldn't believe it. This lady was driving him completely crazy, if last night had been any indication. He'd hardly slept. He kept dreaming of her.

On the other hand, excitement was a slow but sure fire in Lavina's veins, and the beating and pounding of her heart deafened her as his stroking fingertips laid a burning trail down her neck. Pushing aside the open collar of her rugby shirt, he pressed his lips to the pulse at the base of her throat. She gasped and quivered beneath him, caught up in a maelstrom of sensation that urged her to open up to him completely. She held her breath.

Scared of what to do. What to tell him. How to phrase it. How to start. How he'll react…

Oh God… With a wordless sound, his breathing ragged, he caught her face between his hands as his mouth sought hers once more.

Lavina heard a faint shout. It seemed to be in Kiswahili mixed with the Giriama dialect. They were not alone! It seemed to come from a distance, and her senses, already blurred by the champagne and heat, were reeling under Giorgio's voluptuous assault.

He tore his mouth from hers and it was like a wound. She had been kissed so many times before, and had been in several relationships, but never like this. He aroused feelings and responses in her she had never even dreamt of. She heard him catch his breath, then curse softly in Italian.

As she opened her eyes, and before she could focus, a cold, wet nose snuggled in her ear, and a long wet tongue slapped warmly along the side of her face! Gasping, Lavina jerked sideways. As Giorgio rolled off her, she saw that the intruder was an exuberant alsatian looking like a mongrel, his once silky coat turning mangy.

"*Mamma Mia!*" ('Oh my goodness!') "Shoooo, go away!" Giorgio roared at the dog. "Clear off."

Standing amidst the litter of their picnic, the dog cocked its head, gazing expectantly at them with limpid brown eyes. The pink tongue lolled from an open mouth as its once glossy sides heaved in and out.

Lavina struggled into a sitting position, still startled by her feelings. Her whole body was aflame with unfulfilled yearning. To find herself capable of such wanton abandonment was not only deeply shocking, it shattered the image of herself as a self-controlled and level-headed lady, especially in matters of the heart and emotions. Now, who was this stranger under her skin?

Wiping the sweat from her forehead with hands that trembled slightly, she pulled her shirt straight and put the fall of her hair back into the confines of her pony-band. There was no breeze to cool her hot, damp skin. She felt an ache of acute frustration. She felt keyed up, ready to explode into hysterics and perilously close to tears. Biting the inside of her lower lip, she forced herself to take slow, steadying deep breaths and mentally counted up to ten.

There was another shout, nearer this time, followed by a whistle. An African boy appeared over the brow of the hill, with freshly caught fish in his hands, dangling from a bamboo rod.

"Go on." Giorgio gestured impatiently at the happily grinning dog. "There's your owner. What are you waiting for?"

Realising that no one was going to play with him, the alsatian bounded away across the grass and disappeared downhill.

"I like dogs," Giorgio muttered gruffly. "I have several at my residence here, but after today, I don't know…"

Lavina gradually stopped shaking and the edgy wound-up feeling began to subside. She stood up and walked some distance to calm her nerves.

She called out greetings in native Giriama dialect to the boy, asking him if the fresh fish he was carrying was for sale. She could tell it was fresh because of the scarlet gills and fresh sea smell emanating from the boy. It was already gutted and cut into segments, held together by mangrove strings. All the time she was talking to him, he was pre-occupied, his eyes glued to the shiny helicopter.

"*Adzalamukadze.*" Lavina greeted him in Giriama. ('Good morning/ How are you?')

"*Adzalamuka eee. Simanaya wee..*" he replied. ('Fine thank you. How do you do?')

"*Adzalamuka. Gomakumba nigakunguza? Hebu nzoo kuno karibu we. Ni kiboma?*" She asked. ('I'm fine. Is the fish for sale? Please move closer. Is it kingfish?')

"*Eeee... nigakunguza. Ni Kiboma.*" The boy replied. ('Yes..Kingfish. It's for sale.')

"*Sidza'gwei kuona ndege hehe.*" He touched the smooth tail of the helicopter admiringly.

"*Nazona lakini hukooo mulunguni! Ni ya huyu mzungu?*" ('I have never seen an aircraft this close. But I've seen them up in the sky! Does it belong to this white man?')

Lavina nodded in answer to the boy's question. Giorgio resignedly shook his head, looking at them.

"At least I understand a little Kiswahili, but this Giriama jargon!"

He walked a distance away and started picking up the picnic litter and packing their utensils. In a little while Lavina paid for some fish. The boy left, albeit reluctantly, whistling for his dog.

Chapter 8

Saying nothing, Lavina carried the fish. To retain its freshness, she put it into the portable picnic cool-box that had been holding the champagne, and for the sake of something to do, began rolling up the mkeka.

She carried the cooler and they strolled to the helicopter. As he stowed the mat and banana fibre hamper into the chopper with unusual force, he seemed pre-occupied and didn't look at her.

"Right," he said brusquely, "in you get."

Lavina bristled at his peremptory tone. Anyway, it was better that way. Had he smiled or said something tender, she might have been foolish enough to believe it actually meant something.

"G?" she paused, one foot inside the helicopter. He glanced around.

"Yes?"

"Thanks."

"For what?"

His tone was dismissive. Lavina wondered silently what had changed in the space of a couple of minutes.

"For a beautiful day."

She tossed the words over her shoulder and climbed onto her seat.

"Perhaps I'd better make something clear," he said, folding himself into his own seat. To be suddenly so close to him again made Lavina's skin tighten. "Contrary to popular belief, this is not something I do often, though I do have my moments of indulgence." He told her.

Lavina moistened her lips. They still felt swollen from the bruises of his kisses.

"Helicopter rides and champagne picnics?" she enquired silkily with cool sarcasm, deliberately choosing to misunderstand him. His expression hardened and his earlier remarks about disliking the games most people played echoed at the back of her mind.

"What else?" Keeping his eyes firmly on the instruments, he continued the pre-flight checks.

"Well," she began, "If your intention was to impress – " she broke off at his ironic smile. Giorgio Santini would not step one inch out of his way to impress anybody, let alone the proverbial extra mile! He didn't need to. His wealth and reputation always preceded him.

"Anyway," Lavina continued derisively, "as a sales pitch or PR gimmick you certainly do have an edge."

He glanced at her.

"That's the way you see today? As a stunt? A sales pitch? A publicity gimmick?" His tone was completely neutral, giving nothing away.

"What else?" She threw his own words back at him, and though her tone was light and flippant, inside she ached. It was painful to think of his thoughtfulness, of this whole day as simply part of a softening-up process. Yet what else could it be? There was no denying the powerful, almost violent physical attraction that arched between them and let off sparks of fireworks, but deluding herself that it might have a deeper significance could only lead to further heartbreak.

"Even so, it's been quite pleasant." That was the understatement of the decade! He shook his head slowly.

"You're a hard lady to please Ms. Kante."

"That's right sir!" She agreed flippantly.

The look he gave her mocked the lie.

"Don't be too sure yet," he warned smoothly, "after all, the day is still young."

Lavina bit back the cutting retort that sprang to her lips and instead turned her head to look out of the window as, airborne once more, they headed south-west. The light blue sky had paled to a milky haze, and towering pillars of clouds were billowing over the horizon. She turned her head to the landscape below.

After a few moments of mutual silence, he glanced at her.

"Why aren't you married?"

Her eyes widened in surprise.

"I beg your pardon?"

"Well, you look like someone who is married, has been married, or can make a perfect wife."

"What law says that I must have a husband to look the way I do?" she countered.

"Women! I didn't say there is any law, I simply asked why you aren't married."

Lavina shifted uneasily on her seat.

"I should have thought it was obvious. I haven't yet met anyone I'd want to spend the rest of my life with." She finished lamely.

He gave a loud shout of laughter.

"You can't be that naïve."

"What do you mean? Don't you believe in the sanctity of marriage?" she countered.

"Sacred things are far and few in my life. Anyway, to think of a lifetime when demographics show that one in every five marriages here end in divorce? That's insane!"

"The statistics are even more depressing in your Western world," Lavina responded "Where one out of every three unions ends up in court, but trust you to be a pessimist. Why don't you try to be a bit optimistic and look at it the other way round? The demographics are admitting that two out of three marriages do last."

He shook his head wearily. "I call that gambling against heavy odds." He stressed.

"Which is why I'm still single." Lavina said, smiling sweetly. "What's your excuse?"

"Excuse?" His tone made it clear that he considered it beyond him to offer excuses or any explanations for anything he did.

"Alright, your reason then. But I tend to believe that men like you are the ones who led Helen Rowland to comment that love is the quest, marriage the conquest and divorce the inquest!" She conceded reluctantly.

Amusement lit his eyes.

"How do you know I'm not married?"

His question caught Lavina off-guard. She ran her tongue over her lips.

"I see you wear no wedding ring, and I think Lynne happened to mention it once..."

She felt as she had then, as Lynne's words now echoed and reverberated in her mind again. '....wish you two could meet before any other lady ties him down. He is such a caring man and I feel this vibe, like he'll take to you like a fish to water...'

His brows lifted. "Was she matchmaking, or were you interested enough to ask?"

Realizing denial was pointless, Lavina made her shrug elaborately casual.

"I was curious to know what kind of man you were before I met you, because Tim and Lynne kept going on and on about you."

"And now that you've met me, what kind of man do you think I am?"

His voice had deepened to a serious baritone. She felt the subtle shift from frivolity to a seriousness in him. Lavina's gaze fell to his hands. Though large and strong, they manipulated the helicopter's controls with a lightness and subtlety that belied their strength.

The direction of her thoughts sent shivers down her spine. He had handled her body in exactly the same way, his touch raising every nerve, every centimetre of skin, to an exquisite sensitivity that was almost painful.

Yet she could not ignore the way her relationships in the past had ended, especially now that she knew herself pretty well. Just for an instant she was tempted to be glib and facetious, to toss him an answer she could hide behind, but the impulse was fleeting, dismissed even as it occurred.

How could she expect honesty from him if she was not honest herself? Nowadays she was getting used to wearing this social mask, a façade. Everything around her was a farce, so superficial and artificial, trying to hide the pain that was tearing at her insides, a charade of sorts with everyone, apart from the Munges. She didn't have to hide anything from them; they knew it all.

She so desperately wanted to be herself. The only place of refuge, peace, solace and solitude was the beach and her workroom with her art.

So what did she actually think of him? Her tongue snaked out to moisten her lips again.

"Complex," She said softly. "You seem capable of great kindness, and equal cruelty when you need to be. Sophisticated and manipulative, yet startlingly candid, though even that comes out in an arrogant way, a brilliant mind…" Her voice faltered, faded and trailed into silence.

His face, when he turned to look at her, was expressionless. He seemed expert at hiding his emotions behind a blank face, but his gaze at the same time seemed to pierce her very soul. Was that good or bad? She didn't know!

"And do you like me?" He asked.

"Does it matter?" She stalled for time.

"I don't ask irrelevant questions." He answered obliquely.

"So is this the Spanish grand inquisition?"

"If that's how you want to take it."

Lavina looked out at the changing sky. The billows of cumulus clouds had flattened into purple-gray thunderheads. She shivered. She hated foul weather. She mentally ridiculed and rebuked her twinge of unease. She berated and castigated herself at the stirrings of fear due to the darkening clouds. Though the sky had changed and taken on the gray ominous tinge, most of it was still cloudless except for small puffs that looked like cotton wool.

"I'm not sure," she answered slowly. Like was too weak and nebulous a word to describe the tumult of emotions he stirred within her.

"I usually inspire very definite opinions, and sometimes extreme emotions in the people I meet, there is no in-between with me." He frowned, but she could see that the expression was more ironic rather than angry. "I hope you're not simply being polite?"

"I wouldn't insult you by being polite," Lavina retorted. "I'm simply being honest and reserving judgment."

"I should be very grateful, I'm sure."

"You're welcome." She responded crisply.

"Here we are."

Giorgio swung the helicopter around and down in a shallow dive. As Lavina followed his pointing finger, she noticed the unmistakable silhouette of the Galu Kinondo beach strip and to its left some incredible houses.

"This is one of my favourite projects. I finished it last year."

Lavina counted eight luxury homes set some distance apart amid landscaped gardens surrounded by trees culled to admit light, while preserving as much privacy as possible. What drew her attention, as usual, were the private strips of beaches running through every property.

"The houses are built on a south-facing slant and are designed with the top storey set back from the bottom to allow for a balcony cum verandah running the full width of the house. The same also applies to some beach hotels I've designed, so that the guests can have a sea view. The owners of the homes can also watch the sun rise and set all year round, if they feel inclined to do so." Giorgio explained.

"They look like the kind of places advertised on the most expensive of magazines like Homes Kenya and Prime Homes," Lavina murmured, trying to compare such developments in opulence to the squalid villages surrounding them with their conspicuous coconut frond thatches, stippled in poverty.

She gave up. Thinking of the recent economic survey report released by the Ministry of Planning. The five per cent growth in the economy seemed contained to certain quarters only. There was no comparison, none whatsoever. There was too much poverty against backdrops of opulence.

"How much would one cost?"

"To build or to buy?"

"To buy."

"Upwards of one hundred million Kenyan shillings," Giorgio's broad shoulders moved under his polo shirt expressively, "depending on the state of the real estate market at the time of purchase."

Lavina's mouth opened wide as she swivelled around in silent shock despite the seat straps and headphones. She knew such properties had to be expensive, but a hundred million! He shot her a look of amusement coupled with mild impatience.

"It's not all profit, Lavina. You need to remember that just an acre of land costs forty million and apart from the cost of the land, you get your own title deed, and the actual cost of the building. Plus the fact that the people who buy such properties, or for whom they are designed, usually have very specific instructions they want followed to the letter."

"Pure gold taps and a jacuzzi or sauna in the downstairs loo?" she quipped sarcastically and cynically.

"I'm talking about security." He explained patiently. "Why do you think you occasionally bump into Brad Pitt with Angelina Jolie and Naomi Campbell with Flavio Briatore? And yes, some do ask for gold taps, even extremes of wanting diamond handles." He explained patiently.

"I hope the diamonds are from South Africa and not blood ones from Sierra Leone!" Lavina muttered under her breath. He continued his narrative undeterred.

"The first house to the right is owned by a most prominent politician and cabinet minister. Further down is an American billionaire director of a foreign airline who recently commissioned a new route from Nairobi. Next door is one of the most famous super models of our times. The last in the line was bought by one of the world's top earners in entertainment, or rather pop star, but he occupied it for only a couple of months, before selling it to a former president of a western country.

I'm currently working on developing an estate for an oil sheikh from the Emirates, out near Funzi Island..."

Lavina could barely conceal her audible gasp! Funzi Island, a tiny strip of land alone could cost one up to three hundred million shillings! Lavina just felt her eyes widening at the list, which sounded more and more like the who's who of the world. She'd heard of such tales in Malindi, but not from the horse's mouth, because Giorgio was definitely one of them!

The muscles in Giorgio's denim-clad thighs flexed and bunched as he pressed the rudder pedals to swing the helicopter around again.

"All these people are possible targets for kidnappers, hired assassins and hit-men and even nosy paparazzi, not forgetting the dreaded international terrorists. The very latest in hi-tech alarm systems, everything from electronic eyes to heat sensors, CCTV and laser systems to infrared burglar lights, and electric fences, are installed as standard procedure, not just in the houses, but also in the gardens and around the perimeter of the entire estate. Such people are usually looking for more than a home. They seek peace of mind, and Kenya, especially the coastal towns of Malindi and Watamu, are indeed proving to be a peaceful haven compared to most countries.'

Giorgio lifted the helicopter out of its circling pattern and onto a new course. As the silence lengthened, she glanced across at him.

"Aren't you going to ask me what I think?"

He shook his head. "No."

"Why not?"

"I don't need to. Outspoken as you are, if you thought my developments are an eyesore, or worse, a blot on your country's beautiful landscape, I know you wouldn't hesitate to tell me so. But if you find my projects, or rather work, pleasing to look at, then I've proven my point and I rest my case."

Lavina's lips tightened. He was so, so... arrogant! Yes that was the word, so sure of himself!

A sudden gust of wind blew the helicopter sideways and though Giorgio quickly corrected its course, Lavina's stomach felt as though it was still at the back of her throat! In a few seconds, a jagged silver-white flash of lightning split the dark tumbling mass of cloud in front of them. Moments later, a menacing rumble vibrated through the helicopter and a gut-wrenching spasm of fear clutched at Lavina's insides and made her clench her hands in her lap. Her mouth was dry and she couldn't swallow.

Staring straight ahead and flinching as another lightning flash momentarily blinded her, she sensed rather than saw Giorgio's quick glance of concern cast her way.

"There's nothing to worry about." He reassured her.

"O – of – of – c – c – course not." She stammered, agreeing yet not believing him for one moment.

She had seen the wreckage of a helicopter at a crash scene last year, right here in Malindi. It was a high profile case involving some Italians with diplomatic immunity. Media coverage had been rife with headlines about cocaine and heroine and an under-age local girl who had perished in the tragic crash, despite UNICEF's calls to stamp out the vice of young girls dropping out of school to engage in the sex trade. She could still picture the smouldering ashes and metal, the screams of anguish from the wreckage engulfed in flames, and shouts for help. No one had been able to help the unfortunate victims because they were strapped to their seats and unable to unbuckle themselves.

A storm was about to break and here they were inside a plane made up mostly of metal, and they both knew that metal is a good conductor of electricity. Yet he was telling her that there was nothing to worry about.

There was a trickling sensation on her forehead, and when she rubbed at it, her fingers came away with icy perspiration. She was now sweating profusely. She had been in planes in bad weather, but never in a helicopter in a freak storm! Terror loomed large like a great black hellhole ready to devour her. It was taking every ounce of willpower she possessed to resist it. She was holding herself so tightly that every muscle trembled with the effort.

The thunder didn't just rumble. It crackled, drowning the muffled roar of the helicopter's motor, deafening in spite of the headphones. Lavina gasped and shut her eyes, but opened them again immediately. There was nowhere to run. She was trapped. She remembered the scene of the accident again.

It had happened in bad weather. She remembered how the helicopter had burst into flames... Now it seemed she was going to suffer the same fate.

The hysterics took over. She started to giggle. This couldn't be happening. It was coincidence gone mad, something out of a sad comedy or sitcom, a twist in the tale of those confusing South American and Mexican soap operas which had many a Kenyan housewife in their grips, a saga gone awry. She started getting more and more hysterical, laughing uncontrollably.

"Stop that!" Giorgio's voice was sharp. "Lavina! Nothing is going to happen. You're quite safe."

She gulped hard, choking back the threatening hysteria. With all her heart, she wanted to believe him. She willed the histrionics to depart.

As if to mock his words, the sky erupted and exploded in a cataclysm and apocalypse of colour, light, and noise, a cacophony of sound, a dazzling kaleidoscope... The helicopter suddenly rocketed skyward, tossing like a leaf on the turbulent air currents preceding the storm, and then seemed to dip into an air-pocket.

Lavina caught her breath, terrified, her mouth opening in a silent scream. The microphone, being an impediment, or so she thought, however, magnified her undignified shriek. Then, without warning, the helicopter dropped like a stone from the air-pocket back to normal altitude. A strangled cry tore itself from her throat. Was that bloodcurdling scream hers?

She started thinking of her family back in Kericho (tea-growing zone in Kenya's highlands). In case of an accident they would wonder what she had been doing in a helicopter with a mzungu (Kiswahili term for European/Caucasian), stranger. She started thinking of her three beautiful nieces, they would miss her if she died. She had thought that the condition she had was going to be the death of her! Now here she was, staring at death in a helicopter crash! What irony! If she were to be burnt to ashes, her mother, who was from a different tribe and ethnic group to her father's, would insist on visiting the crash scene and carrying a handful of soil to take back home and bury so that her daughter's spirit would rest in peace and not haunt them.

Her gaze was fixed on Giorgio, watching his hands and feet on the rudder pedals as he regained control of the machine. His movements were deft, smooth, but restrained. Then she noticed how his thigh muscles bulged and bunched beneath the tight denim cloth, and the sinews in his powerful arms stood out. She realized that those continuous deft adjustments demanded a strength and concentration that she could barely comprehend. Her calm was restored, because then she knew how much it was costing him to even glance from the controls to her face in an effort to try and reassure her.

As another silver-blue and white flash lit up the cabin, he glanced towards her again, the hard white planes of his face sheened with a thin film of sweat.

"Lavina, I promise you, we are not in any danger, but it will take us longer to get back and it's going to be a rather rough ride."

Instead of listening to his gently soothing and calming voice, Lavina was busy mentally picturing another scene. Scorched earth, crumpled metal, desperate screams, raging fire, smouldering ashes and bodies scarred beyond recognition, and wails of shock, grief, sadness and despair on the faces of the gathered crowd and relatives of the victims...

"I've been at the scene of a helicopter crash. The passengers all died." She gasped out.

Now she had brought the root cause of her fear out in the open. Even the relief of saying these words was short-lived as she felt the subsiding hysteria bubbling back to the surface. Her mouth had the metallic taste only terror induces. She cleared her throat, licked her lips and tried to talk, her teeth chattering.

"Please," she begged unable to hide her desperation. "Let's land. I'm sorry, I just can't take any more."

She shook her head, catching her lower lip between her teeth to stop it quivering; instead she drew blood, and felt the salty taste on her tongue! He looked at her for a long moment, as if debating and deliberating on a decision within himself, then he gave her a brief nod of acquiescence and altered course.

Lavina dug her nails into her palms, drawing blood again, and when a few moments later he said, "Not far now," she allowed herself to hope that they would actually touch down in one piece.

Relief left her weak and shaky.

"Where are we going?" she asked. She didn't care as long as she could get off this metallic flying bird and onto beloved solid earth once more.

"You know, I always wondered why the late Pope John Paul the second kissed the ground every time he got off an aeroplane," she said, her tiny voice still tremulous. "I understand only too well now."

There was a hint of sympathy in Giorgio's amused glance.

"I don't think his reason was quite the same as yours *amore mio*." ('My love.')

Pushing the stick forward, he took the helicopter down and they circled over an elegant maisonette set well back from the curve of the road at the end of a long, winding drive. The house was surrounded by terraced lawns which fell away to a thickly wooded boundary. On one of the lower lawns was a circular concrete helipad.

A slanting ray of sunlight shone through a break in the lowering storm clouds, turning all the front windows to shimmering sheets of gold. She glimpsed a swimming pool and a tennis court at the back of the estate, and she could smell the beach, that special peculiar smell only familiar to one who loves and has lived near the sea for some years. She thought that any minute she would see horses cantering up to them, so tranquil it was. The scenery reminded her of the ambience of the exclusive Kentmere Country Club and the Windsor, both in Nairobi, the capital city of Kenya.

"It's beautiful." Lavina peered out of her window. "Which hotel is this? I don't seem to remember seeing one these sides."

"It's not a hotel." Giorgio brought the helicopter down in a sweeping turn and, hovering over the centre of the pad, he set the chopper down lightly.

"This is my headquarters. I decided to fly here. It's nearer than flying back all the way to the airport, as it was unlikely that you'd hold up through the stormy weather."

Removing his headset, he gestured for her to do the same. With the engine switched off, the rotors had stopped spinning and dropped under their own weight.

"You mean you've turned it into offices?" Lavina asked, her voice seeming loud in the sudden but blissful silence.

Giorgio glanced at his Panerai wrist watch and made some entries in two logbooks which he replaced back in a pocket on the cabin door. Opening it, he swung his legs out.

"Only the ground floor. I've converted the rest into my penthouse."

He was already lifting the basket and cooler from the back.

"We'd better get inside before the rain starts. Would you mind holding these for a minute please?"

Scrambling out, Lavina took the cooler and picnic basket while he locked the doors of the helicopter. She sensed the presence of discreet security personnel who were almost invisible, and if it weren't for two guard dogs who came up to their master and licked his hands, happily frolicking in between his legs, Lavina would have thought they were alone. Knowing she was a stranger, the dogs jumped around her, sniffing at her legs. Some electronic device whirred and she smiled wryly when she recalled their earlier conversation on security gadgets like infrared and electronic eyes.

Then with a look she couldn't decipher cast her way, he took the basket in one hand, letting her carry the cooler, the mkeka clasped under his arm. He took her elbow with his free hand and propelled her towards the front door, the epitome of Lamu craftsmanship, ornately carved Mbambakofi wood and Boriti (Mangrove poles).

Chapter 9

Excuse me for a few minutes, I want to check and see if I've received any mail. Please feel welcome and at home." Giorgio said, leading the way into a small but well-equipped office.

Through the doorway she glimpsed a PC, a fax machine and some other office equipment. She walked further down the hall. A hint of perfume mingled with a flowery, pleasant smell lingered in the air, though there was no one else in the room. She looked around trying to locate the origin of the scent when she noticed the source.

Her eyes were drawn to a vase of red roses standing on one corner of the dining table. It was her soapstone vase. The one he had picked up at the Munges' the other night. She felt an unexplainable prickle of excitement slide up her spine.

There was something blatantly wrong, though, about the vivid splash of the flowers. Lavina sensed that there was something more to their presence than the mere adding of a human touch to a drab hallway, a small potted plant like potpourri would have achieved that. The thought dampened her spirits, though she didn't know why. Giorgio's voice interrupted her train of thought.

"Lavina?"

"Yes?" Lavina turned her back to the flowers, trying to tame her wayward thoughts.

"You were fast." She continued, looking at him quizzically.

"I know new technology takes a while to catch on in some parts of the world, but surely you've heard of electronic mail? Otherwise shortened to email?" he asked sarcastically.

"Of course," Lavina retorted, "I saw your computers. We're not exactly stuck in a time warp here. I meant that you finished so soon, and anyway I don't see why you need all these gadgets here."

Giorgio threw back his head and laughed. Lavina's gaze was drawn up to his thick strong neck, to the dark hair curling at the base of his throat. She recalled how, plastered flat by seawater, the same dark curly hair had covered his taut belly and disappeared beneath his minuscule swimming trunks. Disturbed, she thrust the memory away.

"Oh Lavina! What will it take to convince you? Of course I need all these hi-tech gadgets. I'm running a multi-million Euro business, not some backwater operation. The most up-to-date communication systems are an absolute necessity." His teeth gleamed very white in the gloom of the gathering storm.

She glanced away. Why did such minor, petty and trivial details about him keep on creeping and intruding on her subconscious?

"Competition is fierce. Instant access to information is vital, especially as I have several projects in various stages of development at any one given time. You can add to that the government's Dongo Kundu (red soil) project."

"In that case," she began, and quickly broke off. She wanted to ask him why, if the demands on his time were so many, he was devoting or rather wasting, a whole day entirely to her.

"Yes?" he prompted.

Lavina shook her head. "Nothing. It doesn't matter."

As she watched him stride across the room to draw the drapes on the French windows, she felt weighed down with hopelessness. Would there ever be anything in common between them? It wasn't that she felt inferior in any way, she was used to affluence, and there was a time she once positively wallowed in it, but had never let it go to her head. Yet his life seemed to be on a completely different scale and tangent from hers.

Still holding the emails he had just printed and facsimile papers he had taken from his office, he beckoned Lavina to follow him. The second office was much larger and contained the latest in computers, photocopiers, as well as state-of-the-art architectural drawing boards. Her attention was caught by the large coloured photographs and prints adorning the walls, all framed and protected by non-reflective glass. They showcased aerial views of various developments, some of which she recognized, having flown over them that very day. Some unfinished architectural drawings were mounted on easels.

"Well?" Giorgio demanded as she moved along them. "How do you rate me? Do I qualify as the epitome of architecture?"

"You have more artistic vision than I credited you with. It is beyond my expectations, and though obviously the whole idea is to make money, at least you appear to give further value." She concluded condescendingly.

His eyebrows rose and one corner of his mouth twitched in a mocking grin.

"What a generous assessment." he said sarcastically.

Lavina turned away, ostensibly to examine the rest of the cool, high-ceilinged room, but in fact to hide her expressive face from him, because when he looked at her like that her knees turned weak. She tried to imagine the offices during the weekdays, humming with concentrated activity as designers, architects and quantity surveyors planned and costed the transformation of more acres of redundant arid and semi-arid farmland into carefully landscaped developments of luxury homes. All under the leadership and tutelage of this frighteningly charismatic man.

Who did the perfume lingering in the air belong to? Who had put the flowers in the vase? That was definitely a lady's touch. Conscious of his following gaze, she crossed the room to a large table which held a beautifully constructed miniature three-dimensional scale model of part of a bridge at sea connecting a mainland and an island.

"What is this for?" She asked.

Studying the model, she heard rather than saw Giorgio's approach. He stopped just behind her left shoulder. So sharp and acute were her senses attuned to him that she could feel his body heat emanating from him, though he was not touching her. The musky scent of his sweat triggered off a jolt of response in her own body and her heartbeat quickened.

"A visual aid for the Mombasa (largest port city on Kenya's coast) City Council and the local government ministry's Planning Department." His hot breath fanned her neck. "I'm trying to sell them the idea of a bridge instead of a tunnel for Likoni. The land earmarked for that project borders on an expansive area of extremely outstanding natural beauty with schools and hospitals. Personally, I think they should make sure that the project doesn't detract from all this."

Lavina stared at the model again. No wonder it had looked vaguely familiar. So it was the Kenyan South Coast, the project which was stirring up a lot of controversy and was the cause of much hype and hullabaloo. With every nerve-end screaming at his closeness, Lavina stared blindly in front of her.

"It's very impressive. But, don't you think I should be going home now?"

"I thought you were scared of flying through the raging storm." Something in his voice brought her head around quickly. "And please don't suggest driving, because I hate driving through such foul weather, I'd rather fly." He added.

She stared at him.

"Is that an ultimatum or have we reached an impasse? Because I definitely want to go home, I can call Capital Cabs to…" Before she could finish talking, and as if to add weight to his objection, thunder rumbled across the sky, making the windows vibrate. Lavina jumped. His gaze held hers.

"We'll see about it tomorrow." He paused, his half-smile tinged with irony, "when we take you home."

Her gaze flickered up at him once more, her blood running cold as realization dawned and the full impact and significance of his words struck her like a blow. If he was going to take her home tomorrow, then it meant that she had to spend the night here, in his home.

It was impossible! Out of the question! She hurriedly opened her mouth to tell him so, and just as quickly shut it again. How could she object when she had been the one pleading with him to land at once and not attempt the journey back to the airport?

"Did you say something?" Giorgio enquired, and beneath the silky softness of his voice she detected undertones of cold steel. Was it a determination of sorts? Lavina shook her head in answer to his question.

"Then if there is nothing else…?"

"I've seen enough, thank you." She spoke through clenched teeth.

She did not think she could trust herself to stay under the same roof with him feeling the way she did about him. She felt like bursting into a tirade of accusations and tantrums, but she couldn't, it would be so uncouth and immature. She tried to calm herself again by imagining the pictures she had just seen. She stared at a half-finished painting of the deep sea with Vasco Da Gama's famous pillar in the distance, set up on an easel. So he was also an artist? And a lover and collector of art too, it seemed. She noticed an awesome Jak Katarikawe abstract on one wall. Suddenly his voice interrupted her train of thought.

"You seem surprised, Lavina. And yes, to answer your unasked question, I paint and draw. My use of color tends to be intuitive. I'm currently experimenting and trying to come up with colors that are not obvious. You can decipher my taste from the paintings you see hung here. Peter Elungats' paintings of women. Beautiful. Justus Kyalo's abstracts. Captivating."

She had been surprised by the superior quality of the developments he had shown her, but that surprise had reluctantly turned to genuine admiration. Yet if she openly acknowledged his excellence, it would puff up his already over-bloated ego.

"Then we may as well go upstairs." He gestured towards the front door. "The penthouse has its own entrance around the side of the flat. I try to keep my business life and private life separate, though, unfortunately, that isn't always possible. Just the way it's always hard trying to separate the selfless from the self-absorbed."

What was she supposed to make of that? Lavina wondered as their footsteps crunched on the gravel drive. Was he openly spending time with her because there was something he wanted? People were bound to intimate likewise if they started becoming an item. No wonder the Giorgio Santini of Santini Developments was known as a hard and shrewd man, his business acumen notwithstanding. He gave nothing away, and had a positive knack for knocking his adversaries off-balance or catching them flat-footed.

She wished he hadn't brought her here though. If it was a compliment, showing her where and how he lived, he was bound to have an ulterior motive, and with so powerful an attraction, yet so much uncertainty, the tension was exhausting.

On the other hand, she had to admit honestly that she couldn't have handled flying head-on into the breaking storm. Glancing sideways at Giorgio, she caught him watching her with the same unfathomable expression she had glimpsed several times during the past couple of days when he thought she was not looking at him.

The coastal air was heavy and sultry, the rumbling thunder and occasional flickers of lightning adding to the electric awareness that crackled between them like a high-voltage current, dewing her skin with perspiration and making her shirt cling.

As he unlocked the front door, Lavina loosened her hair from the confines of the pony-band and followed him up the wide, curving staircase with mahogany bannisters, past tall windows that looked out onto sweeping lawns and towering trees, into a large high-ceilinged day room.

"Oh my!" She drew in her breath, her eyes widening as she looked around. An emerald green and gold Chinese rug lay on the gray-green Persian carpet in front of a white marble fireplace. On either side of a Meru (District in the hinterland of Kenya which produces strong oak trees) oak coffee-table were two roll-backed black leather settees strewn with hand-made throw cushions whose presence invited relaxation.

An antique glass-frosted bookcase stood between French windows curtained in pale olive green brocade. She hardly noticed the state-of-the-art flat plasma screen home theatre almost covering an entire wall, but her eyes as usual were drawn to the art.

Gilt-framed paintings and groups of prints hung on the peach-cream walls, and in each corner an arched alcove containing a variety of *objets d'art* glowed softly with concealed lighting.

"Oh my, what?" Giorgio enquired, amused as he touched a hidden switch in one alcove and strains of piped jazz floated into the room. Looking around her, Lavina shrugged helplessly.

"It's so... so big, you could probably fit the whole of my cottage in here, and yet it's – "

She stopped abruptly.

"Go on. Yet it's what?" He prompted softly. She glanced at him, wary, suspicious.

"Tell me," he insisted. She turned, surveying the whole room once more.

"All this space and elegance could be very intimidating, but it isn't." she stated.

"You sound surprised," he observed dryly.

"I am," she admitted, albeit reluctantly. "I certainly didn't expect such a... a... relaxed atmosphere."

"It is my home." He pointed out. "What exactly did you expect?" He demanded curiously.

Lavina gazed around her.

"I don't know, but not this. Not the sort of place that looks like a snap out of a magazine advertising real estate, yet makes you feel like kicking off your shoes, sprawl on the rug with a book or your favourite music and unwind from the pressures of the day."

"Why shouldn't I need to unwind, just like anybody else with a *buon libro?*" ('good book')

"You're not," Lavina lost for words shrugged helplessly again, "just anybody else." She blurted it and then realized her mistake too late.

He continued to gaze at her, his expression unreadable once more.

Lavina turned away, her wariness returning.

"Well, you did ask." She told him defensively. His slow smile made her heart flip over and slip into overdrive. Again.

"That's quite a compliment."

"It's a statement of fact." She responded crisply. The last thing she wanted was for him to think she was trying to butter him up.

Then she caught sight of two ebony carvings of Maasai morans standing side by side on the centre shelf of the nearest alcove. She moved closer. She could recognize her art anywhere. As if reading her mind, he said:

"Those are yours. I got them from Tim and Lynne. By the way, the Mombasa City Council, due to the coming IAAF World Cross Country Championships to be held here in Africa for the first time ever next year, is seeking an exceptional artist to design some animal sculptures for the City Beautification Program. The slogan is Cross Country Comes Home. Why don't you submit a proposal?"

Glancing at him, she indicated the carvings generally.

"I have told you before, my motive is not monetary gain or prestige or recognition. Anyway, I don't suppose you've had time yet to contact the person you said was to —"

He came over to stand beside her, and immediately her pulse rate went a notch higher.

"As a matter of fact I met with Bjorn yesterday. He's the chap I mentioned." Lavina didn't try to hide her amazement.

"How on earth did you manage that? I mean, it was only yesterday."

Giorgio shrugged. "He had to come down here from London on some other business. He gave me a call and I asked him to come and have a look at your soapstone vase sculpture and the two Maasai morans I have here. I must say as I expected, he was suitably impressed. He has this great idea. He wants to —" He stopped suddenly and looked away.

"He wants to what?" Lavina demanded.

"No." Giorgio shook his head. "It's too early. I think it's better not to say anything yet until he's sure he can fix it."

"Fix what?" Lavina grabbed his arms, feeling her own hands tingle as she sensed the strength in the corded muscles beneath the warm skin. "Giorgio, for heaven's sake, you can't drop hints like that and then leave me in suspense. Tell me!"

He grinned down at her. "Alright, alright, unhand me lady."

Embarrassed, she released him as though she had been stung.

"Look at this." He held out his white forearms, though tanned, for her inspection. "If *buona memoria* ('Good memory') serves me right, *mi ricordo* ('I remember') first it was scratches out at sea. Now, fingerprint marks." He mocked her.

"If you don't hurry up and tell me," she warned, glaring at him, trying to ignore the hot, breathless feeling she was experiencing, caused by the laughter dancing in his eyes, "you'll get more than scratches and fingerprint marks, I'll – "

"Or you'll what?" he challenged softly.

"I'll... I'll... I'll probably... throw one of those wooden morans out of your closed French windows!" She finished in a rush, pouting petulantly. His eyes didn't leave hers.

"Tut… tut… all that frustration." He tutted and clicked his tongue jokingly. The deliberate double meaning in his choice of words did not escape Lavina.

"Just tell me. Pleaaase?" she begged.

"Bjorn owns one of the most prestigious art galleries in London. He organizes exhibitions for upcoming artists and sculptors whose pieces are becoming collectable. He said that he will try and see if he can slot you in and arrange a stand for you in his next showing. Mind you, only the elite of society visit his gallery, like the Prince of Wales, the Queen Mother, and the likes. Of course, he'll need more than these three items…"

"That's no problem," she interrupted quickly, "I've got several at home, and I'm sure given a couple of weeks I'll be able to make more. I can also borrow some exceptional ones I've given to a few friends."

An exhibition! In London! When she had only dreamt of trade fairs in neighbouring countries and within the African continent, which in itself was hard due to financial constraints. Incandescent with joy, without thinking, Lavina flung her arms around his neck.

"Oh! Giorgio, Thank you! I didn't think you were serious. I never expected anything like this."

"Nor did I." He murmured softly, the double meaning creeping in again, and lowering his head, he covered her mouth with his own.

As she caught her breath in surprise, he imprisoned her face in his hands. Her lips already parted in shock, offered no barrier to his gently probing tongue, and suddenly the lightning seemed to be inside her, tingling like pins and needles along every nerve.

His kiss deepened, grew more demanding, its urgency re-igniting her own need and hunger. The warm roughness of his hands on the small of her back, the pressure of his lips, the man-odour of him went to her head like champagne, with the same dizzying effect.

Clinging to the corded muscle and hard bones of his shoulders, Lavina felt something open inside her, something she had suppressed for a long time… something like a blossoming flower, and she understood for the first time her power as a woman who really wanted a particular man. The realization awed and thrilled her. Suddenly it was no longer enough to simply receive. She wanted to meet Giorgio's male strength with her feminine subtlety, and give him the same pleasure and excitement that his touch re-kindled in her. She didn't know him, but now she wanted to know him. She relied on instinct to guide her, and realized then that intuition really is the essence of a woman.

Loosening her grip, she slid her fingertips over his neck and threaded them through his hair in a gentle caress as her body relaxed, pliant against his. Something was wrong. She felt him change. As tension left her, so it grew in him. A split second later he grasped her wrists and pulled them roughly from around his neck. Stepping back, he deliberately distanced himself from her.

Moist-lipped and heavy-lidded, dazed by feelings too powerful to conceal and control, let alone contain, Lavina gazed at him, bewildered. It also didn't help that his soft, almost inaudible groan did not match the harsh expression on his face, or the rigidity of a stance that hinted at a fierce inner battle for control, of which he seemed to be a sore loser—

he didn't seem to be taking it too well.

Releasing her, he turned away, crouching to pick up the several sheets of communication paper that he had let fall.

"*Mi dispiace*. Please accept my apologies." He said formally as he straightened up.

"What for?" Confusion clouded Lavina's mind.

"I don't really know what's happening to me – what you're doing to me. But whatever it is, I think it's making me fall madly in love with you. I want to do the right thing. The honourable thing, but I don't think I can handle this."

He raked his free hand through his hair in that certain expression of frustration that she was fast becoming familiar with. He shuffled the papers in his hands into some semblance of order, avoiding her eyes.

"I sense there is something amiss here. I feel like I'm taking advantage of you. One minute you are holding back and the next you're willing, but I can't tell why. Will you tell me the reason?" he asked.

"But you're not taking advantage of …"

He held up his hand and interrupted her.

"I was out of line there. I shouldn't have kissed you."

He glanced at the messages in his hands once more and his remoteness pierced her like a double-edged blade.

"Giorgio —"

She smiled at him courageously, willing him to smile back, but he did not reciprocate. She didn't understand what just happened. The warm closeness had gone. It was as if he had pushed her out of the door practically into the raging storm outside and slammed the heavy Lamu carved door shut in her face, or turned off a light switch.

"Just leave it Lavina. Look, there are one or two things I have to see to. Business matters that can't wait. Why don't you go and have a shower? I'm sure you'll feel more comfortable." He told her.

Logic dictated that he wanted her out of the way for a while. That much was plain. And if she was not to make a complete fool of herself, she would be wise to do as he suggested. Every minute she spent with him made it harder to remember that there was no future in their relationship.

"Thank you," she managed, her throat constricting stiffly with the pain of suppressed tears. His suggestion was strangely intimate, considering they had known each other for less than four days, but the first dramatic moment of their epic encounter had warned her that Giorgio Santini cared little for convention.

She followed him through a short hallway and along the landing. The way he moved, even in jeans and a polo shirt, he had presence, along with a self-possession which set him apart, and when he so chose, made him completely unapproachable. He opened a door and stood back, refusing to meet her pleading gaze.

"This is the guest bedroom. Please help yourself to fresh towels from the linen cupboard. You can take your time. There's no hurry."

He was already walking away as Lavina thanked him again. Closing the door, she flipped the catch to lock it and covered her face with her hands. The tears she had been fighting welled up and spilled over, trickling through her fingers. Suppressed sobs racked her, and her chest hurt with the effort of holding them in. But pride insisted that she make no sound.

Oh God! How were people in her situation expected to deal with their sexual urges? She had to tell him. On no account must he hear it as a whispered rumour from another source. It was obvious that he found her physically attractive and sexually arousing.

But that was all. And with no emotional involvement on his part, she didn't think she wanted to go on this way.

Lavina wiped her eyes with the heels of her hands. Despite what rumours Giorgio may come to hear about her, she had a feeling he was an honourable man, but the thought did little to soothe the pain of his rebuff. Because it wasn't just her body he had awakened. Love was a word she was wary of. She was not even sure that such an emotion existed, especially for her. She had been through so much in the recent past. And rather than risk rejection, especially in her condition, she had shied away from any such potentially explosive situations which threatened her emotional composure and well-being, like this one.

That was until three days ago; until a cruelly ironic twist of fate or destiny had sent Giorgio Santini crashing headlong into her life. She would never forget that day at sea… and then on the beach. When was the right time to tell someone? Was there ever a right time? She wondered what others in her situation would do.

Her head ached from confusion and hurt. A cool refreshing shower might erase the feeling of pressure. Drawing in a deep, tremulous breath, she walked into the bathroom.

Lavina wiped her eyes again and turned to look around her.

Glazed tiles of opalescent turquoise lined the shower cubicle and surrounded the huge bath. A toning carpet covered the floor, and thick white fluffy towels hung on a heated rail.

Kicking her sneakers and socks into a corner, she stripped naked. She adjusted the shower to lukewarm and stepped into the cubicle, closing her eyes as the needle-sharp sprays washed over her clammy body, all the time trying to hold her hair out of the range of the jets of water, as she couldn't find a shower cap.

A shelf inside the shower cubicle held soap and shampoo, both scented with the same fresh fragrance she had smelled on him when he'd come to pick her up that morning. How long ago that seemed, and how much had happened since then.

She stared at the bottles of colognes lined in the cabinet. She knew they cost a fortune. 'Aramis life' by Aramis, 'M7' by Yves Saint Laurent and Hugo Boss… And in the adjacent laundry room she had just now caught glimpses of shirts with the Van Laack label and rows upon rows of twelve-eyelid laced designer Fatelli Rosetti shoes in the rack by the landing. What was she getting herself into?

Anguish stabbed again, and she bit her lip hard. She would not cry. If she needed a reminder that emotions equalled pain, then surely this was it. She could not, would not, and must not allow this to get out of hand.

As she absentmindedly rinsed the lather from her body the room was suddenly lit by a brilliant lightning flash, followed spontaneously by ear-splitting claps of thunder. The resultant vibrating aftermath startled

Lavina, making her jump violently. Soapy water stung her eyes and she gasped, shutting them tight, and swept the plastic shower curtain aside. The smooth silver base of the towel rack was already slippery with lather and shampoo, and she stumbled around blindly, trying not to lose her balance, the soap stinging her eyes. She grabbed for a towel and, with her already precarious balance, her feet shot from under her on the wet tiles and with a terrified scream of fear, she fell to the floor.

As she sprawled on her back, shocked, winded and dazed, half-in and half-out of the shower, the door slammed forcefully against the wall and Giorgio burst in. Turning off the shower, he dropped to his knees beside her.

"*Mamma Mia*! Are you hurt?" he demanded harshly.

"I'm not exactly comfortable." Lavina winced. Pushing her now dripping hair back with a trembling hand, she glimpsed Giorgio's face and was startled by his pallor. The skin around his mouth was taut with strain.

"I meant, have you broken anything? And I'm talking about bones and sprains not the shower curtain or towel rail for heavens sake!"

She made a tiny negative movement with her head.

"I don't know yet, but I – I don't think so." She rubbed her streaming eyes with her fingertips.

"You're crying. You must be hurt." His voice was hard, accusing.

She shook her head again. "No. I got soap into my eyes that is all." Why was he so angry?

"Are you sure?"

"As far as I can tell, I'm okay, but I won't know for certain until..." She started to push herself up.

"Take it slowly." Sliding his arm under her shoulders, Giorgio lifted her carefully to her feet.

"Ouch!!" Lavina bit her lip. "I'm so sorry. I've had this thing about storms and lightning ever since I was baby. A sort of phobia."

"For God's sake!" he snapped, "You don't have to apologize. Just stop trying to hurry."

Catching her breath, Lavina gradually straightened up, mentally exploring her bruised and shaken body as she did so.

"I'm sure nothing's broken." Gripping his arm she reached her full height, light-headed from a mixture of shock and relief. "I expect by tomorrow I'll be stiff and aching all over. You'll probably have to fold me up into two to get me into the car and take me home!"

Letting out her breath in a shaky rush, she grinned up at him mischievously, unaware of how stunning she looked… but then their eyes met and locked. Seconds ticked by as awareness, recognition and memory flashed between them with all the dazzling speed of the lightning outside. Lavina felt her whole body tense with awareness. This was the second time he had rescued her, but now there was not even a bikini bottom to protect her modesty! Here she was, naked in his arms only minutes after he'd made it painfully clear that she was confusing him, and he wanted no further physical contact with her.

Oh God! What if he thought she had done this on purpose? Lavina shrank away from him, her stinging eyes widening.

"Please," she began urgently. "You mustn't think — "

"*Dio Santo*!" ('My God!') "For crying out loud! What the hell is it with you?" he grated, not letting her finish, and his arm tightened, imprisoning her as she tried to pull away. His eyes had a dangerous glitter and a muscle twitched at a point of his jaw.

"Have you got some death wish where water is concerned?" He continued in a harsh voice.

"I didn't get that muscle-pull at sea on purpose, and this fall is no laughing matter either, the lightning and thunder shocked me. Anyway, you shouldn't be in here, I locked the door." She said indignantly.

"*Non me ne importa un cavolo*! ('I couldn't care less!') Then thank your lucky stars, I've just broken the door!" He retaliated. "What if you'd really hurt yourself or knocked your head on the bathtub and been unconscious?" he almost shouted.

"At l-least I'd h-have b-been unconscious in p-private." She retorted her teeth beginning to chatter from the cold.

"God! You're impossible." He muttered.

As they both simultaneously grabbed for the same towel from the heated rail to cover her, his hand accidentally brushed against her breasts. They both froze. Lavina's sharp intake of breath echoed in the pregnant silence, saying it all.

But just then the lightning flickered again, breaking the spell. The moment passed. As another clap of thunder reverberated across the sky, Giorgio thrust the towel into her hands, turned on his heels abruptly, and strode out.

Chapter 10

Dressed once more in the clothes she wore earlier, her hair wet because of the fall and now rubbed so fiercely that it was almost dry, Lavina yearned for her handy portable hair dryer. She gathered her courage and returned to the living room. As she closed the door behind her, Giorgio emerged from what she assumed to be the kitchen, carrying a tray set with tea cutlery, a plate of sandwiches, some bread rolls and pots of various spreads, including her favourite smooth Skippy peanut butter.

He gestured towards one of the settees and, as she sat, he settled himself opposite the oak coffee table between them.

Glancing at the magazines on the coffee table, she realized what a serious reader he was. Spoilt for choice, she flipped through his taste of magazines: African Business, Time magazine, Focus on Property–Kenya's Complete Property Guide, Newsweek, Economist, Architect's Own, National Geographic, GQ, Men's Health... Glancing at his CD rack, she realized that they seemed to have the same taste for jazz and Afro-fusion: Achieng Abura, Joseph Helon, Femi Kuti, Angelique Kidjo, Eric Wainaina, Hugh Maskhela, Youssou N'dour, Salif Keita, Ismael Lo... On the opposite wall from ceiling to floor was a bookcase lined with books on architecture and she also glimpsed titles by Paulo Coelho and Khaled Hosseini who were some of her favorite authors.

She fidgeted, looking for an opening. How should she start this conversation? Taking a deep breath, Lavina tilted her chin a fraction higher.

"Giorgio, I— I— don't you… I mean, you seem to find me attractive, but don't you like me?" She blurted out. Pushing aside the tray, Giorgio straightened up slowly.

"Please. I'd rather know the truth." She insisted quietly.

Dipping his head in acknowledgement, Giorgio looked directly at her.

"The truth? *Ti voglio bene* ('I like you')." He murmured so softly that she barely heard him. "*Si. Si.* Yes, I like you. But that's not what you're asking is it?"

Swallowing, she raised her eyes and met his narrowed blue gaze. His expression was unreadable, giving no clue to his thoughts. She had no choice but to plough on in relation to his question. She had to know.

"When you touch, hold me, and kiss me, I know you experience the same feelings. I sense that you like me, so…" Lavina clasped her hands tightly together. "…I mean why do you push me away?"

Suddenly his eyes were azure glittering slits in a mask of anger.

"Are you serious? I seem to want something more than just a casual fling. Though it will fall into place soon, *a tempo debito*." ('all in good time' or 'everything has its time') "But I also sense that you're holding something back and I want to know what it is."

Giorgio pushed his hands through his hair, the familiar gesture mirroring his frustration.

"I find you extremely attractive. There's something very special about you," he broke off abruptly and Lavina struggled to contain her startled joy at his admission. And then suddenly, surprise lifted Giorgio's eyebrows and he shook his head, his expression perplexed.

"You are certainly different and unique."

"What do you mean?" she asked warily. His lips curled in cynical amusement, but his gaze was still perplexed.

"You haven't hinted at or mentioned love."

She moistened her lips. If only he knew.

"What's that got to do with anything? You've already made it clear that you have no time for the games that most people play."

"Well, nor have I, and talking about love when the issue is physical attraction is one of those games."

Crossing one leg over the other, Giorgio leaned back studying her, his eyes as usual veiled and hooded so she could not read his expression. Typical of him.

"Don't you believe in love? And another question I want to pose to you is, why do you think a man is attracted to a woman and vice versa?"

Lavina shrugged, the movement a little too flippant, revealing rather than concealing her deep hurt. She had suffered so much in the past in the name of love.

"It would be stupid, not to mention self-destructive, to believe in something which only leads to grief and despair. I should know. I've had my share and dose of it. There's no way I'm going to self-destruct now. And to answer your latter question, attraction between a man and woman, I bet, is nature's way of ensuring the continuing propagation of the species."

Giorgio's eyes were twin lasers laying bare her very soul, but she didn't flinch, though inside she was shaking. Should she tell him now? Why was she parrying with semantics and superlatives?

Uncrossing his legs, Giorgio rested his elbows on his knees, a frown creasing his forehead.

"So what do you propose?" He paused, clearly choosing his words with utmost care, "Because Lavina, while a man is quite capable of separating sex from love, a woman attempting to do the same is most likely to end up an emotional cripple. And please spare me the feminist crap!"

Lavina looked at him.

"Breaking news Mr. Santini! Women in the twenty-first century are way past such sentiments! And isn't that being chauvinistic? And presumptuous? Anyway, how would you know? You've never been a woman."

"True." He conceded. "But I've had plenty of opportunity for observation." With a regretful sigh, Giorgio shook his head. "I don't want to pre-empt what you want to say, but after all is said and done, I have this feeling that I'm going to be deeply involved here. Anyway," the merest suggestion of a smile hovered at the corners of his mouth, "I want neither of us to feel used."

Lavina's throat was paper-dry. On the surface it looked as though he was pulling away again, but with Giorgio Santini, appearances were all too often deceptive. She licked her lips and tried to swallow the cottony feeling in her throat and saw his gaze follow the movement of her lips and then move to her throat.

"Well, what do you want then?" She queried softly.

Suddenly, he relaxed as if she had asked the million-dollar question he'd been waiting for all along, and, leaning forward, poured milk into the cups. Replacing the jug, he glanced up and his smile sent darts of excitement and anticipation through her.

"You already know the answer to that. A woman always does," he paused, looking directly into her eyes. "Again I'll say *ti voglio*. I really want you, but on my terms, and as I've already mentioned, sooner or later I always get what I want. *Capisce*? ('Understood?')" he asked softly in Italian, and then calmly lifted the teapot.

"How do you like your tea?" he continued smoothly without skipping a beat. They indulged in small talk for a few minutes. Then restlessly, Lavina picked up her cup and lifted it to her lips.

Giorgio Santini was not like most men. She had sensed that from the start and he was confirming it several times over. 'I want neither of us to feel used.' The echo of his words a couple of minutes earlier, with their undertone of irony, brought an involuntary smile to her lips. Wasn't that usually the woman's line? She didn't want to use him. Such a dirty term.

She had met women who were cheats and consummate opportunists who positively thrived on being conniving, cold and calculating, but she had always wondered... did love ever feature in their scheme of things?

She wanted to share and give, as well as receive. She wanted to discover what pleased him. Was this what love meant? Wanting to be with one person above all others, yet scared at the same time? To learn and to discover? To be close to and to trust?

She started thinking of her grandmother up in the highlands in her smoky hut. The now stooped octogenarian had refused to move into the modern brick house she had built for her. Lavina wondered how her granny would have handled herself in such a situation. A generation of yesteryears, raised in a traditional way of rituals, all those taboos and rites, customs, cultures, no modern turmoils and upheavals, yet disciplined and happy.

Oh, how she yearned for her grandmother's wisdom. She remembered the counselling she had gone through. She was a woman of integrity. She was learned and, above all else she, was compassionate and giving. That was what had got her into the medical fraternity in the first place and later into deep trouble in most of her more intimate and personal relationships. She had to tell him. She owed him that, at least, before things got out of hand.

Lavina sat up quickly, forgetting that she was holding her cup and saucer. The hot tea spilt and burnt her hand slightly. She didn't even feel the hot scalding liquid. She felt rather than saw Giorgio's startled movement forward to hand her a napkin. She put her cup and saucer down and hugged her knees.

Body and soul, she ached for him. Was he feeling the same? It was only since meeting him that she had come to realize how lonely she was. She was almost becoming a recluse.

It wasn't lots of people she wanted around her – she was with people everyday. But she was realizing something; it was one special person that she wanted. Him. She now knew that only he had the power to release her heart from its cold, lonely prison; but dare she tell him? What if she confessed and told him what was holding her back? And what if she also acknowledged the other truth? The other damning truth—that she was falling in love with him? Then what?

Her father had rejected her and made sure that his family had no interaction with her, actually ostracising her because of her current condition. She communicated with her mother in secret. What if Giorgio decided he'd made a mistake and he too walked away? If that happened now, she could handle it. Maybe her survival reflexes would come in handy! She was fast becoming an expert at survival tactics.

She knew that once she committed herself, there would be no turning back.

It was a straight choice: honesty and safety geared towards commitment, or the risk of rejection and re-opening of old wounds and a lifetime of regret. Whichever way she chose, either could destroy her completely. It was the typical 'catch-22' situation. She was caught between a rock and a very, very hard brick wall.

What was she to do? She couldn't deny herself anymore. She had never been one to condone masturbation as a way of self-gratification. It felt sort of dirty, although at boarding school a lot of her schoolmates had been hooked on what she saw as a vice.

She was also not into the latest technology of vibrators and sex toys; she considered it too vulgar! She had been told that many in her condition were having normal relationships, with some adjusting for both partners, that is, if you managed to get a willing partner! What was she to do?

She stood up and walked outside to the verandah, which overlooked the beach and sea. The rain was still falling. By unspoken mutual agreement he followed her with a worried look on his face and stood at her shoulder as she watched the tide approaching the dark beach, rippled like silk by the accompanying wind.

She thought of her friend Anne-Marie. She would make a point of calling her tomorrow. She was the only one she could talk to. They had grown up together, had been in boarding school together and also attended the same campus. Now Anne-Marie worked in Nairobi. She thought of the book of Proverbs in the Bible and her favourite verse three in chapter seventeen '…the crucible for silver and the furnace for gold, but the Lord tests the heart…'.

Was God testing her heart? Was He looking over her shoulder to see if she would tell Giorgio the truth? Did she want to be silver or refined gold? Was this her private hell? A sort of perdition? Dare she let herself stay put in the furnace? Would God come to her aid as He had for the Hebrew lads from Israel, Daniel (God is Judge), Hananiah (God has favoured), Mishael (Who is what God is), Azariah (God has helped). Known to most people as Belteshazzar, Shadrack, Meshach and Abednego in the Bible, after their names were changed by the Babylonian chief priest into names of Babylonian idols and gods. Daniel was thrown into the lion's den and the rest into the hot furnace.

They never forgot their true and real identities. Strange how we forget the things that we should not—our own identities. Even more strange how people seek divine intervention where all else fails.

Her friend Anne-Marie was a born-again Christian and had been drumming into her the rewards of turning spiritual… of getting saved. What had she told her about being weighed on the scales and found to be wanting? '*Mene, mene tekel….*' or something like that. Was that in the Book of Kings or Judges in the Old Testament of the Holy Bible? She needed to read her Bible properly. Something to do with Mordecai and the writing on the wall. Oh God! This was hopeless.

"You have a beautiful place. So peaceful." She intoned like a zombie.

As the daylight had faded into the dusk of evening, the rain had settled into a steady downpour, but now it sounded like handfuls of kokoto (gravel used for construction after being mixed with cement, sand and water) hurled against the French windows.

"Lavina," he said softly. She didn't turn to acknowledge his call. She was so quiet, it was worrying him. He turned her around so that she faced him. "Oh Lavina," he murmured shaking his head. "What is this terrible thing that's eating away at your heart? I can see it in your eyes and I know you're hurting."

To her horror, her eyes filled with tears. He was peering into her eyes using the verandah's electric blue luminous fluorescent tube light and the moonlight as well. She started to avert her head, but in a smooth cat-like movement he caught her chin and turned her face towards him. She tried to resist, but he was too strong. She had no strength or will left to fight.

She stood quite still. The betraying drops trembling on her long, but now lowered, eyelashes.

"Look at me," he said. She gave her head a brief negative shake. "Say it Lavina. I want to hear it! What's holding you back?!" He demanded, his voice soft yet at the same time harsh.

Her eyes flew wide open and she wrenched free.

"Please! Go to hell! A different one from the one I'm in right now! You don't know what you're asking me to tell you! I'm not the type of girl who treats my feet to Remron or Clarks designer shoes that cost thirty thousand shillings a pair! We are two very different individuals Giorgio!" she cried.

After she tore herself free from his grasp, he made no effort to touch her, but simply stood, his hands now at his sides.

"Yes I do. We both know that you need to. The words that you tell me now will be your passport to freedom. I may not know what it is exactly, but I know that it's the key to why you're holding back. It doesn't matter how safe or comfortable you make it, a cage is still a cage, gilt-edged or not. It's time you moved out of it. Out of your comfort zone. And it has nothing to do with money or designer outfits. There's something more Lavina, and I intend to find out what it is that you're holding back! Leave the past behind Lavina."

She felt as though she was literally tearing apart inside. She had been made to understand that safety was the only sensible course. Could somebody really still love her if they found out? How could all this emotional upheaval possibly be love? She had known the man only a few days. Just to see him, to be within his magnetic aura, was enough to melt her resolve like cooking fat in a frying pan.

"Oh what a tangled web we weave…" she quoted Shakespeare under her breath.

"My favourite author." He interjected. When he looked into her eyes the way he was doing now, his gaze stripped her soul bare, exposing all her most intimate hopes and fears. She had nowhere to hide.

Something of her agony must have shown on her anguished face, for, reaching out, Giorgio took her hand and drew her gently into the circle of his arms in a gentle hug.

"I'm sorry sweetheart. I shouldn't push you so hard. You'll tell me in your own time when you are ready to confide in me. I'm a selfish bastard and a lousy host. It's just that—" He bit the words off, his frown quickly replaced by a rueful smile. "You must be starving! Come on. Let's have something to eat. We'll talk later."

"Must we?" Lavina pleaded in a small voice. She was grateful for his consideration and thrilled beyond measure by the endearment, sweetheart, but all too aware that this was only a brief respite. It was not in Giorgio Santini's nature to give up or retreat.

"Eat or talk? The answer to both is yes," he said before she had mustered a reply. "Ignoring a problem won't make it go away. Remember, a problem shared is a problem halved? And sometimes even solved?" His tone was final but gentle. "Serious decisions have to be made Lavina."

"I'm… so afraid" was what she meant to say, but couldn't. Instead she said it!! It just slipped out!! Head bent, she said:

"G. I'm - I'm – I'm HIV Positive." She whispered softly yet urgently in a trembling voice.

There was a deathly silence. She pardoned herself mentally for the pun! She caught her breath as her whole body tensed, waiting for his response to her earth-shattering revelation. Or so she thought. You could have heard a pin drop if it wasn't for the sound of the lapping waters from the beach below.

His hand, which had been lifting her hair and lightly massaging her neck and nape, stilled for a millisecond. She knew it was momentary shock, but in the space of a heartbeat he must have regained his composure, for he continued massaging her neck, and lifted her head so he could look into her eyes, his were ever so gentle.

"Are you sure?"

"Yes."

"Lavina. I'd never deliberately hurt you."

She nodded. She believed him. He wasn't a sadist or a masochist, but nor would he live a lie. Somebody famous or infamous once said that to live a lie is to live in the future, but she couldn't remember who it was now.

"So now we'll eat, and don't tell me you're not hungry." He warned as she glanced up at him.

He squeezed her shoulders gently, all the time thinking how, irrevocably, he seemed to be falling deeper and deeper in love with his African princess, and led her into the living room and back to their abandoned meal.

Chapter 11

After switching off the light, Lavina pulled back the curtains as she always did at her place. Lying on her back in the guestroom's vast king-sized Lamu- and Swahili-inspired carved designer bed, she gazed up at the stars in the dark of night through the rain-streaked skylight glass, smiling wryly to herself.

Again, by unspoken mutual agreement, they had changed the subject and talked of other things, the shift from intensely personal topics had eased Lavina's tension.

From the sanctuary of his verandah he had pointed out Sardinia Two. Lavina was shocked! It was amazing that he was actually a few hundred metres away from the wondrous little isle, which enhances its mystery by remaining visible for eight hours in the daytime during low tide and becoming completely submerged during the high tide. At low tide, when visible, it looks like a silver pebble floating in the turquoise water of the vast ocean. Very few locals knew of its existence, and she wondered how much he'd paid for this particular land to have such a spectacular view.

The isle is not even marked on the Kenyan map due to its insignificant, minuscule size.

It is situated twenty kilometres off-shore near Malindi Marine

Park, and is three square kilometres and only accessible by motor boat. Tourists love Sardinia Two because it is unique in several ways. The beach is pristine white and almost spotless! Water surrounding it in the deep sea is a sanctuary to hundreds of different types of fish and other marine life. Italian tourists who were said to have taken an intense interest in the small spit of sand about three decades ago named it Sardinia Two after the Italian island of the same name. No wonder it has now been gazetted as a Marine Reserve.

Later, she had actually laughed until her sides ached at Giorgio's descriptions of his business trips all round the globe—the disasters and triumphs which seemed an inevitable part of his career. He had regaled her with hilarious anecdotes on the antics of his bustling, but lovingly boisterous Italian family over bowls of traditional meals of hot pasta, noodles and spaghetti back home.

Lavina sighed and turned over, punching her pillow into a different shape. Who was she trying to fool? It wasn't because of the rain, or the distant clap of thunder that she couldn't sleep…

His words kept echoing in her mind. '…I want you, but not on your terms… and sooner or later I always get what I want.' And later, after she'd told him of her status, '…I'd never deliberately hurt you.'

She'll have to call her mother tomorrow. This was a triumph. She had actually voluntarily admitted to a man she was attracted to that she was HIV positive. That is, apart from the Munges and her immediate family.

She was forced to admit. She liked him. She liked his dry humour and the way he mocked himself as well as others. Also, despite all her expectations to the contrary, she respected him. He had high standards and refused to compromise. They kept clashing, certainly, but that was to be expected from persons of different temperaments, and she was learning a lot from him.

He was opening her eyes and her mind. Financially they were poles apart, yet they had remarkably similar views on what constituted quality living. Despite the inevitable tension, she enjoyed being with him.

Perhaps 'enjoyed' was the wrong word or too mild a term, because during the time they were apart, she relived every moment they had spent together, like she was doing now, and always looked forward to their next meeting. The more they were together, the more she wanted him to touch her, to fill the newly recognized emptiness at her core and make her complete.

Being close to him made her blood sing. She felt different, vibrant, sensual, more aware of all the subtleties of body language and eye contact she had never noticed before. The one thing she craved most of all was his understanding, and she thought she had seen that in his eyes after she told him of her sero-status.

Surely the pleasure of a physical relationship with no strings attached, no emotional demands or hang-ups was most men's ideal or so she had been told? He had to be different. Just like the way he spoke impeccable English, maybe because of studying in the UK. Yet here in Malindi, they were used to Italians talking in broken English: 'You robba me!' instead of 'You stole from me!' and '*Stupido!*' instead of 'Stupid!', and '*Bandito!*' when referring to thieves. Lavina smiled as she restlessly turned over again.

Turning once more and onto her side, Lavina curled into a ball, drew the sheet over her ears and fell into a fitful sleep thinking of his kiss when he had wished her *della buonatte* (Goodnight).

Chapter 12

It seemed like minutes. Waking with a start, for a moment she didn't know where she was. Realization brought her upright with a jerk, and she winced at the soreness in her back and side. She looked at her watch and grimaced. It was already morning!

Tossing and turning until the early hours, and then dozing fitfully, she had overslept. It was ten minutes to nine! A loud rap on the bedroom door had her grabbing for the sheet, and she realized it was this sound that had woken her.

"Yes?" She croaked.

"Breakfast is ready!" Giorgio called out.

"Give me ten minutes!" She yelled back and crawled stiffly out of bed.

It took nearly double that time. Drying herself and getting dressed drew strong protests from bruised muscles – she was paying dearly for yesterday's fall in the shower.

There was a knock on the door again. She opened it a crack, and Giorgio thrust a white polo shirt through the opening.

"Put this on and no arguments, your tee-shirt must be very dirty by now." That forestalled any protests she was cooking up!

She had to grit her teeth as she combed her hair and plaited it back in one long matuta[27]. She had no intention of facing Giorgio Santini looking less than tidy. As she put on his polo shirt, big as it was, it almost reached her knees, she felt a strange sense of *déjà vu* as his special scent clung to her.

Lavina pulled a face at her reflection. Though the quick shower had refreshed her and given some much needed awakening, it had not erased the tiredness in her eyes, or the fine lines of strain at the corners of her mouth. It would be easier once she was back in her own home with everything familiar around her. She would then have enough privacy to mull over the decision she had made.

A haunted image stared back at her from the mirror.

"Come on girl!" She told her reflection, "You can do better than that. Where is your pride? Your spirit?"

Giorgio was sitting at the breakfast bar that divided the kitchen from the living room studying a report as she walked carefully into the kitchen.

Freshly showered and shaved, his dark hair still wet, he looked cool, formal and devastatingly handsome. Navy blue trousers had replaced yesterday's jeans, definitely a Gianfranco Ferre design judging by it's soft look, a white shirt with a light blue strip, and one of those silk ties which were the current rave countrywide, in a print of pearl gray.

As she hesitated in the doorway absorbing every detail of his appearance to store in her memory, he looked up, and after one swift appraising glance he pointed to the high breakfast bar stool next to him.

"*Buon giornio Lavina. Come stai oggi*? ('Good morning Lavina. How are you doing?') And a double wow! That shirt looks better on you than it does on me, but then anything, even a sack will make you look super!" Before she could think of a rejoinder he continued, "So. How are we today? We look decidedly fragile." He observed.

She started to shrug, which provoked an immediate protest from her bruised back, forcing her to abandon the familiar gesture.

"You've probably got a lot to do today, and I don't want to hold you up so I'm ready to go as soon as—"

"Thank you for your consideration." He inclined his head gravely. "But we are not going anywhere until you've eaten."

"Don't worry about that," Lavina said quickly. "I can have something when I get home."

"Listen Lavina, I don't enjoy cooking, but breakfast is a necessity, so I've become quite an expert." He paused, "the juice is already prepared." He indicated the refrigerator. "If you'll get that out, and while you're at it, get our fish from the freezer. Dinner is on you tonight. I hear you're quite an expert. I'll do the toast. The coffee is ready, and I've got the eggs and some bacon keeping hot."

In spite of her bruises and all the tension bottled inside, Lavina started to laugh.

"You really are out of this world, you're so understanding." She spluttered, shaking her head. "Even after the news I gave you last night you're still incredible towards me."

His eyes narrowed to glittering slits.

"I can be much more than that," he said softly, "as I intend to prove to you in the not too distant future, but first things first. Let's eat. *Bon Apetito.*" he whispered in Italian, wishing her a good appetite.

As Lavina took her first mouthful of crisp, lean bacon and creamy scrambled eggs, she closed her eyes.

"That bad, eh? I'm only an amateur you know."

Lavina swallowed. "Mm...," she nodded, her tone dry, "The way Picasso was only an artist."

Giorgio's eyebrows climbed. "I'm not sure I like the comparison."

"Then stop fishing!" she retorted. "Compliments have to be freely given to be worth anything, and I was about to say, if I'd been given the chance, that these are some of the best scrambled eggs I've ever tasted, and that includes my own."

"Coming from you, that's quite a compliment judging by what I've heard." Giorgio remarked. "Anyway, eat while the food is still hot."

"Yes, sir." But she needed no prompting. The first mouthful had made her realize just how ravenous she was.

"No, thanks." Lavina shook her head moments later as Giorgio offered her the plate for her fourth slice of toast. "I'm full, I'll burst."

She flexed her shoulders carefully and heaved a deep content sigh.

"That was delicious. I rarely have such a breakfast these days. My appetite has gone down. Nowadays I don't eat much in the morning, just a mahamri[28], a salad or small snack will do…"

"Perhaps that's a habit you should reconsider." He suggested as he looked dubiously over her slender figure. "And breakfast is also a time for bonding…." he stressed his double meaning and drained his cup.

"More coffee?" He lifted the jug from its stand.

"I'd love some." She saw him glance at his gold Philip Patek wristwatch. "Are you sure you have time though? There must be things you ought to be doing."

"There are," he agreed seriously, "but you won't let me do them." That double meaning creeping in again! Lavina jerked around to face him.

"Careful," he warned as she winced. "Remember your back."

"It's not easy to forget," she muttered, gingerly swivelling on the stool. "What do you mean, I won't let you? I'm the one who's just told you I'm HIV positive…" she ground to a halt.

"Indeed you may be," he interrupted with infuriating calm. "But my choice of phrase is deliberate. The decision, the choice is still yours. I've admitted I'm into you. Seriously you really blow my mind away and I want you, HIV status notwithstanding. How many couples manage and yet one of them or both have the virus? Lavina, I want you to move in with me, I've never felt this protective about someone before. Who knows? We might just be lucky and turn into a discordant couple."

She tried to muffle her audible gasp, but instead ended up almost screaming!

"What?" she paused almost dramatically and then opened her mouth to continue, but just then there were footsteps in the passage outside and a female voice called out Giorgio's name in sing-song. Before he had the chance to answer, the kitchen door opened.

"Oh, dear, I apologize," the woman who entered said.

"What do you want Gabriella?" Giorgio enquired pleasantly, but Lavina detected an undertone of chilling anger in his voice, a sort of icy calmness that brought out goose pimples on her arms.

The European woman framed in the doorway seemed quite unaffected. Her cream linen two-piece suit and chocolate camisole had the expensive simplicity of a designer label. From her smooth blond bob, her Panerai watch to her Italian Tod's pointy tipped shoes which were currently the ultimate in hand made Italian craftsmanship, she radiated sophistication.

Lavina rightly guessed that the woman was Italian like Giorgio. Even her lilting voice reminded Lavina of Maya Solano, the Italian soprano who had visited Malindi last year to entertain the Italian community during the celebration of Italian day.

"Good morning Giorgio."

Her greeting and smile addressed to him alone was a tacit reproach. And Lavina instinctively knew there had been, maybe still was, something between Giorgio and this woman.

"I'm so sorry to interrupt. If I'd known you had a guest...," she made a vague apologetic gesture with one elegantly manicured hand.

Lavina sensed that she was trying to antagonize Giorgio, and that it wouldn't have made the slightest difference whether he had a guest or not, she would still have walked in unannounced as though she owned the place and had every right to barge in. Maybe she did, Lavina corrected herself.

"Gabriella, you're early today, how come?" Giorgio said this sarcastically, as if trying to forestall and counter any more queries. Gabriella, shaking off the question, said:

"We were worried. Is everything all right?"

Lavina wondered whom we meant. Giorgio raised one dark brow,

"Why shouldn't it be?"

"I've been trying to reach you for the last, like, twenty minutes. When you didn't answer...."

"I didn't answer because I haven't switched on my office desk extension yet, and my cell phone is still off." Giorgio said.

"I didn't know that. I was concerned. We thought you might have been taken ill or something."

"How thoughtful, but as you can see I'm in excellent health." Rising to his feet behind Lavina, who had been listening with interest to this exchange, he rested one hand casually on her shoulder.

"Lavina, this is Gabriella Donatonni, my PA. Gabriella, Lavina Kante."

"Good morning Miss Kante." The woman inclined her head, but the practised social smile never reached her brown eyes, which remained unnervingly blank like one-way glass. "I hate to break your tête-à-tête, but there are one or two things which require Mr. Santini's immediate attention. I'm sure you understand."

Lavina made as if to stand up, but Giorgio's hand tightened on her shoulder, preventing her from rising, and signaling her to remain right where she was.

"Crisis this early on a Monday morning, Gabriella? What's happened to your flair for organization and management?"

Giorgio's dry enquiry brought two spots of hot colour to Gabriella's contoured high cheekbones. Lavina drew herself up and knew that the lady would never forgive her for having witnessed Giorgio's rebuke.

"And haven't you learnt to put a leash on that libido yet G? Still bringing in all the stray cats…" Gabriella, who seemed to Lavina not to be one to lose ground, quickly responded. She positively purred the words, but Lavina sensed an underlying vindictiveness and malicious intent to hit way below the belt. A dark look spread fleetingly across Giorgio's face.

"Gabriella you'd better shut up…" He trailed off, a sort of threat hanging in the air.

Lavina wondered what had been or was between the two.

"Or else you'll what? You don't have the balls to do anything to me!" She sneered almost derisively.

Giorgio sighed, eyeing her.

"I don't need to use my balls to do anything to you. I have the letterhead to do that most effectively." He paused for effect, letting the firing threat hang in the air, and then continued: "…or I can make it impossible for you to renew your expatriate work permit or alien ID, or both, which are about to expire…"

"Giorgio! There is no need to be so melodramatic about it, I didn't mean it to sound the way it did." Gabriella responded hurriedly as if trying to pacify him.

"Melodramatic? One of these days I'll show you what real melodrama means…" He drifted off meaningfully.

"Anyway, *per quanto mi riguarda*! ('On my part/for my part!') I run this office like clockwork," Gabriella continued with icy calmness defending herself. "I can hardly be blamed or held responsible for other people's disorganization. Mr. Tony Kamunde just phoned to say that he must have a decision this morning instead of tomorrow evening as previously agreed, he's just talked to the minister. The government delegation wants a site meeting with the committee at Dongo Kundu. I also need to know if you intend to go on appeal concerning the Galu Kinondo beach strip, and the site and project manager at the Olkaria Geothermal Power Station called concerning the specifications of the steel beams that you promised to deliver within— "

Giorgio raised his hand.

"Whoa! Point well taken. I'll come at once." He looked down at Lavina, "Sorry about this. We'll take a rain check on our interrupted conversation, but I'll be as quick as I can."

He gave her shoulder another tiny squeeze.

"Decisions. Decisions. Decisions." he murmured softly so that only she could hear, giving her a conspiratorial wink. "They rule my life. If I'm not making them, I'm waiting for other people to do so. Like you." And before she could think of a suitable reply, he was striding nonchalantly towards the kitchen door.

Gabriella followed him, and as the kitchen door closed behind them both, Lavina began stacking the breakfast dishes. With so many demands on his time, no doubt Giorgio would want to leave as soon as possible. The least she could do in return for his hospitality was tidy up. Besides, if she kept busy, she wouldn't have time to think, to wonder.

A couple of minutes later the door opened behind her and she glanced around, surprised that he was back so soon. But it was Gabriella who came in. Without a word, she stalked over to the breakfast bar, picked up the report Giorgio had been perusing and returned to the door.

Fully expecting her to leave, Lavina was startled to see her close the door and then lean against it. The polished smile had vanished, and Gabriella's flinty expression was as hard as the peach varnish on her French manicured long talons as she hissed:

"If you think that by sleeping with Giorgio he'll ask you to marry him and then he'll end up financing your business, you're wrong madam sculptress."

Stunned and speechless, Lavina could only stare at her. It wasn't surprising that Gabriella knew who she was, considering the number of her works in the house that Giorgio had been bringing over, and obviously he must have talked about the artiste behind the work. What really shook her was not simply Gabriella's assumption that she had slept with Giorgio in order to get him to marry her, but also the remark that implied that she was nothing more than a gold-digger, an implication that she was little more than a prostitute. A whore. A call girl. It galled and hurt her.

"As for any ideas you might have about a future with him," Gabriella continued in her sneering voice, "Forget them. No one will ever tie Giorgio Santini down. He values his freedom way too much. In any case – " her painted mouth curled derisively, "what could you possibly offer a man like him? All he wants is to use you, and he'll try every possible means of persuasion to do so." Her lips thinned in a bitter smile. "Giorgio can charm ice-cubes into a fire and sell snow to an eskimo! I bet he found getting you into bed a real bore. I see you are already down to the basics of wearing his shirts!"

Lavina wondered at all the acerbity. All the bitterness. Is that what had happened to Gabriella?

Lavina opened her mouth to voice her vehement protest that her relationship with Giorgio was nothing like the picture Gabriella was painting, that far from wanting to get married, she didn't even want to think of wedding bells and nuptials, and that despite their profound attraction to each other and the chemistry that seemed to arch between them, she didn't want to sleep with him because she had her own reasons.

But one look at the Italian woman's cynical expression made her realize it would be a total waste of time and precious breath. Gabriella simply wouldn't believe her.

"You may be an African beauty Ms. Kante, but I've seen even more beautiful women come and go here. Even some *putas*, but still I can't grasp what he sees in you…"

Instead of replying, Lavina picked up the jug and poured herself another glass of juice.

She was so proud that her hand remained steady, it didn't occur to her that her need to lubricate her dry throat would be seen as a gloating snub, until she glanced up and glimpsed the venom in Gabriella's eyes.

Lavina swallowed.

"I don't recognize the Giorgio Santini you've just described, but if he's what you say he is, a man who uses people and discards them as soon as he's gotten what he wanted, why would you want to go on working for someone so ruthless and unfeeling?"

Gabriella was saved from having to reply by the sound of Giorgio's footsteps outside. Gabriella moved quickly away from the door and slightly raised her skirt up above the knee. Extending one shapely leg backwards, she half-turned, pretending to ostensibly examine her calf upwards towards the back of her thigh.

Puzzled, Lavina watched as the door opened and Giorgio walked in. Gabriella had stationed herself in a strategic position so that her silk-clad leg was the first thing he saw upon entering the kitchen. Lavina then realized it was an excuse for having delayed with the report that he'd forgotten to pick up and had sent her to get!

Hardly breaking his stride, Giorgio sidestepped past his assistant.

"Another ladder, Gabriella?" He enquired with cool irony, "You really are unlucky with tights."

Smoothing down her skirt with a sensuous wriggle designed to draw attention to the curve of her hips and outline of her thighs, Gabriella flashed him an arch smile.

"Stockings, Giorgio, stockings. You know very well I only ever wear stockings, not tights, darling." She drawled.

Catching Giorgio's eyes, Lavina quickly looked away, embarrassed at the sexually loaded remark. Gabriella's earlier attitude should have forewarned her that she was the real definition of vindictive. What she had not expected was to actually be a witness to such a scene.

"Of course. I can't imagine how a fact of such paramount importance slipped my mind." He rasped with a sudden cutting sarcasm. "And I will not tolerate such blatant indecent exhibitionism in my home."

Beneath her makeup Gabriella blushed and then grew pale. Lavina said a silent prayer for being an African, no visibly vivid blushes for her, thank God! In a slightly miffed tone, Gabriella retorted back, pouting petulantly,

"Blatant? It didn't seem to bother you before."

"That's enough Gabriella!!" He returned harshly. And then, after a minute, "...Well," Giorgio paused thoughtfully, "You're the one who jumped ship and refused to bail me out remember? You also know by now that I'm not one for half-measures and don't suffer fools easily either."

Silently, Lavina came to the conclusion that the two certainly shared a history.

"You came back for the report." He suddenly snapped, all business-like again. "May I have it?"

Gabriella lifted the folder.

"I was just abou—"

Giorgio cut her off mid-sentence.

"Then I suggest you return to your office and get on with your work, which will leave me free to do mine. Unless you have any other questions?"

"No." Gabriella's half-smile was polite and demure. "Everything is quite clear now."

Her words were laced with double meaning. She turned her cold, one-way, glassy, blank gaze on Lavina and gave her a nod.

"Ms. Kante."

Lavina gave her a brief nod of acknowledgement, but inwardly heaved a silent sigh of relief at her departure. Having been through so much emotional upheaval herself in the recent past, Lavina was acutely sensitive to strong emotions in others. She was sure that behind the expressionless façade, Gabriella was shocked and seething with anger at the way Giorgio had spoken to her. Especially in the presence of a stranger.

Lavina wondered. What had made him so angry?

"Gabriella is a brilliant PA," Giorgio remarked after she had left them alone. "I would not have kept her on otherwise. She's never been one to make *buon giudizio* ('good judgement') on other personal matters."

Otherwise? Typically he was not denying his affair with Gabriella, but what he was not making clear was how things stood between them now, and that was one question Lavina could not, would not ask! Was he trying to explain his actions?

"Anyway, I thought you Kenyans adore everything imported? Gabriella is that and more. Just joking." And then added as if an afterthought, "The other problem is that she's completely self-absorbed. Any conversation you initiate inadvertently leads back to her! She's also the kind of woman who doesn't think of sex solely as a token of love or affection."

Though one corner of his mouth tilted upwards, there was no humour in his expression.

Lavina's head snapped up, her eyes widening in confusion and dismay.

"Are you suggesting – ? You surely don't think that I – ?"

"Of course I don't!" he retorted angrily. "In spite of your bravado and desperate attempts to prove otherwise, I've realized you are a sensitive and emotional woman. Far too sensitive and emotional to resort to battering your body. Ever."

Lavina stared at him, overwhelming relief followed by shock at his insight.

"You keep doing that," she blurted.

His dark brows climbed. "Doing what?"

"Making statements about me. You're so definite, so sure of what you're saying, yet we only met a few days ago. You don't even know how I got infected. You don't know me well enough to judge me or —"

"Who says I don't?" he responded, his eyes gleaming. "I saved your life, remember? Lavina, there are moments when I'm sure I know you better than you know yourself."

"That's exactly what I mean." She raised her hands in frustration. "Don't you think you're being insufferable and a wee bit patronizing?"

"Probably," he agreed, "but that plus my *braggado'cio*, and my arrogance are all part and parcel of the Santini charm and fascination."

Lavina raised her eyes to the ceiling in mock desperation, letting out an exaggerated sigh.

"This is hopeless."

"On the contrary," he countered swiftly. "Not only do I have high hopes, I also have a great deal of grit and determination. Which is why anyone who knows me well enough will tell you..."

"You – always – get – what – you – want – in – the – end." Lavina finished for him in sing-song. "So you've said many times. In fact, you seem to think that if you say it often enough, whatever you want will actually happen. Chant *abra-cadabra* and it will miraculously appear!"

Giorgio's hooded smile got her nerves quivering.

"I know it will mia cara, and I'm not just thinking of myself."

"Oh, I see, you've got my interests at heart." Lavina gazed at him, hopelessly torn.

"Yes, as a matter of fact I have." He answered quietly, all serious again.

He shouldn't say things like that. It was cruel, but the words were a balm to her aching soul. And she wanted with all her heart to believe him.

"What should you care what happens to me?" She challenged, "I'm not important to you." Lavina sighed as she looked down at her jean-clad figure. "And I'm a very *kawaida*, very simple Kenyan lady. No Manolo Blahnik designer knee high boots from London for me—"

"*Kawaida*? That is Swahili for ordinary isn't it? A lady who is a sculptor? You are nothing of the sort my dear!" Giorgio sighed. "Anyway you seem very marriageable."

Lavina stared at him blankly, suddenly thinking of Gabriella's uncalled for accusations.

Instead she asked, "What's marriage got to do with it?"

"Even in these liberated times it's still the ultimate security for a woman." Giorgio stated.

"Oh please, Giorgio! I think subconsciously you are a male chauvinist still rooted deeply in the neanderthal age!!"

Pausing for breath, Lavina was about to add a caustic retort about the divorce statistics and the ability of women to earn their own living and pay their way, but did not get a chance.

"I'm talking about emotional security," Giorgio interrupted her thoughts, seeming once again to read her mind. "Most men have mixed feelings about marriage. They see it as a haven and a trap, a release from the hassle of hunting for a mate and helper, and yet a restriction on their freedom, all at the same time."

"So if a man asks her to marry him, a woman should be eternally grateful for his sacrifice?" Lavina's voice had a cold edge to it.

"That's not quite how I'd have put it," Giorgio said dryly, "presumably her reactions would depend very much on how she felt about him. The point I'm making is that, whereas a woman is basically monogamous, a man isn't, and that's since time immemorial." He raised his hand before she could interrupt. "We are talking biology, not choice." His mouth quirked in a sardonic grin. "Nature's little joke ensuring that since the beginning of time men and women have stormed out of caves, castles, grass-thatched mud huts, ancient Tudor-style mansions, manyattas and, igloos, you name it, carrying spears, clubs, riding boots and snow shoes yelling – I just don't understand you!!"

Lavina could not help grinning at the comical scene he painted with his last comment. Strangely, she remembered the Flintstones, television cartoon characters from her childhood. And also Rupert bear and Casper the friendly ghost. She wondered if she'd ever have her own children. A twinge of regret flitted across her face as she thought of Makena introducing her to her favourite cartoon the Power Puff Girls, who protect their city against evil, as she in a child-like manner had pointed out to her the three toon girls of Blossom, Bubbles, and was it Buttercup, or Butterfly? It seemed like this generation was in the middle of a cartoon revolution, not gentleness any more, but more brashness in the form of Samurai Jack and the smooth talker Johhny Bravo. Not forgetting their obsession with Harry Potter and his school of wizardry with strange titles like The Order of the Phoenix and The Philosopher's Stone!

Picking his Gianfranco Ferre suit jacket cum blazer from the end of the breakfast bar, Giorgio put it on.

"Hey!" Giorgio waved his hand in front of her face, "And don't worry about Gabriella, she's just jealous, that explains the leg show. It was purely symptomatic."

Lavina stared at him. What was he saying? Why should the Italian lady be jealous of her? Suddenly Gabriella's near vitriol-like verbal attack on her the moment Giorgio had left the room sprung into her mind. As she replayed the words, realization dawned.

Giorgio looked at her puzzled face.

"Lavina, you are completely unaware of your beauty, aren't you?" He smiled warmly. "Carry the fish, put it in the cooler. You owe me dinner; what did you call the fish in coconut milk? I remember now, *samaki wa kupakwa*. Time we got moving, we've both got work waiting for us."

Giorgio decided to fly, saying it was faster. He did not talk much during the flight, what with so much on his mind. Lavina was glad for the silence. The sun was shining, the air fresh and cool after the storm, and the views from the helicopter were spectacular.

After a few minutes Lavina no longer noticed the view as her thoughts turned inwards. No matter how hard, how fiercely she tried to deny it, the hope that Giorgio's interest in her wasn't entirely based on physical attraction stubbornly refused to die.

Chapter 13

As they touched down at the airport, Lavina was surprised to see it looking exactly the same as when they left. So much had happened to her in the last twenty-four hours or so that somehow she expected everything to have changed. Giorgio glanced sideways at her.

"What are you smiling at?"

"Myself," Lavina admitted wryly. "I really am a total idiot sometimes."

"No," Giorgio shook his head, looking mockingly thoughtful. "I wouldn't say total. Though with a bit more practice you might become a complete idio – ouch!" He grinned as Lavina thumped him playfully in the ribs before he could finish.

"I am so, so, very, very sorry," she cooed in an exaggerated and sweet reconciliatory tone, "My elbow must have slipped."

"Well." He drawled. "The passenger's code of conduct states that beating up the pilot is not an acceptable option." he announced, sliding the logbooks into their pouch and removing his headset.

"Then the pilot shouldn't ask for it," Lavina retorted, half turning towards him so that she could hang up her own earphones.

"There are penalties you know," he warned, the gleam in his gaze skewering her like a butterfly on a pin.

Her heartbeat quickening by the second, her tone wasn't at all what she had intended. Instead she sounded both nervous and eager. Trying to regain control of her treacherous responses and of the situation, Lavina raised one eyebrow. She went for skepticism.

"Such as?"

His slow smile made her breath catch in her throat. Then before she could move, his hand snaked forward and cupped the back of her head and his mouth was on hers. Warm and gentle, his lips moved on hers with a subtle delicacy that forced a soft, wordless sound from her throat as excitement raced like tiny flames along every nerve, flooding her body with heat. He raised his head.

"In matters of disciplinary action," he murmured, his voice slightly hoarse, "The pilot has discretion."

Lavina swallowed. She felt dizzy, as if her body didn't belong to her.

"He chooses the punishment?"

"Yeah." He replied, looking at her meaningfully.

She ran her tongue over her lips in anticipation, the taste of him lingered and she wanted more. She saw his eyes follow the movement.

"Can I appeal?"

Desire hardened his features.

"You can," he whispered, "God knows you can!" Then with obvious reluctance, he released her but still held her gaze.

"There isn't time right now to explore the situation of your appeal as fully as I would like to, however, you can be sure that the moment circumstances permit, it will have my full, loyal and undivided attention."

While his choice of words and tone of voice were formal and businesslike, the expression in his eyes made Lavina melt. She shivered in delicious anticipation tinged with a frisson of fear.

Carrying the cooler and her backpack, she followed Giorgio through the airport's reception area and out to the car park. She waited while he opened the trunk of his car and took out his laptop encased in the slim tan designer portfolio case. Unsure whether the goose pimples on her arms were due to nervous tension or the new freshness in the air, Lavina was glad of her warm cardigan which she had carried in her backpack, and which she now drew over her head.

As they turned out onto the highway, his cell phone beeped softly. He flicked it open, at the same time attaching his hands-free kit. It was the first of several calls. Giorgio listened more than he talked. His questions were brief and his replies even briefer, but during the drive all the way from the airport, on the highway and down the road where the lane led to the Munges' residence and her cottage, Lavina began to realize just how complex Giorgio's business empire and the wide-ranging interests were. He even held one conference call.

They drew up to the Munges' stately gate. Giorgio slammed his door and came round the front of the car to join her.

"I'll walk you to your door."

"You don't have to," she began. "I've already taken up a lot of your valuable time..."

"Surely that's for me to say?" he reprieved gently.

Lavina drew in a shaky breath, determinedly thrusting her fears aside.

"Listen," she said, "You're late for work and I believe you should be in demand at your office right now, by the look of how we left things with Gabriella. Why don't you come and have dinner with me tonight before we proceed to the mayor's Christmas ball? You've shown me your work and your way of life. Let me show you mine. Then maybe you'll understand why our lifestyles are completely incompatible."

Giorgio laid one hand lightly against the side of her face and looked deep into her eyes.

"I understand far better than you think. Thank you for the invitation." He stepped back.

Lavina searched his face. What did he mean?

"You will come a bit earlier then?"

He nodded.

"I should be delighted."

He turned to go, half raising his hand in farewell.

"Until this evening then."

Lavina went to her cottage, still feeling the warm imprint of Giorgio's palm on her cheek.

Once in the cottage, she headed straight for the phone to place a long distance call to her mother in Kericho. She preferred the fixed land line whose charges were more bearable. The tariffs of the cell phone service providers were kill-joys!

She knew her mother, so, bracing herself for recriminations and determined that she was not going to be browbeaten, she picked up the receiver. She asked about her sister and nieces and was glad the whole family was fine. She hastily rushed into explaining to her mum that she had met this Italian gentleman who was interested in her, that she'd told him she was HIV positive, and that he still seemed interested in her moving in with him.

Lavina was startled when her mum, instead of the usual tirades and probing questions, opened her end of the conversation by suggesting that she think seriously about accepting his offer, that is, if she sensed that he really cared about her.

"B-but I thought, I mean, mum! I thought you'd be shocked."

"I know, I know. But Lavy, this is your life and you need someone to love you. So long as you are both careful, you know what I mean, precautions and all that stuff."

"Just a minute mum, but I— " Lavina tried to break in.

"No buts." Her mother's raised voice thundered down the line, drowning her objections. "Sentiment carries no weight here. Given the way you're talking about him, he seems like a caring man, considering the present state of your mind. You said he's Italian, right? They are usually very strong-willed people. It is most unlikely that he will withdraw his offer. In fact there is a strong possibility he will really pester and pursue you."

Her mother had been an executive housekeeper at five star hotels along the Kenyan coastal strip for many years, she should know.

"Mum, I don't really know anything about him apart from what Tony and Lynne have told me, and they seem to approve, but—"

"Lavina, for God's sake!" her mother shouted in their tribal dialect.

Lavina jerked the phone from her ear as her mother's voice exploded through the line. They had barely talked for a couple more minutes, when her mother abruptly said, "Lavina honey, God bless you, I have to hang up –" her voice faded.

Lavina flinched as her mother's receiver clattered down with a bang, giving her no chance to tell her about the exhibition Giorgio's friend Bjorn was trying to arrange for her in London. As she held the receiver bemusedly, she could only guess why the sudden interruption; her dad must have walked into the room. She was actually persona-non-grata at their farm in the lush and evergreen tea-growing zone of Kericho in the highlands of Kenya.

Ever since her father had disapproved of her relationship with Raval and she refused to heed his warnings, and after things had gone drastically wrong and her subsequent sero status, he had actually ex-communicated her from the rest of the family.

She could hardly believe what had just happened. She was used to her mother being pompous and mildly overbearing, but this had been different. There was an over-protectiveness in her voice and manner that she didn't understand and identify with, but found deeply reassuring.

Feeling decidedly shaky, she hung up the phone, taking several deep breaths to calm her jittery nerves. She deliberated on whether to go to the main house to see Lynne, but decided to go to her workroom instead. She spent the whole morning chipping and smoothing away at soapstone and wood, trying to finish one sculpture or starting on another carving and before she realized it, lunch hour had come and gone, and it was already five in the evening.

As she tidied up and then had a shower, she held Giorgio's polo shirt to her face and wondered what would become of them.

It suddenly struck her that though she had invited Giorgio for a meal, she hadn't the faintest idea what they were going to eat. Considering various alternatives helped her overcome the after-effects of her conversation with her mother. Then she remembered the fish and her promise to Giorgio, but there was still no escaping the pressure crowding and clouding her mind. However, she got the fish out of the refrigerator.

She quickly got to work, she cleaned and gutted the fish and then removed the scales.

After sorting the rice, she deftly grated one coconut for the fish. She decided to finish with the fish and deal with the rice later. Soon she was through and the cottage was tidy.

The savory aroma of fish in coconut milk spiced with Kitunguu saumu[29] and other condiments wafted from the traditional jiko la makaa[30] where it was simmering. It was too early for the rice.

Pulling on a clean pair of blue jeans and a white spaghetti top, Lavina tied her head with a white and blue bandana. She had no idea when Giorgio would arrive. Neither of them had hinted at or specified a time. Everything was ready apart from the rice. All she could do was wait. That was the hardest part. She couldn't settle down.

Leaving the door open so that he would know she hadn't gone far if he happened to drop in before she was back, Lavina did what she always did nowadays when she needed time to think and space to breathe or to reflect and do some soul-searching. She walked down to her beach.

There was a faint hint of the forest smell after the storm drifting over the beach. There was an almost eerie silence from the direction of the kaya forests to the right, the forests whose name means 'homestead' in Digo dialect and are revered by the locals because of the significance in their history and culture as the resting places for the souls of the departed. Anyone caught desecrating the grounds could even face death. The sacred forests are off-limits and taboo except for a select few, a group of elders called 'Wazee wa Mvaaya' who meet in special council sessions they call 'Thome'. The Kaya forests had recently been named a World Heritage Site at a recent UNESCO convention in Canada.

She had learnt that there are fifty Kayas in the coastal region and had caught glimpses of Kaya Kinondo, Kaya Tiwi, Kaya Fondo and Kaya Waa, *not forgetting Kaya Bombo where it was said the local youth involved in the 1997 land and ethnic clashes in the South Coast had hidden and taken oaths*, among others. She had once been accorded the honour and privilege of visiting one Kaya with the Munges and learnt a few facts.

Permission to enter the forest may or may not be granted. The locals believe that before entering the site, one has to tie a black piece of cloth around the waist. This is because the spirits recognize the colours and have to respond to them. White and red are also eligible.

At the entrance, there is a shrine where one has to offer prayers. This is for safe guidance through the entire journey and a sign that the spirits are watching over you. Nothing should be dropped inside or carried outside of the sacred site. All cell phones have to be switched off and any head gear removed. Those entering are instructed to make sure they harbour no ill motive against anyone, they could not be told the reason though. Only that the spirits alone know what will happen to those who break the rules.

One of the rare species of trees found there is the Chinese Cycard, on which dinosaurs are said to have dined, and the Strangler tree which produces different kinds of fruits in different seasons....

Lavina came back to earth from her memories. To the left was the gazetted Arabuko Sokoke forest, a tourist attraction with fauna and flora so beautiful it rivals other tropical rain forests in the world of eco-tourism. That's why Lavina had been saddened by the heading she had seen in a local daily last week... ENCROACHMENT A THREAT TO UNIQUE COAST FOREST.

Though Lavina welcomed the silence, it was different. The sense of timelessness, which had made her beach so special, had been shattered. It would never be the same again. Standing at the water's edge, she tossed sea-shells and pebbles into the gentle swell. She thought she saw one or two baby turtles scuttling into the water. She wasn't surprised. The Munges stretch of beach was an area protected by the government for turtle conservation, and it was a nesting place for the turtles which were threatened with extinction. It is believed that turtle oil is an aphrodisiac and this belief contributed to the endangering of the species.

The sun was low over the forests, its slanting rays turning the billowing banks of cloud into flame and gold in the dazzling contrast to the wine-dark sea. The approaching sunset was a fiery display of orange. Tonight there would be 'Omotienye bwe egekondo', as she used to call the orange sunset with her paternal grandfather, up in the highlands of Kisii, when she was not chasing fireflies or following him up the hills of Tabaka to harvest soapstone, or towing after her grandmother to watch her harvest river-sand, or her cousins preparing ballast to sell to masons. She had never asked, though she'd always wondered why the orange sunset was referred to as 'Monkeys moon.'

She started reminiscing on how she would hover near her grandmother when she was preparing 'amarwaa' the traditional brew. She and the other village children would feed on 'chinkara', the roast barley which would be fermented into beer until their stomachs got bloated, and they would still come back for some more despite the discomfort they would suffer for days.

Pushing her hands into her jeans pockets, Lavina gazed at the breaking waves. This time last week, Giorgio Santini had been a prominent name. But it was only that to her; a simple name. Then, in the space of a day or two...

She recalled that heart-stopping moment when, recovering from the shock of his rescue from her 'attempted suicide' and agonizing spasm of muscle-pull, she had looked at him properly for the first time. Vague impressions coalesced into vivid reality of black hair, bronzed skin, a tall powerful physique, and glittering blue eyes that cut like lasers through every defense she raised against them. She could even hear his voice; deep, resonant, quite authoritative, but with an underlying note of amusement and self-mockery.

What a strange irony that he should save her life, only to change it beyond imagination.

She had never talked to anyone the way she talked to him. Just the way he said her name made her feel special. She could hear it in her head, even now. It was so clear, almost as if he were right here, right now.

"Lavina?"

Startled, she swung round. He was here... crossing the white sand towards her, his suit-jacket hooked on one finger and slung over his shoulder.

Remaining where she was, Lavina watched him approach, drinking him in—his lithe stride, his wind-ruffled hair, the gleam of his white teeth as he smiled a greeting.

"I didn't find you at the cottage. I had to go up to the Munges, and Lynne guessed you'd be down here. She's worried sick because you haven't called or gone to see her today. She also said that she had wanted to talk to you about the mayor's dinner. We tried reaching you on your cell phone, but it was off. Why don't you put it on voicemail or a divert?" He asked, bending to kiss her cheek lightly. "But at least I got your number. I've saved it in my phone book."

He scrolled through his phone just to make sure, then he leaned back, studying her more closely.

"I take it you haven't had the easiest of days?" She looked away, shrugging her shoulders.

"You could say that. I talked to my mum today, and she gave me food for thought."

"Anything I can do?"

She raised her head to meet his gaze, overwhelmed by an anguish she did not even attempt to hide.

"Yes. Go away and leave me in peace."

His features hardened, but his gaze remained compassionate.

"You know I can't do that. Anyway, how is your family?"

"Ok." She nodded wearily.

Giorgio put his arm around her shoulders and in silence they walked slowly back across the beach. The warm weight of his arm was comforting and as she leaned her head against his shoulder. He kissed the top of her covered head. Lavina didn't know whether to laugh or cry. This man was turning her life upside down and she loved him for it!

She paused and, gazing around, was swamped by memories. Standing behind her, Giorgio let his jacket fall to the sand. He held her shoulders.

"Lavina have you thought over my proposal – about moving in with me?"

"You don't understand," she cried, whirling round to face him. "I can't! I'm so scared."

"Lavina!" he was impatient, "Why should you be scared, when I'm going to be here for you? Anyway, I'm the one who should be scared because every time I see you, I feel like I've been struck by lightning. Even when I went back to the penthouse and found your shirt, which you forgot in the bedroom, I felt like I'd been struck by lightning! I don't know what you've done to me!"

Oh God! Lavina thought to herself, she'd felt the same way just holding his polo shirt!

But instead she said:

"Well, up in the highlands my people say that lightning doesn't strike the same place twice, so maybe your feelings are a premonition or an omen of bad things to come?" Lavina replied, trying to break away, but he held her fast.

"Listen, don't give me that crap! I realize it's a big step, but I want you with me, I'll take care of you sweetheart."

"You would say that!" she flared, "I've told you I'm HIV positive, what happens when I get full blown AIDS? What then? You ditch me? And don't call me sweetheart!"

Lavina had a sudden vision of Gabriella, Giorgio's glamorous and sophisticated PA.

"Look at me." He demanded.

She shook her head. His grip tightened, his fingers biting into her shoulders. She could tell from his quickened breathing that she had made him terribly angry. Well, that was too bad, she was very angry, hurting, confused and frightened!

"Look at me," he said again, and before she could refuse again, he grasped her chin, forcing her head up. "Clinging to memories and reliving the past all the time will not undo anything or turn back the hands of time. And I've told you I'll take care of you. I'm willing to spend a million shillings a month on your medications and anti-retrovirals alone. Anyway, you look as healthy as a horse, it will be years before you get full-blown AIDS and you might not even get full-blown. And tell me, why shouldn't I call you sweetheart?" he posed.

"Because its too confusing." Lavina whispered, blinking furiously to dispel the threatening tears which, despite her valiant efforts, continued to well up until they spilled over.

"I can't—" Catching her lower lip between her teeth, she shrugged helplessly.

Folding his arms around her, Giorgio cupped her head and pressed it against his shoulder.

"Don't fight me darling. There's no need. I want what is best for you."

"Are you really, really sure? You don't know what it feels like taking the test month after month, hoping against hope that this time it will turn out negative only for it to still be positive." Lavina mumbled against his shirtfront, feeling his body heat and the roughness of his chest through the thin material.

"Come on Lavina, give me some slack here. Why shouldn't I be sure *mia cara*?" he enquired softly, his lips brushing her forehead. "I feel like I've been hit by a sledgehammer. It's the first time I'm falling in love and I want it to be for keeps," he said. "Anyway you never know, miracles do happen. That next test may just turn out to be negative."

When she kept quiet, he repeated again,

"Why do you think that I'm not sure?"

"Because— because—" Lavina swallowed hard. "Because although you call me loving names and use all these endearments, I haven't the faintest idea what you really feel for me."

She felt his mouth curve in a brief smile.

"Lavina!" he reproved, "Don't play reverse psychology with me! How can you say such a thing? You know perfectly well what you do to me. Even just standing here like this – *Dos Santos*!!"

His arms tightened fractionally and he broke off. The response of their bodily reactions to each other made further explanations unnecessary.

"I don't mean… that." Lavina murmured, "I mean—"

"I know what you mean," he said as she struggled to find the right words. "But it cuts both ways. You haven't told me either." Cupping her face between his hands, he looked into her tear-washed eyes.

"Tell me Lavina," he urged softly. "Tell me what you really feel."

"I— I—" she whispered breathlessly. "I— I— can't. Almost everyone I've fallen in love with has walked out on me. Something always goes wrong. Could it be a jinx or a curse? You will too."

She gazed hopelessly and helplessly into his eyes, praying for his denial, yet knowing she would not believe it.

Giorgio felt like he was drowning in those eyes with their exotic African slant at the edges. His face changed as different expressions passed over it fleetingly like clouds across the sun. Then he held her close once more, and though being in his arms was the greatest comfort she had ever known, somewhere deep inside she was screaming with terror. For now she knew he must be uncertain, because she had something in her that made her unlovable, or so she thought.

She started talking in a slow halting voice.

"I remember when I found out I was HIV positive. My world collapsed, but I've always been practical. I went for counselling sessions and had time to learn how to deal with such a blow. When you rescued me at sea, that was not the first time I'd tried to kill myself. In Mombasa, friends and foes alike were pointing fingers. I remember once at the highrise building where I was going for the counselling, a friend of mine worked on one of the floors. That day I went in to say hi, but I sensed it, I wasn't welcome. It was like she didn't want to associate with me, I mean, not even hello. Oh God, Giorgio, I was so devastated…"

She went on to recall that chilling scene to Giorgio. She had gone up eight floors to see her psychiatrist, thinking of what an impossible burden she had to live with. When the doctor left her alone for a couple of minutes, she'd wiped the moisture from under her eyes, blown her nose and gone to the window, aware of the faint padding sound her feet made on the thick carpet. Drawing the drapes, pulling aside the curtain, she rested her forehead on the cold windowpanes. Eight stories below her was the hustle and bustle of Digo road, the main avenue snaking through Mombasa's CBD[31].

A peculiar sense of floating outside herself came over her. Her breath slowed, filming the glass, her bitter self-recriminations faded, and there was only the distant pavement glinting and beckoning seductively at her. Until that afternoon her infrequent considerations at suicide had always been along succinct, logistical lines, but that afternoon, gazing down from eight floors up at the shimmering square cuts of pavement stones, her normally acute mental processes and faculties were distorted and thoughts floated like insubstantial wisps of clouds that could not be grasped.

These are slide-up windows, she thought with sudden clarity. There are no grills. It's so easy to open one and just jump out and end it all. But then the doctor came back, and the moment passed. She wondered whether it was through divine intervention that she did not jump through that window? What was God telling her?

The doctor never guessed what had been going through her mind as she stood gazing through his window. If he would have known, maybe he would have thought his therapy sessions were in vain after all.

She bent her head forward and she was crying once again as Giorgio held her...

"Oh Lavina! I'm so glad I was on the beach that day, I promise you, I'll never give you reason to think of death again."

His voice was a harsh whisper. His arms tightened around her until she could hardly breathe, and she realized that he was in the grip and throes of some powerful emotion, which had made him forget his own strength. Dare she throw caution to the wind and label the emotion 'love'?

They were standing just a few metres from the sacred Kaya forest. Were the Milungus[32] of old going to intervene on her behalf? She could faintly hear ngoma[33] beats of sengenya[34] dancers in the distance, maybe there was a wedding in the offing somewhere.

After a few moments, Giorgio loosened his hold, but made no move to let her go.

"*Mia cara*, parting with people you love is an unavoidable fact of life. That's why Charles Dickens said that life is ever a series of partings. It can happen for all sorts of reasons, but fighting shy of feeling because of the risk of loss is totally self-destructive. People who avoid emotional commitments spend their lives searching for something to fill the gap, they chase after money, possessions, and power, yet wonder why there's no sense of fulfillment. They turn to alcohol, drugs and sex to try and blot out the loneliness, I should know. Despite being brought up in a large Italian family full of love with huge family dinners and large bowls of pasta," he chuckled ruefully at the memories, "In relationships I've always been a wanderer, normally bailing out when things become too thick, but this time – God! I know what I'm talking about." Giorgio muttered against her hair, "And I don't want to see that happen to you."

Lavina looked up quickly, but before she could question him, he grinned and she sensed a deliberate change of mood.

"I thought you invited me for a meal. Something certainly smelled nice when I peeped into your kitchen looking for you. We better hurry if we are to make it for the mayor's ball."

With one arm around her shoulders, he propelled her up the path towards the cottage.

"I've brought a rather good bottle of wine." He announced, "to help us celebrate the good news."

"What good news?" Lavina demanded, her own mood lifted by his upbeat one and obvious pleasure at what he was about to tell her.

"Bjorn phoned today. He's managed to fix a date for your show, sometime next month at his London art gallery."

By then they were already in her kitchen. Lavina gulped.

"My work on display?" She handed him a coconut and a small metal bar. "Please crack it for me, into two neat halves."

"*Si, Signorina.*" He replied and went about the task obligingly. Shaking his head, Giorgio laughed as he watched her arrange some items on the counterpane working space.

He looked around properly for the first time. He hadn't done that when picking her up on Sunday morning or earlier in the evening when he came calling.

"This is neat. Bamboo recliners, water hyacinth sofa seats, banana fibre stools, mangrove love seats, uteos[35] on the walls for decoration, and your own carvings and sculptures – wow!"

"I'm glad you like it, no polished chrome seats for me sir!" Lavina replied mockingly.

Above her kitchen sink he stared at the quote hanging in gilt frame.

'IF I CAN BRING OUT OF THE STONE WHAT EVER IS IN MY MIND,
THEN THE SCULPTURE IS CORRECT.
FORM IS THE ABILITY TO PHYSICALLY EXPRESS EMOTION'
Dominic Benhura

"You seem to be a real fan of Benhura." he commented.

Actually the Zimbabwean sculptor is my role model and mentor in absentia! I would love to meet him one day. Last year he presented a stone sculpture to Nelson Mandela for his office in Jo'Burg and was commissioned by the UNDP to produce work titled 'Peace'. Benhura says that his motivations for being a stone sculptor is the love of it and that somewhere in his heart he always felt that stone was his future. His pieces in Opalstone and Springstone are awesome. Just the way he brings out family and women's issues in his pieces endears many to him. He says his work celebrates the things he holds dearest and are his motivations and inspiration and they are his five children, his wife and his culture. Some men prefer his bull sculptures. You know, macho stuff!"

Giorgio moved to the next quote on the opposite wall...

'STONE HAS MANY POSSIBILITIES. I'M ALWAYS TRYING
TO SEE WHAT COMES OFF A STONE AND I'M ALWAYS
CURIOUS ABOUT WHAT I'M GOING TO DO NEXT.
DIFFERENCE BETWEEN SKILL AND CREATIVITY
IS THE DIFFERENCE BETWEEN CRAFT AND ART'
Dominic Benhura

Giorgio listened to her for a while and then said,

"Lavina, you have this smoldering passion when you talk about art and I would love to explore how deep that passion goes!"

Lavina ignored his comment and went on.

"I have several of his pieces here. Come let me show you. I bought some when I went for one of his showings in Zimbabwe and some are presents. This one is called Our HIV Friends. Its sculpted out of Springstone. Playing Sister, Proud Mother, Playful kids, Baby Steps, Lady of Peace, Apple of my Eye, Come Close, Up in Arms, Playing With Mama."

Above the pieces was another intriguing quote…

'ALL MY PIECES COME FROM THE SKETCHES I MAKE WHENEVER I GET AN IDEA FOR A SCULPTURE. I DON'T DREAM MY PIECES, THEY DON'T HAVE FAIRY TALES BEHIND THEM. THEY COME FROM MY MEMORY AND EXPERIENCE.'
Dominic Benhura

"Of course I do have several favorite Nairobi-based Kenyan artistes, though, like Sane Wadu and Irene Wanjiru, especially her wood sculpture piece 'The Cave Where Woman Was Born' and also Maggie Otieno and some of her pieces like 'One Eyed Dream', 'Private Journals' and 'Melody Maker.' There is also Gakungu Kaigwa's 'African Dream, Mother and Child' the one of a woman carrying a machete with a baby strapped on her back. My interest in contemporary art was actually born years ago as a small girl when I got to know veteran gallery owner Elimo Njau of Paa ya Paa Art Gallery. He was a friend of my grandfathers."

Giorgio stomach grumbled and he grinned sheepishly.

"Hey! What's that smelling so nice, and what is that you're cooking it on?" he enquired.

"It's *samaki wa kupakwa*.The fish in coconut milk I promised you, and that for your information is a jiko la makaa, I thought you've been in Kenya long enough to have seen one? It uses charcoal fuel."

She grabbed a mbuzi[36] from a corner and squatted over it, taking the halves of the coconuts from him and starting to grate one half. After grating both halves on the traditional grater, she took the kifumbo[37] and proceeded to squeeze and sieve the tui[38] of the grated coconut into a separate bowl. She then squeezed out some more milk which she diluted with water to boil for the rice.

She took the fish from the jiko and kept it on top of the table.

"So, that's how you grate your nazi[39]." He remarked.

She added more charcoal in the jiko and placed a saucepan with the diluted coconut milk on it to boil for the rice. She had already washed the rice, so when the water boiled she added some salt and then the rice. She stirred the rice with a mwiko[40]. She gave Giorgio some tangawizi[41] to grind for her using the kinu[42], explaining that it was for her tea. Giorgio did as told, but kept staring at her in amazement.

When the rice was almost cooked, she added the tui on top without stirring. She took a newspaper centre and wetted it. She used the wet paper to cover the rice and then covered the saucepan with a sinia[43]. She put the saucepan of rice on the floor, quickly reduced the coals which she had heaped on the sinia before returning the saucepan to the jiko. She had created an oven of sorts, a method used by the locals to cook rice.

Giorgio busied himself with her magazines as she set the table. He flipped through 'MSANII' which is Swahili for artiste and 'RAMOMA', an acronym for Rahimtulla Museum of Modern Art, another magazine from the Godown Arts Centre and Domicic Benhura's Sculpture Diary.

In a while they were at the table.

"Now that's what I call perfectly cooked and yet fluffy rice." Giorgio said after his first spoonful, "....umm the taste of the coconut is incredible, it's so sweet, and I've never tasted fish like this before. How do you get the skin so crisp and yet the inside so tender, the flesh just slides down my throat and ummm so coconutty too. What on earth did you do to it?"

"You can't expect me to divulge all my trade secrets," Lavina chided, thrilled beyond measure at his admiration of her cooking. "I'll tell you this though, I don't care if you call me old-fashioned. You won't get the same results with your micro-wave or electric oven."

He burst out laughing.

"Lavina, you're priceless, do you know that? I noticed you have an electric cooker and oven, but you'd rather use the jiko. You have a blender and food processor, but you'd rather use the kifumbo, mbuzi and kinu. On top of all your other attributes, you're an excellent cook, a brilliant sculptress and carver and a laboratory technician."

He let out a low whistle. "You're priceless." He said again.

Laughing, she pulled a face at him.

"Stop it! You're making me sound like an antique. But I admit sometimes I'd give anything to have a mud floor, three firestones for my hearth, and an earthenware pot for even better results. Life would be less complicated."

A whimsical look came into her eyes. Seeing the look in her eyes, he leaned towards her across the table and took her hand.

"You're certainly very rare. My antique. My mermaid." He said softly. The look in his eyes made her heart skip a beat.

They continued with their meal. As they shared the bottle of wine, Giorgio's dry wit reduced Lavina to helpless mirth and laughter after he commented on some of the habits and traits of people he had met through his business dealings. When they were through, he insisted on washing up, while she made the coffee. She carried the tray into the living room and set it down on a low table. Coming up behind her, he rested his hands lightly on her shoulders.

She spent the next half hour showing him her different works in soapstone and they discussed the different types of wood she used, from Malakoti and Jacaranda to Rosewood and Ebony.

They went through her finished range, including a maasai couple immortalized in red oak, a group of gazelles in black walnut, the Big Five[44] in blue gum, a mahogany animal salad bowl comprising entwined carved giraffe and buffalo lining the rim, ebony wood sugar dishes, a set of salad spoons with handles of giraffe heads in cast iron, a Turkana maiden sculpture fabricated in steel and resin, soapstone chess board and pieces painted black and white, colourfully painted soapstone paper weights in mixed media, flower vases and sugar bowls, cow-horn earrings, bracelets and chokers.

She explained how she was now interested in experimenting with glass works, and Giorgio was awed at the tour of the workshop and then came down to earth reluctantly.

"Bjorn said that he can get up to one thousand US dollars per piece for your endangered animal species carvings and up to one thousand five hundred US dollars for your soapstone sculptures or wood carvings of the Big Five per group at a special show-casing of your art."

"What?" Lavina was stunned.

"Yes!"

He then tried to bestow a brotherly kiss on her upturned surprised mouth, but the contact released a great rush of emotion in Lavina. As his arms tightened around her, she captured his face in her hands, revelling in the roughness of new beard growth on his jaw as she poured all her love, hope and need into the kiss.

Something intruded, a sound, familiar in tone, was nagging at the edge of her consciousness. She had heard that sound before. She tried to ignore it, but the sound went on and on, a high-pitched bleep, insistent, demanding.

She opened her eyes and in that same instant Giorgio tore himself away, cursing under his breath in Italian as he grabbed his blazer from the back of the bamboo recliner cum love seat and reached into the inside pocket to get out his cell-phone. He pressed a button and the bleeping stopped. He talked rapidly for a minute or so in English interspersed with smatterings of Italian.

"What is it?" Lavina asked, anxiously standing up and clutching the back of one of the water hyacinth fibre settees for support. Her heart was racing and her legs felt weak and shaky.

Giorgio's face was flushed and beneath his shirt his chest heaved as he struggled to control his ragged breathing. His hair was ruffled and spiky where she had run her hands in it.

"I'm sorry sweetheart. I have to go, but I'll be back in an hour's time to pick you up for the ball."

"Now?" Lavina could not hide her disappointment.

Snatching up his jacket, Giorgio quickly put it on, then raked his hands through his hair in an effort to restore it to some semblance of order. He came towards her.

"I have to get back to the office," he explained. "I left strict instructions that I was only to be called in regard to some two very extreme circumstances, that's why I didn't switch my phone off or put it on call-back."

Bending down, he kissed her cheek.

"I promise you it's a matter of great urgency. Why don't you start dressing up? Let's take a rain check on where we've reached and I promise I'll make it up to you later. There are also some very delicate and sensitive issues we need to discuss. *Capisce*?"

Lavina nodded and hugged her arms across her midriff, trying hard to hide her shakiness.

"With whom did you leave the instructions?" she asked, more out of determination to try and make a go at normal conversation than any real curiosity. But when he glanced around in surprise and said, "Gabriella," her stomach clenched into a small and painful tight knot. No wonder the Italian words interspersing his phone conversation. He traced the contours of her face with his fingertips.

She wanted to walk him up to his car, but he wouldn't hear of it, insisting she stay indoors. His deep kiss went a long way towards softening the blow of his hasty departure.

As she dressed, Lavina found comfort in his final words, '…some very delicate and sensitive issues we need to discuss…' What did his caring attitude portend? What did this relationship herald? More heartbreak? She was HIV positive for heaven's sake, and he didn't seem to care!

Her head was now besieged with images of Gabriella. Gabriella who worked with Giorgio and wanted him all to herself, and seemed to warn off anyone who presented even the vaguest of threats. Giorgio had told her that Gabriella rented an apartment in Malindi town. So Lavina didn't have to worry about her sleeping over at Giorgio's because of work. He said it was urgent, to do with work. If she was falling in love with him, she had to start believing in him. Trusting him. After all, why would he lie?

She switched on her cell phone, which had been off since she'd finished cooking and gone down to the beach. She checked her voicemail, only to find a couple of text messages from earlier missed calls, Lynne and Giorgio, maybe from when he'd gone looking for her and got her number from Lynne.

Glancing at her Gucci timepiece, she decided it was time to start dressing, but first opted to text Lynne, asking her that they link up at the mayor's ball and that she would be accompanied by Giorgio. As she pressed the 'send' button, she smiled wryly to herself hoping that she wasn't putting the cart before the horse, praying that Giorgio didn't stand her up.

෨෴෴෴

Two hours later.

Giorgio could still not help staring at Lavina. She took his breath away. It had taken them half an hour of fast driving to reach the Lion in the Sun Beach Hotel owned by Italian billionaire and Formula One mogul Flavio Briatore, the venue for this year's Mayor's Christmas Ball, but he was still thinking of how he'd felt when he'd seen her standing like an African queen regally at her door in the flowing Moo Cow African evening number of tan coloured batik with giraffe print against the backdrop of her cocoa coloured creamy skin. The multiple layered cow-horn choker and dangling earrings she'd crafted herself lent a new definition to ethnic chic. He'd concurred right there and then with whoever had said that the African woman was the most beautiful of women.

While Giorgio signed the guest book at the foyer, Tony Kamunde, who had been monitoring their arrival, smoothly interrupted and requested a dance from Lavina, barely giving her a chance to append her signature and put her purse on their reserved table.

She didn't have a chance to refuse as he dragged her to the ballroom. Halfway through the dance Lavina stared at Tony. He was certainly out to spoil her evening with his snide comments! She'd thought she was going to have a wonderful time at the Mayor's Charity Christmas ball, after the lighting of the town's Christmas tree lights. She let her mind wander just to block out Tony's boring tirade.

She had even heard through the grapevine that Hollywood celebrity

Brad Pitt, who had separated from his wife Jennifer Anniston of the 'Friends' sitcom, was here with his companion Angelina Jolie of 'Tomb Raider' fame who had been his co-star in their latest movie 'Mr. and Mrs. Smith'. It seemed that Angelina Jolie was in Kenya in her role as goodwill ambassador to the United Nations High Commission for Refugees, working on a documentary as part of an MTV initiative aimed at sensitizing its audience on poverty in Africa due to premier in the USA soon. 'The Diary of Angelina Jolie & Dr. Jeffrey Sachs in Africa' also featured Professor Jeffrey Sachs, the UN Special adviser and economist, whose most recent book 'THE END OF POVERTY – How we can make it happen in our lifetime' caused him to be named one of the most influential leaders in the world by Time Magazine. The documentary featured Sauri village in Nyanza, a province in Kenya, as the first Millennium Development Goal village in Africa.

Lavina came back to earth, jolted by another of Tony's caustic comments. She stared at him in shock. How dare he?

"Come-on Lavina! Don't give me that look. Giorgio is extremely rich. He's almost a billionaire for heavens sake!"

"Tony, haven't you heard the joke doing the rounds in town, that in Malindi multi-millionaire only means that finally you can afford to buy your own house?" Lavina said sarcastically, then added, "Anyway, are you saying that women fall for only that, his money?" she asked, one perfectly shaped eyebrow lifting.

"He's the kind of man who makes a woman drop into his arms and not care why he's got them open." Tony countered.

"Hasn't it occurred to you that by now he might have developed an immunity to gold diggers?" Lavina posed.

Tony stood silently for a moment, his enigmatic stare searching Lavina's face.

"And have you suddenly developed an immunity to millionaires? Because to me and almost to everyone else included in Mombasa's who's who list, since Raval, you have just gone ahead and netted an even bigger fish. I just hope for his sake that Giorgio is very, very immune. I have a gut feeling he's going to need every single anti-body he's got, because you madam, who pretends to be miss goody-two-shoes when all along you've always been a perfect latter day Delilah, shamelessly peddling your body to the highest bidder, left some very nasty rumours circulating back in Mombasa about your immune system!"

Every vestige of bravado left Lavina's very being as the tears welled in her eyes, she couldn't believe that this was the Tony who not very long ago had confessed that he would follow her to the very ends of the earth! She lifted up her chin as she answered him.

"Well, they aren't rumours Tony. And for your information, Giorgio loves me all the same." Her tremulous voice wavered.

"What!" Tony bellowed, almost shouting. She wondered if he'd been expecting her to deny her HIV status. "I just don't know how anyone can love you, leave alone trusting your motives, behaving as you are, as though you never did a wrong thing in your life. I don't trust that beautiful face of yours or that equally majestic body. I don't, most especially, trust your morals. I'd say they were as bad as an alley cat's, but that would definitely be unfair to some of the felines! I have to talk to Giorgio and give him a piece of my mind, he must be out of his Italian head for once!"

He thundered to a halt.

Lavina felt as though she might be sick right there and then in front of him, and certainly the hot stinging sensation in her eyes heralded that tears were not far away. She blinked hard as she opened her mouth to say something in her defense, but no words came out, just a peculiar little croak that might or might not have been a denial of his ruthless, harsh and certainly vindictive summing up of her character, leave alone his critical analysis of her circumstances. She wondered if this was what people meant when talking of slander or character assassination.

"You bastard!" she was shocked. Was that her voice? And still she continued, "Let me remind you, *dunia ni duara*[45]!"

"Yeah," He drawled nonchalantly, "and it usually comes round full circle!"

There was no escape from the crowded dance floor, but she painfully inched her way through the crush of the bodies in the ballroom and, almost suffocating, managed to push past him and ran out of the room, not noticing that some of the patrons were staring at her tear-streaked face. He made no move to stop or prevent her rush out, but only stood immobile watching her as she made her flight outside.

Once outside, she stopped for breath. For a moment there she felt as if the top of her head was going to fly off. The ballroom had been stifling. The heat combined with the cigarette smoke and heavy scents of perfumes, colognes and Tony's bland accusations had nauseated her.

She took the stairs made of bamboo to the other end nearer the edge of the free-form swimming pool. She slipped off her evening sandals and sat down, dangling her feet in the cool water. The tears were still streaming down her cheeks, and she was trying hard not to sob.

The sea smell drifting in from the beach combined with the smell of chlorine from the swimming pool, as always, gave her a heady intoxication. It acted like a soothing and relaxing balm for her frayed nerves.

She loved the Lion in the Sun. It was one of the modern beach hotels on the Kenyan coast. Its ambience was one of the best atmospheres she'd ever encountered, and always thought of it as the ultimate in tropical settings. It was only comparable to Hemmingway's further up the road, The Eden Roc and the pioneer traditional one like Nyali beach hotel in Mombasa. The shadowed coolness as the lights were dimmed at night made the poolside a private and romantic place.

There was a noise behind her. She held her breath, it was the sound of a step and it made her heart leap. She wasn't alone, but the subtle whiff of the Hugo Boss cologne 'Boss In Motion' assailing her nostrils allayed her fears, letting her know that it was Giorgio. By now she knew and was pretty certain that he lived by the book to the cardinal rule of colognes and scents of less is more. Out of the corner of her eyes she saw his tan coloured pointy-tipped twelve-eyelid laced Pierre Cardin shoes come into view and her peripheral glance caught the swing of his cream Valentino jacket gleaming in the moonlight. Tomorrow she guessed it would be a black Hugo Boss suit with creased gold cufflinks, a Phillipe Patek watch that she knew cost four thousand american dollars, an equivalent of more than a quarter of a million Kenyan shillings and Prada shoes... His Monte Blanc gold pen near his lapel also caught the moonlight and strangely she wondered again what she was getting herself into, because she knew that classy pens like Monte Blanc don't come cheap either. No wonder people were always talking about her hooking up with rich blokes.

"What happened?" his words were harsh and clipped.

"Nothing."

"Tony said something to upset you, what was it?"

She winced at his peremptory tone.

"Nothing. Really."

She stood up from the edge of the pool. He took a step closer.

"If I have to go back in there and choke the truth out of him I will. Because the last time I looked you were dancing with him, and the next minute you rushed out here! I have a good mind to go in there and *ha fatto una capa tanta!*" ('talk his head off/give him a tongue-lashing!')

She stood silent, and he turned on his heel as if to go back inside and execute his threat.

"He thinks that we're having an affair, or I'm hanging out with you because you're loaded…"

The words were husky, low and barely audible, but they halted him. He turned.

"But you and I know that's not true. Don't we? Yet it upset you so much you came flying out here like a frightened dove? And for you to have tears in your eyes?"

She shook her head.

"No? There is something more sweetheart, isn't there?" He guessed astutely.

She stood watching him, knowing that the wheels in his keen engineer's mind were working and turning at a furious rate.

"Let's see," he said with a cool thoughtfulness. "I think I can re-enact that scenario without too much trouble. It doesn't need Sigmund Freud or Einstein to do that. He makes a pass at you. He gets the cold shoulder treatment. *Si? Te nami?*" ('Yes? Am I right?') He queried. "He accuses

142

you of sleeping with me for my money and then suggests that there are rumours circulating about your HIV status."

Her anguished face gave him his answer. He swore softly and lapsed into Italian.

"That bastard! That self-righteous swine. When are your people going to learn and discard this notion about HIV and AIDS? When are you going to stop treating your very own who are infected and affected like they are pariahs and with contempt while at it? I'm a foreigner and yet I love you, so long as we're careful and understand the methods of transmission."

His hands were clenching ominously at his sides and his knuckles had turned white and his face pale red with fury.

"Please. Just forget it." Implored Lavina.

He took a step closer.

"Nothing he says can hurt me, though I have to work with him on a daily basis at the sites. I know how to deal with him, after all, at the end of the game, the king and the pawn go back to the same box, but it matters to me that he tries to hurt you all the time with his insinuations. I worry about you. Remember, you're supposed to be leading a full and positive life. I don't know how you're going to manage with the likes of Tony hovering around like scavenger vultures. I assure you of my love though. And I'm also going to make long term provisions for you."

"*Si Amico*! ('Yes Sir!') Thank you G. I'll try not to forget that." She promised huskily.

He held out his hand.

"Then don't give him the satisfaction of knowing that you're out here hiding in the dark. Come with me. We'll soon shock them into silence with the direction our friendship will take."

With that he pulled her into his arms and gave her a tender kiss, his hands warm and intimate on the small of her back. They went back into the ballroom together, but Giorgio's mind was on the surprise he was already planning in his head for her in about a week's time above the Tamarind Dhow, the world famous floating restaurant anchored at the Severin Sea Lodge in the North Coast of Mombasa.

Chapter 14

The door to her workroom was pushed open and Makena came tumbling in with her beach bag. Lavina was momentarily taken aback, and then she remembered her promise to go to the beach this afternoon. She managed a smile and turned around on her stool.

"Hello Makena." She said while blowing the white dust off the sculpture she was holding.

"Hello aunt Lavina."

Makena was far from shy. She was intelligent and lively, and at this particular moment conspiratorial as she closed the door behind her and tip-toed across the room to Lavina's work table.

"Mum said that you're busy and that I stay up at the house, but I told her that you really promised me the beach today. So I've just sneaked out."

She stressed, grinning cheerfully, revealing her missing milk-tooth gap. Lavina's heart warmed to her.

"Yes Makena, I really did promise you the beach, no need to sneak around, let me just give your mother a call and then we'll be on our way."

Makena's eyes widened happily.

"Ok," she said equably and followed her into the other room which served as bedroom cum living room and kitchenette. Makena sat on the bed and bounced up and down as Lavina talked to her mother on her cell phone.

Lavina went into the bathroom to put on her bikini under her jeans and tee shirt. She was out in a few minutes, locked the door and they were soon on her moped driving along the pathway leading down to the beach.

Makena was a talkative child and somewhat of a little minx, and very mischievous. She had, inevitably perhaps, been spoilt rotten. Probably for the lack of a sibling for close to six years, but at least she wasn't a problematic child. Now they had a new addition to the family, her two-month old brother Munyi.

Lavina and Makena had become fast good friends. There had been no difficulty in breaking the ice with the small girl when Lavina had come for refuge at the Munges. She was now chatting happily about friends at her kindergarten.

They rode further down the stretch of beach to a public spot, and parked near a couple of other mopeds. The large motorcyle look-alikes were fast becoming the preferred mode of transport in Malindi and the beach environs, though environmentalists and marine scientists were up in arms against them saying they were a threat to the barrier reef and marine life.

Lavina settled down on a mat she had carried after removing her outer clothes and helping Makena out of her dungarees. Heavy eyelids drooped as Lavina enjoyed the warmth of the sun rippling over her bikini-clad body, and soon she allowed the face of Giorgio Santini to drift before her eyes and block the sunshine.

Somehow, insidiously and against her will and better judgement, the wariness she felt against him had given way to something warmer that she was reluctant to face, name or admit to herself. After the other night, and having told him her HIV status, he still showed her that he wanted her and cared for her, even after he had been over to her place for dinner. Dare she believe him?

She had wondered once, a few days later when he had shown openly his affection for her when they were with Tim and Lynne, how he would be as a lover. The thought had shocked her, sending as it did searing pangs of aching and longing through her. Come to think of it, had he been seeking the Munges approval of his courtship of her?

"Aunt Lavina, why don't you come and help me with my sandcastle?"

The impervious, childish voice pushed aside such unwelcome and intrusive thoughts.

Remembering that it was unwise to allow a young child to play on the beach unsupervised, she flicked open her eyes and looked down at Makena. The little girl wearing her two-piece swimsuit of gay multi-coloured lycra that showed off the smooth baby roundness of her limbs, was kneeling beside a huge pile of sand watching Lavina with her head tilting questioningly on one side.

They smiled at each other with a tenderness and warmth that needed no words and Lavina thought for the thousandth time how beautiful Makena was, the absolute image of what Lynne had looked like at that age, through glimpses gained from their family photo album.

"You don't really need my help, do you?" she murmured. "I'm feeling very lazy!"

"Then can I have an ice-cream instead, please?"

Lavina laughed as she reached for her tiny leather pouch in Zebra print.

"Blackmailer! Alright, here. I'm watching you Don't go talking to strangers."

She turned and sat hugging her knees, and monitored the little girl's progress as she threaded her way through the sparse crowd on the beach to where the ice-cream man had parked his push-cart. She watched as Makena came skipping happily back, picking her way across the sand clutching a large, but swiftly melting, cone ice-cream.

She sat herself down at Lavina's feet and said nothing, concentrating at licking away contentedly, yet at the same time watching the sea with its vast assortment of oddly shaped beach craft as well as the more conventional triangular shaped sail yachts and the windsurfers.

"Why didn't you buy the cup ice-cream? It's tidier." Lavina commented, looking at the ice-cream dripping down Makena's hands.

"Aunt Lavina, you know I love the biscuity taste of the cone!" She replied, starting to bite on the beloved cone after licking her fingers.

When she had finished and allowed herself to be cleaned up, Makena laughed cheekily and said.

"Alright! Now help me build a sand-dolphin. I'm bored of sand-castles!"

Laughing at the trick, Lavina dropped to her knees and began to dig, scrape and pat the sand into the desired dorsal shape. When was the last time she'd done this? Years ago....

Finally, exhausted, she smiled faintly and stretched out in the sun again, enjoying the feeling of sheer physical well-being. When she opened her eyes, it was to look into the kindly eyes of a large and middle-aged European woman who was standing near them. She remembered greeting her earlier down the stretch of beach. The woman was with her husband, and Lavina guessed their two grandchildren.

"*Tu Parli Italiano*?" ('Do you speak Italian?') The lady was addressing Lavina.

"*Si, io parlo Italiano, malto bene!*" ('Yes I do speak much Italian!') Lavina replied.

They had all exchanged pleasantries in English earlier when she'd met them in the shallow waters when she took Makena to paddle and splash around a little. The woman was again now speaking to her in English.

"I was just testing your Italian for a while there. We've been here on holiday for only a week now and it seems that everyone in Malindi speaks Italian. It's simply amazing, the parents, grandparents, children, househelps and even the school dropouts and beach boys!"

Lavina heard her own voice make a polite, meaningless comment in return. A dreadlocked beach hawker with a beach boy in tow, on seeing a white lady with Lavina came closer, knowing he could make a killing by selling a curio or two. The hawker, knowing that it was criminal to harass tourists on the beach, held out several bead necklaces.

"*Quanto la vende quester?*" The lady asked about the price.

"*Vendo a ottocento soltanto* ('800 shillings')." He replied.

Lavina knew that, being one of many tough street and beach hustlers, he had hiked the price by a few hundred shillings. She intervened, knowing it was unfair to exploit the innocent tourist. The lady haggled with the hawker for a couple of minutes and finally capitulated to half the price.

"*Va bene* ('OK')." She said and bought the necklace and gave the hawker a thousand-shilling note. She held out her hand asking for her "Cambio", that is, her change.

As Makena came back, the woman's next comment made the suns rays go down in her heart.

"…no need to ask what the relationship is between you two my dear, I've never seen a mother and daughter so alike."

Just as suddenly as their arrival, the four-some Italian family was waving goodbye.

"*Ciao* ('Bye')." The two children echoed their grandparents.

"*Ciao tutti.*" Lavina and Makena replied.

As the woman walked away, Lavina stared at Makena's sand-dolphin with a whimsical look on her face… building castles in the air, the incongruous thought sneaked up on her consciousness. Life seemed just like that, as fragile as that sand creation, and not as stable and guaranteed as it once was.

It was almost five o'clock and she used the excuse to get Makena dressed. She hastily pulled on her own clothes and packed their things.

As they said goodbye to the elderly couple and other children, Lavina thought with a cry that was almost audible in its intensity …if only it were true! If only Makena were my daughter! If only Giorgio was my… But that treacherous thought she could not allow to finish even in her mind, despite the desperate longing to belong, to be part of something and someone to whom she was important and by whom she was needed. She must never, never entertain such thoughts about Giorgio. I am HIV positive for heavens sake, how can I even contemplate such destructive thoughts?

"What's wrong Aunt Lavina?" Makena asked, her voice coming from beside Lavina.

"You've gone all funny and quiet."

"Have I now, baby? I'm sorry. I was just lost in my thoughts."

"I wish you wouldn't think then. Grownups go all moody when they start thinkin' I don' know 'bout what!"

Despite her sadness, Lavina had to laugh at the succinct comment laced with childish reasoning and wrong grammar.

"Alright. I won't think then! And you should say thinking and not thinkin' and don't instead of don' and about, not 'bout!"

"Deal!" Shouted Makena cheekily. "Race you up the beach!"

The nerve! Thought Lavina as she raced after the child.

Moments later Lavina parked the moped beside Giorgio's jaguar, also in the Munges driveway, when they reached home. As they entered the house hand in hand, Giorgio, who was with Tim, looking as though he was about to leave, looked at their silhouettes framed in the doorway. He looked elegant, sophisticated in a gray suit, and handsome, somehow sleek and untouchable with his tanned skin and curious blue eyes.

Lavina smiled uncertainly, remembering the way he'd dropped her off at the Munges to sleep-over after the mayor's ball, only to find him in her room at the Munges' in the morning. He was an early bird and had come to invite them for deep-sea fishing in his glass-bottomed boat. They had not talked much, but now she replayed that morning's scene in the Munges guest bedroom in her mind. She had opened her eyes to find that she was looking directly into Giorgio's eyes.

"My goodness! What are you doing here?"

Angry and disturbed, she had sat up in bed and hitched the covers around her shoulders, but not before she saw his eyes flicker over the smooth ebony skin under the straps of her night gown.

Cooly, he had stood and studied her, a slight smile lifting his lips.

"Lynne thought I might have better results waking you up than if she did!" His eyes had gleamed wickedly. "Seems she was right".

He sat down next to her on the bed. Her heart rushed up to the base of her throat and started beating in a heavy, slow rhythm that made breathing difficult. He let his blue eyes make a lazy tour of her bare face and tousled hair, and then made a detour back again. She could feel the quick warming of the blood in her veins.

"What are-are- are you doing in here?" she stammered.

"I was… umm… let's just say, curious."

"About what?"

"I wanted to see what you look like before your shield is in place."

"I don't know what you're talking about." She'd bent her knees to hug them to her, effectively disguising the shape of her body under the covers.

"Oh yes, you know perfectly well what I'm on about. The shield that you present to the world…"

"Giorgio what do you want?"

He'd lifted one dark eyebrow.

"Do you really want to know?" He teased. "You'll find out one of these days…"

And then he walked out. And they had a wonderful day at sea with the Munges.

Coming back to earth, she now wondered if she should dare and risk herself to a daily dose of Santini charm. Now, unwilling to commit herself until she gauged his mood, and only saying in a soft, slightly diffident voice,

"We've been to the beach."

"So I see." His voice was lazy and relaxed, and she guessed his mood was reasonably affable and she relaxed. She saw his eyes travelling over her body, from her sandy feet encased in raffia slippers decorated with Maasai beads, up her bare arms which glowed with health.

She let herself glance at Makena who had run up to her dad and flung herself at him. As he bent to pick up his daughter, she wrapped her arms firmly around his neck, hanging on as if for dear life.

"Had a good day, my princess?" he asked in the loving tone he reserved strictly for her.

"Super! We went in the sea and I swam a bit with my ring and floaters, and then aunt Lavina helped me build a large sand dolphin.

She bought me an ice cream."

Before her father could respond to her news, she squirmed down from his arms and went over to Giorgio. She stood before him arms akimbo,

"Uncle G, why didn't you join us at the beach? You promised yesterday that you would."

"I got tied up sweety, but wait for me tomorrow at two, I'll pick you up and Aunt Lavina, so that she can also teach me how to build a super, duper sand castle!"

This said tongue in cheek, as he looked over Makena's head at Lavina, who turned her head away.

"Super! Duper!" Shrieked Makena. "Did you hear that Aunt Lavina? Another treat tomorrow!"

"Yes I heard. Off you go to mama Karisa for your bath and supper, mummy must be through with feeding baby Munyi."

Again Giorgio's eyes dwelt penetratingly on Lavina's face and she felt embarrassed beneath his scrutiny.

"I have to rush, I'm having dinner with a prospective client in twenty minutes time. I'll see you tomorrow Lavina." He said, though in a subdued and preoccupied tone.

He went out with Tim, conversing in low tones. Tim had dropped a newspaper clipping on their way out. Lavina bent and picked it up and as she straightened to put it on the shelf in the alcove the headline caught her eye and she found herself reading it.

'COURT TOLD OF WRANGLES OVER BEACH PLOTS'

"An investor who purchased property in Manda and funzi Island in Lamu worth millions of shillings, allegedly from a former District Commissioner, has been summoned to appear in court on charges of acquiring public land through fraudulent means. The whole issue came to light when the Italian investor started having problems with the locals over their access to his beach by passing through his private airstrip which he'd built. The investor has been citing interference by the locals' cows and goats to his landing and take-off rights..."

She glanced at the date in the left hand corner where it was not torn.

It was today's date.

Oh my God! No wonder Giorgio seemed so low. Dear me, this is so bad. I wonder how he's going to handle it. She went to the kitchen, then out through the back door, and strolled to her cottage in a pensive mood.

Chapter 15

She was sitting cross-legged and looked so comfortable, completely unaware of his presence. She held a sort of sharp paring knife in her right hand, and as Giorgio stared at her unobserved, the block of wood in front of her, after a short while of chipping here and there, began to take on the distinctive shape of a female figurine.

She kept wiping her brow. It must be taxing, yet it looked like child's play in her hands!

A pair of pliers, pieces of wire, fine brushes and paint, colourful Maasai beads, and red Maasai shuka cloth were cluttered around the small workshop floor.

Sensing she was not alone, she looked up and when she found him staring at her in awe said,

"I'll never forget the first time I completed a Maasai. I painted him and dressed him in his red checked shuka! I was so happy coz I used to spend hours on one piece only for the hands, legs or even the head to come out wrong. I was a quick learner though." Lavina said. "Right now, locally there is a demand for my set of Big Five animal wooden serving spoons, which include one for the salad. The set makes a good wedding present. The only problem I have is waiting for my supply of jacaranda wood from Nairobi. I like it because it produces the best carvings, it is soft and dries quickly once the carvings are finished."

He took the wooden block turning into a figurine from her hand.

"Who is she?"

"A Turkana maiden." She replied and chuckled at his incredulous look. "Wait till you see how she'll look tomorrow when I am through. That's why I have the beads, cloth, wire…." She trailed off, indicating the array of accessories scattered all over.

"You're incredible, you know that?" He asked.

"Yeah. I do." She replied.

"Not very modest, are we today?" He teased. He walked over to stare at an unusual flower vase with a sexual connotation.

"It resembles part of the female vagina, Lavina." He commented.

"Yes I know. Its from Kitengela Glass Works. You only notice the connotation if you have a sharp artistic eye. I have an eclectic taste and I always buy other artist's pieces when I sell one of mine! I saw a piece like this one at an exhibition at the residence of Mary Collis, the mzungu artist who is a second generation Kenyan and also the RAMOMA Chairperson. Remember, Rahimtulla Museum of Modern Art? And I ordered a replica version!"

She happened to glance at him and remembered his promise—the beach! He was in cut off faded jeans and a white Dolce & Gabanna tee shirt.

"Have a seat while I tidy up." She invited, "I'd completely forgotten about your promise to Makena."

He seemed not to hear her. Instead he was staring at her. At her huge eyes with their almost oriental tilt at the corners, the light from the open windows picked out the pale blue sun-dress she wore. She seemed almost ethereal and not substance at all.

He moved towards her so that his legs almost touched hers and she had to strain her neck to look at him. He was breathing very unevenly, he raked his hand through his hair in the now familiar gesture of frustration.

"Damn you." He said. And then repeatedly let out a string of fast-flowing Italian swear words, "I'm up to here with you!" He used the local people's action of touching his chin with his thumb as a sign of being fed up with something. "I'm not going to let you get under my skin. I don't know what you've done to me, I didn't sleep properly again last night. I think—"

She raised stricken eyes to his, and he saw the haunted, miserable look in her enchantingly bewitching eyes that she had been trying to conceal. The look seemed to be his undoing and changed whatever he was going to say. He sighed heavily.

"God! I'm sorry sweetheart, don't let a mood of melancholy like that fall on you, it's not the end of the world. We'll make this work out. I promise you, I won't press you into anything you don't want or aren't ready for. But if you feel at any time that you want to put our relationship on a different footing, give the word. Ok?"

"Alright." She whispered, smiling as the haunted look left her eyes.

"Fine. Get yourself and Makena ready, we'll be off in a few minutes. Carry your swimming gear, I know a quiet and secluded place where we can swim without being invaded by too many holidaying tourists."

If it hadn't been for the shadow cast by her constant thoughts of her sero-status, hanging ominously like the sword of Damocles over her head, she knew she would have thoroughly enjoyed the outing. They were completely spoilt for choice. Giorgio was in his very best mood: considerate, amusing, cheerful and relaxed, keeping right off any personal level of involvement with her. In fact, only very occasionally when she became aware of his eyes on her, did Lavina realize the depth of desire that burned beneath that amicable surface.

She could not help but be aware that it was she, Lavina, and not any other woman who had aroused these feelings in him. But this did not make things any easier for her. She was glad that Makena was with them and thus acted as a buffer between them. The effort of entertaining and looking after the child took both their minds off more personal things.

True to his word, Giorgio did indeed know a small secluded bay which they shared with only a handful or so other people.

For a while Giorgio helped Makena with her sandcastle building and at around four Lavina unpacked the picnic basket Mrs. Karisa, the elderly house-help, had packed for them. She laid out the various tempting delicacies for inspection. Ham sandwiches, beef samosas, shis kebabs, bhajias and Makena's favorite, Farmer's Choice Nyamabite, all washed down with freshly squeezed home-made mango and pineapple juice, fruits which were always in season and in abundance in Malindi.

Makena, knowing the drill well, rested for a few minutes for the food to be digested or to settle down well in her stomach, as her mother normally put it. In a while she was up and changing into her swimsuit.

She went back to her sand creations while Giorgio stretched out on the mkeka they had carried, his hands behind his head, and dozed contentedly. Lavina, sitting near him on the mkeka, watched him covertly and thought about what a pretty little picture of a contented family they must look to the other people on the beach, though Makena was not half-caste a point-five or pointy as children of mixed parentage or blood especially between a white person and an African were referred to locally.

Giorgio opened one eye sleepily.

"What was that in aid of? You just sighed most dispiritedly."

"Did I? I didn't mean to. I think it was caused by too much food."

"More than likely," he countered, "do you intend to get that delicious looking swimsuit wet? Lavina, by the way, I almost forgot, will you be able to accompany me to Nairobi next weekend? I've been invited by the Italian Institute of Culture for a homage to Verdi and Bellini, you know, stars of Italian Opera, at the Village Market. Doctor Carlo Calli the Italian Ambassador to Kenya will be the guest of honour. Will you please go with me?"

"I really can't. There is an important assignment I'm putting finishing touches to for a client. Maybe next time?" Lavina offered hesitantly.

"Ok." He agreed, "But maybe I won't go too. I just thought you would appreciate the art and a change is as good as a rest... Maybe next month for the Rhino Charge? It's in aid of completing the fencing of the Aberdare forest. It will also be a good way of touching base with Glenn Edmund. Remember I told you about his school of road safety and precautions for car-jackings? I'm interested in knowing more about that."

She stood up.

"I might be free for that one. Remind me again towards the end of this month so that I don't take any bookings for urgent carvings! Let me take Makena in. The food must have gone down by now. Makena, *uko tayari sasa ukaogelee*?" ('Are you ready now for a swim?')

While they played together in the warm shallow waters, splashing and laughing, Giorgio propped himself up on his elbow and watched them, the frown between his eyes not caused entirely by the scorching sun shining down. His thoughts were turning at a furious rate and he had just made up his mind. He loved her, he wanted her, and by heavens he was going to have her!

After a while he got up and stripped off his shorts and tee-shirt, having swimming trunks beneath. He joined them, delighting Makena by taking her up on his shoulders and plunging with her into the deeper waters.

Lavina stood at a distance, watching from the edge where the small waves washed over her feet. Though she longed to plunge in after them, she remained on the shoreline, a slender pretty figure in her white swimsuit, and waited for them to come out.

When they did approach her, Makena still high on Giorgio's shoulders, he seemed to have forgotten that he was to keep his distance, for he smiled intimately at Lavina, taking her hand and kissing her firmly on the mouth with salt-tasting lips.

"Why didn't you join us?"

Lavina, on the other hand, while her body trembled with delight because of the kiss, managed to smile and shake her head.

"No, thanks Sir. I didn't want a reenactment of my last beach encounter with you!"

"You make it sound like a tantalizing title to a thrilling box office hit movie or a New York best selling list novel. Don't let muscle pulls scare you from the beach forever darling. But I also don't want a repeat of the damsel in distress routine coz I'm no knight in shining armour and nor am I prince charming!"

No mention of suicide attempts this time around, she noted. Thank God.

They walked back up the beach, each holding Makena by a hand, while the little girl swung in between them chattering on happily.

There was a heavy, almost embarrassed silence between the two adults. Once their eyes met briefly and Lavina, almost shyly, still feeling his kiss upon her lips, looked swiftly away. By that simple gesture, the lightest and most circumspect of kisses, Giorgio had aroused her as all the passions in the world could not. It was as simple as that to admit it.

They reached the place where they had left their things and she sat down swiftly, her back half turned to Giorgio, suddenly breathless and scared to look at him. She had sensed a shifting and changing of his mood.

She could not also explain her feelings except that somehow things were rising to a crescendo, a climax of sorts or a penultimate nadir. Something had to give, and soon.

"Uncle G, can I go and climb over those rocks?" Makena asked in her bright, happy voice. "If I take my bucket I might be able to catch some crabs."

"Alright, but *fai il bravo mia bambino*" ('be careful my brave little child'). Giorgio agreed equably. "But mind where you step. Those rocks can be very sharp. Put your shoes on, the crabs might find your tiny pink soft toes very, very delicious!" That elicited giggles from Makena.

"And don't get out of our sight…" Lavina added hurriedly as they watched her go running across the beach towards the rocks that spread across the beach at intervals and out into the sea. No doubt there were numerous rock and coral pools there with crabs, shrimps, and sea urchins. It was only when Lavina smiled at her childhood memories of the beach that she became aware of how close Giorgio had moved to her. She turned her head and looked directly into his eyes. He was smiling apologetically.

"I didn't keep my word, did I?"

"What?" She was genuinely puzzled.

"Remember? I promised I'll keep away from you? I intended to, honestly. But God! You looked so beautiful standing there waiting for us that I couldn't resist kissing you. I'm sorry."

He didn't look particularly sorry, Lavina thought, turning her head to look out to sea. He leaned forward, pushing her heavy, lustrous hair back from her face, while the other hand rested lightly on her shoulder. As he spoke, the fingers of his hand gently rubbed against the smooth flesh.

"Tell me something Lavina. You said that you contracted the virus a couple of years back. How come you have managed to remain so glowingly healthy?"

"I follow a strict balanced diet, no junk food and no stress, 'till you entered my life!" She paused, "and I also avoid alcohol, drugs and cigarettes. But I believe I'm what people have come to refer to as a carrier…"

Giorgio stared at her.

"You know *Mia Cara*, I'm finding you to be a complete phenomenon. You look delicate yet you are strong to have gone through what you have."

Lavina answered him, but looked away.

"I guess I have developed this obsession with self-preservation. I detach myself and watch from a distance. This attitude has helped me go through situations that would normally push a sane person right over the edge and drive some people up the wall, across the ceiling and down the opposite wall."

She was talking too bravely and flippantly, and so he forced her head round and looked into her eyes and he saw the unshed tears shining brightly, but he smiled.

"Don't *mia cara*. It doesn't matter, I mean the past. I say we forget it and so we should. Baby let me ask you, you said that your family knows of your status, what about Tim and Lynne?"

She nodded silently. No wonder they loved her so, he thought silently to himself.

"I must admit you have me twisted up into a terrible muddle of strings…"

Listening to his words and thinking of her love for him, a hopeless love made all the more tender and painful because she knew that it will come to nothing, the suppressed tears at last overflowed.

"*Mios Dios*! Don't cry! *Mia cara*, I've told you my feelings for you are too strong to be fickle. I love you. There! I've said it! The plain truth. There's no need to consult anybody about us, but I want you with me. I'll take care of you. It's only for you to say the word 'yes' right now, is it so difficult?"

"Giorgio... I... I..."

"At least admit that you aren't completely indifferent to me."

He touched her smooth cheek. He looked far into the depths of her eyes, her very soul, she thought.

"I want you to move in with me, I just love you. I know what you are thinking – 'that cowboy mzungu is crazy, he's HIV negative, I'm HIV positive and he wants to sleep with me!' Let me assure you that it has nothing to do with sex. We can go for tests tomorrow and every other day after that. Maybe I'll still be negative and you positive or vice versa, but my feelings for you won't change. We can work this out, we'll use as many condoms as you want. I just want to be with you, protect you and take care of you. Is that so hard to understand?"

He voice was gentle but implacable. He vowed to himself that he was going to get his answer now.

"If I thought we did not have a chance, then I wouldn't be so patient, but we do stand a good chance, because of love." He added emphatically. "That is why I'm trying so hard. It's not that I want to wear your defenses down. You can't look me in the eyes and tell me that you don't care at all. Can you?"

If he only knew how much she loved him.

"No," she whispered brokenly and flicked her tongue over her suddenly dry lips.

"I do care, so very much, and I've loved you ever since the first moment we met, but I'm so scared. You don't know how it feels. It's like stepping into the unknown. Uncharted waters. I'm sick, for heavens sake!"

He brushed her hair with his lips, so relieved at the former part of her answer that his insides trembled. His emotional reaction frightened him, but he forged ahead bravely.

"Baby, did it cost you so much to admit that? Now then, what's your real answer going to be? I can't stay away from you another night. Will you move in? You know Lavina, we belong together and we are going to end up together. So we can either drag this thing out, dot all the I's and cross all the T's, shed a few tears and eventually get married, or we can fly out to Nairobi, then drive up to Kericho to see your parents and then get married. There are no two ways about it…"

"Ok. I'll move in after a couple of weeks, but I'm scared of disappointing you. My friend Ann-Marie is coming down from Nairobi in two days' time and I need to talk to her about this. We've always shared everything."

Shock rippled through him. Did he just hear right? At last!

"Do you know how happy you've just made me? And how happy I'm going to make you Lavina?"

"I don't know if I'm doing the right thing. I feel like someone who doesn't know how to swim and has just dived into the deep end of the pool and made the worst decision of my entire life…" she murmured helplessly, and as he leaned towards her, she blindly lifted her head so that their lips met and clung. Then they parted reluctantly.

"I've told you about Ann-Marie before, haven't I? Lynne and I were in school together with her. I would like you to go with me to pick her up at the airport." she explained.

"That's alright with me, at least I'll get the chance to meet this much talked about paragon of virtue and epitome of elegance." quipped Giorgio.

Lavina went on to brief Giorgio about Anne-Marie's latest job.

"She now works for the government as a research executive with a new organization formed to deal with the endemic that HIV/Aids has become. She's currently working on building up this guide for policy makers and program managers. Something to do with integrating STD, HIV and AIDS services with family reproductive health programs."

She came to a halt when she saw the questioning look in Giorgio's eyes.

"Did you enlighten her about your HIV status?"

"No, I didn't. That's not something I can tell her over the phone. I need her down here so that I can gauge her reaction deep down." Lavina countered.

"Don't worry, from the way you and Lynne talk about her, she is one hell of an amazing lady. She seems to be compassionate, and she must be real close to you if she can drop her busy schedule to be down here with you."

She was living dangerously, but somehow in the last few minutes, the point of no return had been reached. She sat there as if in a dream, a sort of trance, listening to his calm voice explaining that she had to tell her family and the Munges immediately of her decision to move in with him; that he also had to call his family in Italy; also that Bjorn would be in town next week concerning logistics for her London exhibition and they had to arrange so many things.

He had moved away from her and was lying again on the mkeka, eyes narrowed against the sun. Lavina indulged in the luxury of looking at him, her adoring eyes absorbing every aspect of his appearance, the wisp of dark hair that flopped a little over his strong, broad forehead, the finely moulded mouth relaxed and yet mobile as he spoke.

Her eyes dwelt lovingly on the smooth tanned skin of his chest with its liberal covering of black springy hair. Around his neck he wore his usual thin gold chain and medallion. The impulse to reach out and touch him was almost overpowering. She clenched her hands into fists and wondered what she had done to deserve such a person to love her.

He sat up again, pulled her close and bent his head to find her mouth. Just for a moment Lavina relented and their bodies, warm from the sun, clung together in a long, hard embrace. She fell back onto the mat and he bent over her, whispering urgently in disbelieving tones, echoing what was going on in her mind.

"God! I can feel it in my guts that *mia madre* ('my mother') is going to love you just as I love you! I don't deserve you. Do you really love me?"

"Yes," she returned brokenly, "I love you."

The sun was again blotted out by his head. This time he gently moved her hair away and let his mouth explore her neck and the curves of her shoulders. Lost in delight, Lavina touched the hair at the back of his neck, letting her fingers dig into it. He held her tighter as he talked while kissing her.

"I promise you that you won't regret this because I love you *con tutto il cuore* ('With all my heart.')."

They were interrupted by Makena's tiny sing-song voice demanding in Italian. "*Parini! Aqua! Bibite!*" ('Juice, water and snacks.')

Chapter 16

Malindi.

Giorgio was tired of this intense conversation he was having with Tim in his study concerning his upcoming court case against the inhabitants of Funzi and Manda islands in Lamu. Nevertheless, Tim continued patiently with his explanation:

"…the atmosphere is still volatile you know. Intrinsically, so much of tribal land such as Manda and Bajuni was designated as crown or state land long before independence, yet others were declared game parks and forest reserves, including Galana and Arabuko Sokoke…"

"Even the Arabuko?" Giorgio interrupted.

"Yes, and you better do some more reading and research at the archives with your lawyer before you guys go to court, or one of these days you may just end up at the international court at the Hague! I know some of our Kenyan officials may mislead you, many rarely do any reading themselves! I'm telling you this as a mayor who reads! Anyway, historically there were no squatters here at the coast before 1885. The introduction of the Protectorate and Kenya Colony drew distinct divisions between the Seyidia, the native reserve that was for the Nyika tribes and crown lands. Consequently, rather than take the bull by the horns, the squatter issue is being misinterpreted and allowed to cause unnecessary friction and insecurity here at the coast. Victimizing the minority never helps and never solves anything. I've always believed that there should be an honest investigation into the causes of land alienation.

After all, fingers have been pointed at prominent families from upcountry as having grabbed land, aided by the first government of this nation, from indigenous owners.

Thus, the monster that has become the issue of absentee landlords and the political bickering of our leaders is not helping even a bit, and issuing of unenforceable land title deeds as a leverage for buying votes in next year's general election..."

"For heavens sake! For *prodotto economico* ('productive economy') of this country they need to do something *pronto* ('immediately') about this land issue! All I did was innocently buy land from a corrupt DC! Still, I believe I have *buona condizione* ('good condition') and *buone probabilità* ('good probability') of winning it. Anyway, let's talk about something pleasant for a change..." he raked his hand through his hair dejectedly.

Realizing he was using too much Italian, and though he knew Tim understood the language, his mind automatically switched to the love of his life. Lavina didn't have to do anything to make him happy; just her presence did it. He couldn't explain it three months ago, and he still couldn't explain it now. His feelings for Lavina did not come from reason.

Reason would have told him that he and Lavina were too different to have a lasting relationship. She had explained to him how she contracted the virus, and he understood, yet Lavina was hot-headed, almost to the point of being stubborn. Had circumstances made her that way? There was something about her, something fragile and pure that was in contradiction with her volatility; something that touched him as he had never been touched before.

She was a dynamic package of TNT nevertheless! She seemed to have grown different in the few months that he had known her. He could tell that her first instinct for brashness of brushing away any man who tried to get close was waning. But he didn't know what had replaced it. He also didn't want to try too hard to find out, he liked the new her.

He suddenly thought he heard his mother's voice, admonishing him as it used to.

"Fool me once, shame on you. Fool me twice, shame on me."

He had asked Lavina to marry him, hadn't he? And she had refused, though she had agreed to move in with him in a months time. Still, he was going to propose again soon. Thinking of Gabriella, he certainly hoped that he wasn't about to become the fool twice.

Tim's voice interrupted his train of thought.

"You're thinking of her. I mean Lavina. I can tell. She's something else, isn't she?"

Giorgio just sighed.

"*Non posso* ('I can't') leave her alone! *L'amo!* ('I love her!') I don't think I'll stop chasing after her till I have a ring on her finger just the way she has one through my nose!"

Tim chuckled at the description of Giorgio being led around love-struck by a bull-ring through his nose.

"I know you told me that she turned down your marriage proposal, but has agreed to move in with you. So, have you asked her again? And don't you think that you are putting the cart before the horse?"

"Tim, I'm so used to having her around me now!"

"Giorgio, why don't you then just buy a pet? Marriage is more than that, you know!"

"Tim, I don't really care whether she keeps saying no. We have the same taste in music and even the books we read. Just the other day I'd finished reading Ngugi's Magnum Opus 'The Wizard of the Crow' and was going out to buy Wangari Maathai's 'Unbowed – One Woman's Story', only to find Lavina had finished reading Maathai's and was going out to buy Ngugi's! It was uncanny. I tell you Tim, I do want to marry her and not just live with her. She has to become *mia moglie* ('my wife'). I really need the whole package even if it comes with this latest strange predilection that she has of challenging the smallest suggestion I make…"

He wondered if she was being deliberately provocative; trying to push him away.

"Giorgio, I think Lavina has passed through the worst scenarios anybody can think of. But I still think you should give her some space."

Giorgio stared at him.

"Will you cut to the chase and say what you want to? Space for what Tim?"

"Space to hurt. She is still healing from her past. Love is supposed to conquer all isn't it? It means sacrifice, compromise and giving it your all. In the end you have to convince her to marry you! She really needs you, she just doesn't realize it yet. And lately she's become too accident-prone for her own good. Anyway, you have my blessing."

"Tim, stop looking at me like I'm Superman, Saint Francis of Assisi and Sir Galahad all rolled into one! Although I can assure you that even though I'm not your average knight in shining armour or prince charming, I will try to take care of her the best way she lets me."

Tim raised his glass in a silent salute of encouragement.

In the day room Lynne looked lovingly at Lavina. They were discussing Ann-Marie's expected arrival any time from Nairobi. They had come a long way, the three of them. From their adventurous days at school, and being referred to as Alexander Dumas' Three Musketeers and sometimes Achilles as Pataclus friend, the genesis of today's often quoted line of an Achilles Heel.

Lavina suddenly blurted out:

"Oh Lynne! I don't really know what I'm feeling! It's too soon, three months. I didn't want to be falling in love at such a time as this, yet I don't know why I have such strong feelings for him…"

Lynne stared at her friend with a strange look in her eyes.

"Are you trying to suggest that love has a set time? Shall we synchronize our watches then…"

"No Lynne! What I mean is that to love someone and to be in love are two different things, I should think."

"Well, I don't wanna split hairs with you over love Lavy. All I know is that you've just got to trust your instincts sometimes."

"Oh Lynne! I'm wary of instincts and emotions nowadays. I remember once Rawal called me a nasty shrew and a vindictive bitch because I went to confront his Somali lover to know how long he'd been playing us. I told him I wasn't a bitch and if he insisted on calling me one, then he better get the definition right, and I wrote it down for him."

Lavina took a pencil to demonstrate to Lynne. She tore a page out from a notepad, scribbled something on it and handed it to Lynne. On it was written: <u>Babe In Total Control of Herself</u>. They burst out laughing and after a while Lavina resumed talking.

"He certainly didn't like the definition one bit, especially when I told him that's how the sisterhood view the word, yet I couldn't help but wonder at the time, can passion be the ultimate betrayal?"

Lynne looked at Lavina.

"Lavy, can you please refrain for once from laying guilt-trips by the dozen on your own pathways? At least for today? Pleassssse?" She implored.

"It's just that I don't know what to do. He wants us to get married but I think it is wrong and too early."

After a few moments of silence Lavina continued.

"You saw how angry he was at me last week at the jetty after the deep sea fishing. He'd broached the marriage subject again, and I rebuffed it. I've promised to move in with him next month though. I don't blame him, but it hurts to know that I'm responsible for his anger most of the times."

"Don't worry," Lynne said. "He'll probably be that way for a while, but he'll come around."

Leave it to Lynne to respond to a rhetorical statement with reason. It was another trait that Lavina admired in her. She had always been the more reasonable and more sane of her friends.

"I wish I could be as confident as you are."

"You'll be fine, Lavina. Don't worry so."

Lavina smiled.

"What did I do to deserve such a good friend as you?"

"Just being you, a loving friend and a companion for life. Incidentally, I was just now thinking of Anne-Marie. When did she say she'll grace us with her precious presence?"

Lavina smiled at the majestic picture of Anne-Marie Lynne was rosily painting.,

"She said maybe in a day or two. Let's wait and see if she'll be granted leave from their cramped calender…."

Chapter 17

Nairobi.

Anne-Marie sighed as she took a bite of her lettuce sandwich that she had packed for lunch as she thought of her life. It was hardly a life. Her job dominated her entire days. She was on a treadmill of sorts; workshop after workshop; talk after talk; seminar after seminar; symposium after symposium. She was beginning to agree with the latest statistics indicating that Kenya was truly the country that leads the world in the number of workshops held annually!

She was glad of the few days that she had been granted as part of her annual leave. She intended to go down to the coast to check on her two friends Lynne and Lavina. It had been quite a long while since the three of them linked up.

She stared at the Nairobi skyline as the matatus with all their madness zoomed about and around her on the highways. She thought of the new minister in charge of the sector trying to enforce his new rules on seat belts, speed governors, and driver and conductor certificates, complete with primary color with yellow stripe for signifying public transport.

Anne-Marie wondered if it was the end of the road for the matatu art and culture exemplified in Nairobi's gaily and at the same time violently decorated matatus or mathrees and manyangas as the expressive youth had labelled them. The old school failed to realize that the flamboyantly painted matatu was real art. It was cool to the youth. Someone should have the good sense to sequester one and put it on display at a museum. How can we let a whole street culture just disappear into thin air?

At least Gidi Gidi and Maji Maji had the good sense to capture one for posterity on their music video of an overloaded, wildly painted matatu, heaving 'I'm Unbwogable!'. Maybe it was garish to others, but this was real art. We can't afford to maintain such a culture for the intellectual delectation of elites who ride in off-road four-wheel drives. To Anne-Marie, the matatu art was the most authentic example of Nairobi's changing aesthetics. They should let well alone and let matatu art stay, but insist on the yellow line and other regulations for safety.

Anne-Marie smiled to herself, knowing that, painted or not, the matatu is a symbol of national madness she loved! A display of fine works of art using different colors. Many a time she had brought expatriates working with her to the 'Car Boutiques' of the youthful artistes. The foreigners found it most intriguing that they were hand-painted and not spray painted—a phenomenon that even the elite Kenyans have caught on to, calling it 'souping their rides.'

Anne-Marie prayed that such an artistic institution did not get lost in government rhetoric!

She wondered silently in her heart if it was so hard to see the industry as a refined and highly evolved urban art form, unique and intrinsic to our country? On the backs of the matatus the larger-than-life paintings of our own Genge music luminary Jua Cali, side-by-side with portraits of American musicians Jah Rule and Beyonce, coupled with slogans that brought smiles to our faces, the encouraging anecdotes that make one's days and lift one's spirits...

The nicknames of the matatus alone will let on that the minds behind the art are highly learned artistes! EQUIVOCAL, AMALGAMATION, BOURGEOISIE...

Some thought it to be idiocy, but to Anne-Marie it was our youth expressing themselves less violently and not derivative of the white man's regimentalisation.

It was a passing of a forgettable era of street-cred-driven, graffiti-laden road terrors!

But we loved riding in them as we came home from school! Our government should let well alone, look at the jeepnies in the Philippines… It is all about freedom of expression, creativity and cultural development. We should not destroy a show of what is modern and uniquely artistic in traditional Kenya.

Anne-Marie sighed as she thought to herself that flamboyant to her was a representation of the fullness of life, with its twists and turns. The colorful rides added a funky element of fun and creativity to Nairobi and its environs.

Our government will surely regret the passing of the order which was in disorder! Art on wheels made the streets colorful and gave them character! These youth were not dissident elements in Kenya!

As jobless sheng-speaking youth trek in the rain or scorching sun as they have missed a 'sare' (free ride on the matatu courtesy of a buddy conductor or driver), maybe to attend a Kwani? Reading session at Kengeles, the colors of the matatus bring them back to life and to the ones who can afford the fare the conscious hip-hop of Ukoo Flani Mau Mau and their Kilio Cha Haki album topping the list on MTV and Channel 'O' and sneak previews in matatus with DVD players of Kenyan ghetto life movie Hip-Hop Colony soon to premier in the US!

As Anne-Marie came down to earth from her musings on Nairobi's skyline and street culture, she thought of her friends and how she missed the deep sea fishing, swimming with the dolphins and water skiing. She drew in a deep breath of the fresh air floating freely in her favorite place.

Nestled deep in Nairobi's up-market Karen suburbs the Resurrection Garden was a tranquil sanctuary that had become Ann-Marie's haven for prayer. It was an elaborately landscaped retreat, whose main feature was the History of Salvation represented by life-size mosaics. Laid along the walkways were large bronze art panels that portray The Way of the Cross and The Last Supper.

Anne-Marie never ceased to marvel at the 'divine' artworks of Giuseppe Audino, whose bronze panel sculpture 'Resurrection' is so real that you can almost reach out and touch the brutality of the Roman centurions.

A shiver went down Anne-Marie's spine as she vividly recalled scenes from Mel Gibson's box office hit 'The Passion of the Christ' starring Jim Carviso as Jesus Christ. Carviso had brought the reality of two thousand years ago to the screen and it was uncanny to note that the lead man shared the same initials with the character he was portraying down to the same age of thirty three.

Anne-Marie did what she always did, she went around slowly. The panels of the 'Way Of The Cross' were creations of Luciano Finocchiaro of Cantania, Italy. The last of the panels were blessed by the late Pope John Paul the Second at St. Peter's Square in 1988. Inside the chapel, where one can book a confession, were stained glass mosaics designed by Italian Albano Poli. The life-size mosaics that adorned the 'Salvation Way' were creations of Mr. and Mrs. William Bertoja, who prepared them in their studio in Friuli Mosai, also in Italy.

It was so peaceful. Anne-Marie loved escaping the fast and noisy city centre. As she left the pristine enclosure of The Resurrection Garden, she felt ready to face another harrowing and stressful week. But first, she just had time to catch Cajetan Boy's movie starting at six, as she glanced at the city clock to her left. It was a family saga aptly titled 'BACKLASH' that she had watched a while back at the FCC (French Cultural Centre) as a play, but wanted to watch the screen adaptation too. It was an absolute must-see, her colleagues who had watched it had told her. It also ran along the theme of HIV-AIDS, around which her current job revolved.

She was an ardent fan of Cajetan and she had seen his other plays and knew that he was an exceptionally gifted playwright. The drama and play junkie in her salivated at the thought of another of his masterpieces. She had been made to understand that he had already turned 'BY ANY MEANS NECESSARY' into a movie and another on the plight of housegirls entitled 'BENTA' was in the offing.

The harrowing week ahead could wait for an hour or so and crossed Mama Ngina street and headed towards the 20th Century Fox Theatre.

Chapter 18

"Wow! Malindi here I come! This is good! A smooth road in Kenya for once with no potholes. Humming along to Kristin Ndela's latest gospel hit single *ikoo Njia*[46]! This is intoxicating, the smell of the sea and not Nairobi's polluted air!" Anne-Marie chuckled. "And this smooth baby to drive. Thanks for letting me have a feel of this latest BMW series Lavy."

The minute she got out of the airport and saw Lavina's ride, she had insisted that she let her drive the smooth wheels and Lavina give her directions to their residence.

"Wow!" Ann-Marie exclaimed again as she stared around at the Arabuko Sokoke forest on either side of the road. "No more HIV case studies and AIDS statistics, even if only for a week!"

"Well," Lavina interjected softly as if she'd been waiting for such an opportunity to edge in a word, "One of your soon-to-be case studies and statistics is sitting right here beside you!"

The words were sharp and cold like shards of glass. They pierced Anne-Marie's brain like flying shrapnel from a shattered explosive, as she had seen discarded hand grenades, relics from the colonial times, and buried land mines explode in Kenya's arid and semi-arid northern frontier districts of Turkana and Lokichoggio with devastating effects on victims who ended up dead or maimed for life, with amputated limbs.

The shock of Lavina's words sank into her very being with a ring of finality, and Ann-Marie's grip slackened involuntarily on the steering wheel. She trembled with dread, hoping against hope that she had misheard her friend, or misunderstood…

A car horn blared, hooting ominously. Roused from her shocked stance, she lifted her foot from the accelerator. Tyres screeched behind her. And more honking! Dear God! This was the blind corner bend near Kijipwa police station and she was almost three feet into the other lane and another car was trying to go around her! She jerked the wheel and shot a panicked glance into the rear view mirror. A large lorry filled with sacks of charcoal loomed behind her, much too close!

People say that your life flashes through your mind just before you die. Ann-Marie now thought that this was a prelude to death. We're gonna die…. she thought desperately as a panorama of incidents from her childhood and early teen life zoomed at supersonic speed through her mind. She rammed her foot down on the accelerator. With a wrenching motion the big truck whipped around her and overtook her! Whew! What a close shave! Kenyan drivers and their lack of patience!

The danger was over. At least she hadn't lost control or landed in a ditch. But it was very narrow and up close. At least they both had their seat belts on. Her heart pounded at a furious rate, and she could see the murderous look the driver of the truck, a man, kept throwing at them from his rear view mirror.

Reaction washed over her, making her hands slick and sweaty on the wheel. Her moment of inattention might have killed them both!

The cream coloured lorry moved on, but not before she caught another glimpse of the truck driver's furious expression, but he at least had the courtesy to slow down and look into his rear view mirror, check on their state to see that they were okay before continuing on his way.

She was sorry that she had put their lives at risk. She had several close shaves herself on her research trips as she traversed Kenya's regions, especially on the so-called 'black spots' on the Mombasa-Nairobi highway and the Naivasha-Eldoret road. This time she was really at fault, so she decided to pull over and take a breather.

Taking the key from the ignition, she sighed wearily.

"So much for the smooth highway!"

She turned slowly and stared at Lavina, who was crying, the tears trickling down her cheeks, and she was shivering violently.

"Sh… sh… It's okay Lavy, please don't cry."

Ann-Marie hushed her up as she held her.

"But please don't ever do that again—your statement a few minutes ago. What you said. What did you mean?"

Lavina was now sobbing uncontrollably and she tried to talk through her hiccups.

"Oh God! Ann-marie… Hic! hic! I am… hic! Sorry. I know I gave you a shock, but that's just what I… hic! Mean… hic! Sob! Sob! Hic! Hic! I'm HIV positive and I'm so scared that I'm going to die…"

Ann-Marie, in her profession, was used to such revelations which sometimes seemed to be bone-chilling, but after a while one got used to them. She knew that her reaction was due to the fact that Lavina was her dear childhood friend. Both of them grew up together, literally glued at the hips together, including Lynne, like siamese triplets.

Ann-Marie composed herself, mentally enlisting the counsellor within her to take over.

"Lavina, honey, you first need to change your attitude. Think positively and speak life into your situation. You are the only one who can determine if you are going to die or live. You need to have a will to live. How did it happen? Can you tell me?"

Lavina shook her head and took the Kleenex tissues Ann-Marie had plucked free from their box on the dashboard, and was holding out to her, blew her nose, and wiped her tears.

"I… I… can't talk about it right now, but maybe later I can tell you all about it. Please drive on."

"Alright, I'll let you off the hook for now." Ann-Marie conceded as she once more engaged a gear and started up the highway.

They decided to have a pit-stop at the Total petrol station ahead to fuel and have the oil checked. As the station's efficient pump attendants cleaned the windscreens too, they went into the station's convenience store for hotdogs.

Chapter 19

Ann-Marie had been in Malindi for close to a week now and today she had insisted on going water skiing. They had been out for deep sea fishing twice, so they decided to indulge her. They converged on Giorgio's boathouse, after changing into swimsuits at his beach residence. Giorgio said that he would get the boat and meet them all at his private jetty.

He soon came by. In the boat were several pairs of blue fibre-glass skis and tow ropes. He was the first into the sea, the low powerful hum of the boat making a bubbling sound in the water.

They all went on board and Lynne threw the yellow nylon rope to him. He caught the rope, propped the tips of his skis up, and squatted in the water.

"Ready!"

Tim, who was at the wheel, pushed the throttle forward and with a low growl the speed boat surged ahead. Giorgio came up smoothly. Leaning back, he weaved from side to side, crossing the boat's wake. One hand lifted in a skier's salute as he grinned at them.

Tim twisted the wheel slightly, guiding the speedboat away from the path of a sailboat that was gliding over the water on their starboard side. He gave the two young fishermen a high-flung wave. They recognized him as the mayor.

A deft turn of the wheel brought them back to the jetty. Giorgio scrambled aboard, as Ann-Marie was so anxious to hit the water. As Giorgio crawled out of the water and shed his skis and life jacket, he listened to Ann-Marie requesting Lavina to ski-double with her. His eyes flickered with concern over Lavina.

"Are you ladies that good?"

It had been many years and Lavina was not convinced that she wanted to double-ski with Anne-Marie, but Giorgio's voice, soft with challenge, immediately stiffened her resolve.

"I haven't water-skied for a couple of years, but it should gradually come back to me." Lavina responded.

"Before or after you break your neck?" His voice was softly mocking.

Irritated, she replied sharply.

"I can take care of myself. Please pass me that extra tow line and another pair of skis."

"And two life jackets too Giorgio." Quipped Anne-Marie.

As the two ladies prepared themselves, zipping on life jackets and putting feet into skis, Tim passed the wheel of the powerful boat to Giorgio, as it was his turn to act as observer, and joined his wife at the helm.

The ladies both gripped tow-lines and as they splashed into the water, Lavina tried to forget Giorgio and enjoy the warmth of the sun's rays on her head and the water's fine spray. She had always loved skiing. It gave her the feeling of being very young again, a feeling of that glorious sense of freedom and speed and sensual pleasure she'd loved as a teenager.

The onset of the easterly monsoon winds which compete with the receding harmattan across from the Sahara seemed to be a week ahead of schedule. The ripping sensation of the wind slashed through their hair as the waves hit the sides of the speedboat.

Anne-Marie lifted her hand and sketched the thumbs-back sign in the air, and Giorgio, knowing the sign, circled and headed back to the private jetty.

They skied conventionally side by side until Ann-Marie suddenly leaned her upper body away and tilted her skis towards Lavina, cutting the water and gliding so close Lavina felt a slight spray from Ann-Marie's skis. Anne-Marie swung away, controlling her path with her powerful legs. Lavina glanced at her and saw her broad grin. Her smile was contagious, and Lavina answered it with one of her own, but she suddenly wasn't interested in anything showy.

Their first round had been wonderful, but now she was beginning to remember that she hadn't skied in ages, and she could feel the pull of the boat in her arms and legs. She had to concentrate all her energy on staying on her feet. She wasn't afraid of a fall, she'd had plenty of those before. But skiing double meant that Lavina, as she was a bit upfront, would have to be submerged when the speedboat slowed to pick her up again.

Ann-Marie moved her grip higher on the rope, letting the triangle dangle under her wrist.

"Let's criss-cross," she shouted, "now!"

She skied towards her and Lavina had no choice but to also ski away from Ann-Marie's destination. Ann-Marie ducked under Lavina's rope and passed by her with a loud swish of moving water. Lavina was not exactly steady, but she managed to change places with her friend and stay on her feet. She had to, or risk a powerful collision!

At another signal from Ann-Marie, Lavina crossed her path again, while Ann-Marie ducked under her tow rope and went back to her side. Ann-Marie repeated the actions until Lavina felt her knees begin to tremble and her arms ache from nervous strain, but Ann-Marie seemed oblivious to Lavina's fatigue.

"Stay where you are," Ann-Marie shouted, Lavina was only too glad to comply. Suddenly she was beside Lavina, her voice raised to carry over the sound of the water and that of the boat's motor.

"Remember piggy-back skiing?"

Lavina shook her head, knowing she was too tired for piggyback, but her protest either went unnoticed, or Ann-Marie thought she was shaking her head to signify that she had forgotten, but was willing to be reminded!

Ann-Marie skied close, but before Lavina could move away or stop her, she slipped out of her right ski and stepped on the back of Lavina's ski. Her weight shifted and then her other left ski also drifted away, and she was behind Lavina, sharing her skis, her extra weight making them cut deeply into the water. She dropped her towline with one hand and put her arms tightly around Lavina to grasp her rope. They were now locked tightly together.

"Isn't this beautiful? Gosh! I've missed this!" She laughed into Lavina's ear.

Giorgio had to swing the boat around to carefully avoid the path of another powerboat coming across in front of theirs.

"Ann-Marie, please don't give Giorgio the around-again sign. I can't go another round." Lavina said weakly with fatigue.

Her arms felt as if they were being pulled out of their sockets. She saw the white churning waters in the other boat's wake coming crosswise towards them, and there was nothing she could do to avoid the turbulent waters.

Her skis tipped down into the turbulence and then up again on the crest of the wave, and in a desperate attempt to compensate for Ann-Marie's extra added weight, she leaned forwards and inevitably lost her balance and fell down on the incredibly hard surface of the water like someone who'd made a bad dive, her hand clinging to the tow rope with a death-grip.

The sea water surged into her face and all around her. An intolerable pain shot through her arm. Someone shouted, telling her to release the rope. She threw it away and then finally realized that without it, Ann-Marie was the heavy weight that was pushing her under the surface of the water…

Chapter 20

She was underwater. She thrashed about in angry confusion and tried to get her head up to breathe. Her arms seemed useless. She surfaced, but went under again. She closed her mouth to keep from ingesting the sea water and told herself not to panic.

Why this feeling of déjà vu? Why did events similar to those of her first encounter with Giorgio start cropping up? Surely this was the ultimate karma... Her problem was not swimming this time around, but breathing. Why did the life jacket seem to push her down instead of keeping her afloat?

She struggled, fighting to get free of the tangle of hard, unyielding plastic material under her arms, when suddenly, a hard tug at the nape of her neck brought her head out of the water. She opened her mouth and gasped, sobbing in cool refreshing ocean air.

A hard muscular arm clamped itself around her middle.

"Lavina!"

The voice was harsh and strained but compelling. She opened her eyes.

"Giorgio ——" he floated in the water next to her, his shoulders beaded with water.

"Damn you! You could have been killed."

"Don't." she said, in an instinctive attempt to protect herself from his harsh words.

"Let go of me. I'm ok now."

He made a disbelieving snort, but he released his painful grip on her hair. But now his free hand slid down to wrap itself around her waist and draw her into his arms. She raised her arm to fend off his watery embrace.

"Ouch…!" Her drawn out moan of pain brought him even nearer, his legs tangling with hers.

"Don't move," he commanded her sharply. "You might have broken your hand."

She bobbed in his arms, confused and shaking with nerves. Every inch of his hard, wet flesh seemed to be touching her.

"Is she alright?"

Ann-Marie's distraught face bobbed above the water a few metres away.

"She's alive," came the rough answer. "No thanks to you!"

"I'm sorry. I didn't think she'd fall—"

"You didn't think at all!" Giorgio shot back, harsh condemnation in his voice.

The engine of the boat throbbed in the water.

"Cut that motor," Giorgio ordered Tim urgently. "There's a ladder under the rear seat."

Lavina heard the metallic sound as Lynne fastened the short metal ladder to the side of the boat and Tim cut the engine.

"Lay back in the water." Giorgio ordered Lavina.

She could take care of herself. "No—"

"Do as I say right now!"

She was too exhausted to battle with that hard determination. She relaxed back, floated and kept her eyes and mind on the blueness of the sky as his arm shifted to clasp her around the waist, just under her breasts. He gave a powerful kick with his legs and they began to move through the water.

It was then she knew that she hadn't escaped injury. Pain knifed through her right arm from elbow to shoulder. Despite her slight discomfort, when they reached the ladder, she lifted her head and said,

"I can manage."

She grasped the cool metal rungs with her uninjured arm to hoist herself up. From underneath her, a warm hand fit around her petite bottom to embarrassingly boost her upward. She wanted to resist, but was in no position to.

A still shaken Ann-Marie helped her over the side and settled her into the front seat.

"You okay, Lavy?" A worried frown appeared between her brows.

"I'm fine Ann-Marie, just shaken up a bit."

She sank down and cradled her right arm, more aware of the pain that was becoming a constant ache from elbow to shoulder. Lynne disappeared below deck and reappeared with an icepack that she gave Lavina to hold to her arm.

Giorgio climbed into the speedboat, his body dripping water. He snatched up a heavy beach towel, but instead of drying himself up, he stepped to her side and wrapped it around her shoulders. Don't. Her mind cried. Don't bother about me. Not now. Please just go away and leave me alone. But he didn't hear her silent plea, of course, instead he slid into the bucket seat beside her, taking infinite care not to bump into her.

She tried to order her mind to be reasonable, knowing that if she stiffened, he would certainly suspect that his nearness disturbed her. She willed herself to relax, even though her nerves reacted to his presence like an alarm clock that has been triggered. She was so intent on keeping herself under control that when a hand touched her tentatively from behind, she was startled. Ann-Marie, a contrite look on her pretty face, was looking her.

"Lavy, I'm so terribly sorry that you've hurt your arm. I got carried away coz I've not done this for quite while…"

"It's okay Ann-Marie. I was wondering about how fit you are and I've just remembered that your latest project was somewhere in Turkana or Lokichoggio, that explains your fitness, eh? Survival of the fittest in the forgotten Northern Frontier!"

That brought a chuckle from Ann-Marie. Giorgio was speaking to Tim.

"Take us back to the jetty so that we can go home and pick Lavina's clothes. Then I'll take her to the emergency room."

"Giorgio, I don't think I need medical attention. A massage with Deep Heat will do the trick."

His eyes sliced over her.

"That arm has to be X-rayed."

She leaned back in the seat. She was cold in the warmth of the sun, shocked and weary, but at least safe from her own unruly heart.

"I suppose you're right," she agreed diffidently.

By the time they docked the second time, the pain in her arm had become unbearable and she no longer cared that Giorgio was at her side, helping her out of the boat. She was only dimly aware of Ann-Marie apologizing once again and Giorgio cutting her off with a curt direction to go home with the Munges.

To Tim he said,

"Take the boat and pick up the skis Ann dropped. We'll catch up with you guys later on."

No one questioned any further his right to order them about. They walked away together and a few minutes later, as Giorgio propelled Lavina across the manicured lawns of his residence and through the sliding french doors, the revving of the Munges car driving off reached their ears.

"Can you walk upstairs?"

"Why should I?"

He gestured at the glass wall behind them and a mocking smile curved his lips.

"I thought you might not want to change in full view of the shamba boy and cook, but what the hell, if you don't mind, I'm sure I won't either."

"I see your point. Fetch my clothes from the room I used to change with Anne-Marie and I'll use the downstairs washroom..."

The amused light in his eyes faded. He put the palm of his hand against her back, urging her forward.

"Don't be ridiculous. You can't get out of that one piece swimsuit with an injured arm all by yourself."

His eyes played over the sleek fit of the one piece swimsuit, and new frissons of alarm tingled through her. Though she knew he was being reasonable, her reply was curt.

"I'll manage."

He grasped her uninjured elbow and propelled her forward. She climbed the stairs beside him, her heart pounding with a fierce resolve. He was the one behaving ridiculously if he thought she would just let him undress her as if she were a rag doll or clothing store mannequin. She had to find a way to convince him she could manage.

At the top of the landing, before she could protest, he pushed her into the guest bedroom she had used with Anne-Marie earlier that morning to change.

"I don't need your help."

"Why not?" he countered just as coolly. "I assure you, your body holds no mysteries for me." He drawled the next words with sardonic humour, "I have seen a woman's naked body before."

She didn't want to be reminded of his past lovers at this particular moment. She lifted her arm to ward him off, but pain stabbed her elbow, and she gasped audibly.

Moving with the speed of lightning, he peeled her suit down over her breasts, hips and legs and was kneeling at her feet with the bit of wet silk draped around her ankles before she fully realized he had stripped her. She found herself wondering how the legendary Ruben or Picasso would have captured and immortalized this scene onto canvas.

He lifted first one dainty foot and then the other out of the wet lycra and tossed the piece into the bathtub. As he straightened, silence seemed to hum in her ears. His eyes swept over her naked curves for a brief moment. Then his eyes returned to hers. She met his look steadily, her breathing shallow and forced.

He made a low sound in his throat and turned away to rip a huge terry towel off the heated bar with unnecessary force. She remembered the fall she'd had here. It was then that shuddering reaction swept over her. She did want him to see her. Wanted him to touch her. Wanted him to want her...

He seemed to regain control of himself and swathed her in the towel and began to rub her dry, his hands hard and impersonal on top of the soft terry cloth. Try as hard as she could, she just couldn't emulate his detached attitude. His nearness and his warm breath on her bare neck made her nerves begin to vibrate again at a newer, higher frequency. And all for a silly reason: because he had just now seen every naked inch of her, and seemed unaffected. His cool, almost clinical attitude was upsetting her.

All of a sudden she was angry with herself for the turn her thoughts were taking, for this acutely aching desire she felt for him. She shuddered briefly and his hand touched the smooth bareness of her throat to tilt her head back and force her eyes to meet his.

"You're in shock." He stated matter-of-factly.

She wanted to laugh hysterically. The impulse to destroy his cool control made her ask huskily, the desire thick in her voice,

"Is that what it is?"

His eyes travelled over her face, searching each feature, silently questioning the raw, low sensuality throbbing in her words. She returned his look honestly. The answer he wanted was expressed plainly there in her deep, bottomless, black eyes for him to see. It had been so long, she couldn't take it any more.

"Giorgio," she murmured, unable to keep his name from leaving her lips.

He groaned softly, and hard hands flattened themselves against her back and forced her against his taut body.

"You do pick the most inopportune times, don't you?"

His mouth came down with a punishing kiss that swept her mind clear of everything but his warm, nearly naked body against her own. He demanded her response and she couldn't deny him. She couldn't deny him access to the warmth of her mouth. She gave herself freely, meeting his passion with a fierce need of her own. A shudder and tensing of his muscles warned her he was going to end the kiss. His lips against her cheek, he murmured,

"You are so warm and real. Lavina, I –"

"No. Don't talk."

She shook her head. Words were an intrusion. She wanted his mouth on hers again, wanted that feeling of complete wholeness, wanted to know that her lips were as enticing to him as his were to her.

"Don't talk." She repeated and pressed against him. "Please… kiss me again."

He gazed down at her, not moving, his body tense, his facial bones hard against his tanned skin. He was fighting the sweet enticement of her swollen mouth, the heady invitation in her husky voice. She pressed closer, her now naked breasts brushing the dark springy hair that grew on his chest, her hand tracing the warm contours of his mouth.

His resistance collapsed. Hungrily, as if those few seconds away from her had intensified his desire for her, he took her lips with a warm, persuasive tenderness, an evocative possession that made all else evaporate from her mind, but the thought that she wanted him more than she had ever wanted any man in her entire life. In his arms, any time he so much as touched her, she felt fulfilled.

His hands a delight on her bare back, his tongue making erotic forays into the depths of her mouth, she was complete as she had never been before. She let her own hands discover the smooth silk of his back, and felt the sheathed muscles underneath move as he adjusted his hold to ensure her comfort.

This time when he lifted his head, she also moved to maintain her contact with him. Her mouth sought the firm line of his jaw, traced down his throat and wandered lower to nestle in the soft hollow.

He groaned,

"Lavina, I'm warning you. I'm going to reach a point of no return—"

The vibrating sound of his voice lay just under her lips, increasing her desire and erotically tantalizing her like the purr of a kitten.

"Giorgio –" she raised her eyes to him.

As he read the message of sweet surrender and submission, fire leaped in his own, lighting the indigo to purple flames. An aching need centred deep within her, clamouring for the releasing appeasement only he could offer her.

His hands started moving with erotic ease over her breasts. They moved to her dark nipples, then skipped over the taut buds that protested the loss of his caress. She gasped a second later when he bent over and his lips trailed over the taut line of her throat. She buried her fingers deep in the dark, silky hair at his neck, feeling as though each strand was a silken gift for her alone. His tongue resumed teasing her breasts. Then suddenly, without warning, his mouth covered one swollen peak possessively.

She gasped with delight and clutched his dark head as aching need centred deep within her and radiated outward in ever-wider circles. He moved to suck on the other breast… Her hands wandered lower down his spine, found his swimming trunks and then traced the straight line of his spine, found the firm, taut curves of his butt. He moved closer and lifted his mouth to kiss her again. This time his tongue claimed hers boldly, thrusting against hers, taking pleasure from her as if he was one of the Somali pirates terrorising sailors off the high and deep seas of the East African coast. She moved her hips in silent provocation, and with a deep-throated groan, he echoed her movement sharply, tightening his grip on her hands.

Pain shot through her arm. She cried out in surprise more than distress. She had been so absorbed in pleasure she had forgotten her injury. Giorgio lifted his hands from her at once.

"*Dos Santos*! My God! I must be crazy!" He pulled away.

She stared at him in agony, need and desire, but he braced himself mentally and pulled away from her. He disappeared into the bathroom and came back with her clothes.

"Stand up straight and lift up your arms slowly." He directed.

Dear God! How could he be so calm? Inside she was still trembling with a powerful emotion, but she did as he said.

Even though he was gentle, she still winced with pain as he slid her tee-shirt over her shoulder.

He made her sit down on the bed and put her feet into her jeans with the same silent control. How could he turn his emotions on and off like this? Like a tap. Like a light switch. Even more like a propelled automaton? Is that how savvy businessmen managed to keep on top of things?

He helped her off the bed and to her feet with consummate care.

"Will you be able to walk down the stairs and wait for me as I dress?"

"Yes. Of course I will."

Minutes later they were in his car heading for the hospital. The coastal air was heavy with humidity and Giorgio turned on the car air conditioning. She realized she had forgotten to borrow his comb. She ran a hand distractedly through her unkempt hair, which though wet, was still ruffled from his lovemaking.

The numbness and shock wore off, and in its place came a sick self-loathing. This was so unlike her. She sighed listlessly. Why had she made her desire for him so obvious? She felt like a puppet controlled by unseen strings. She had given herself away completely. She wished she had never met this man. She felt depressed and degraded, and her state of mind hadn't changed when they reached the hospital.

She was well known at the hospital due to her frequent visits for repeat HIV tests. The emergency room of the private hospital, with the smell of medicine floating in the air as usual, was neat and clean. The doctor, who was familiar to her, was cheerful and philosophical.

"You're very lucky Lavina. Nothing's broken. You've dislocated the joint at your elbow, but it's already back in place. Keep your arm supported with this brace for the rest of the day and don't do anything strenuous, and that includes carving!" and he looked at her meaningfully. "You'll have pain tonight, but you'll feel better tomorrow. I'm just giving you some painkillers for today and tomorrow. This gel, you'll start using the day after to heal the swelling."

They were silent on the trip to the Munges.

"Thank you for taking me to the hospital G."

"Now, I really am convinced that you have a death wish where water is concerned! And that reminds me, when are you moving in so that I can take care of you? You promised in a month's time and the month is already over. Are you going to postpone it again? Or shall we first get over with your London showcasing of your art? We can't go on like this. *Mai in vita mia (*'Never in my life') have I met such a stubborn person like you!" He said bluntly.

Lavina just stared at him.

Chapter 21

A drop of cold water hit her face and then another and another. She opened her eyes cautiously and saw Anne-Marie leaning over her with a cupped fist, the water glistening on her knuckles. She pushed her hand away and sat up.

"You haven't indulged in that trick since high school." She drawled drowsily.

Lynne, who was standing beside Anne-Marie, smiled as Lavina propped herself on the bed.

"I'm just remembering how after preps you used to be the first in our dorm to jump under the blankets, and always the last to wake up. You gave me a struggle those four years. Remember how at the crack of dawn I often had to pour cold water on you and also turn on your harsh overhead fluorescent tube light to get you scuttling out of bed before old Mathe came at you with her cane!" She chuckled at the fond memories and pet name of their dear matron at boarding school.

They stared at each other sombrely as they reminisced about how far back they had come from. Lavina was the first to break eye contact and looking away, feeling shaken at the depth of her being in wanting so much to confide in Anne-Marie. Anne-Marie saw the flickering need in her friend's eyes. She leaned over impulsively and hugged her.

"Oh Lavy! Are you avoiding me? Two days ago after our water skiing and your small accident, you promised to talk to me about this issue, but you seem to have developed a propensity for going on long solo drives! Talk to me please. You know you can pour it all out."

Her voice held tinges of a stronger emotion, more than simple curiosity or concern. Lavina could discern the care and love in her tone. She could see the compassion in her tender eyes. It had always been like this. It was her undoing and the final straw. Heart-wrenching sobs started shaking her body from deep down within, the dam just burst and the pent up tears were like a deluge.

Anne-Marie just held her tightly and they were both crying. In a few minutes Lavina's night dress was soaked. All she could hear was Anne-Marie's gentle and soothing words of comfort as she held and rocked her to and fro, telling her it would be ok. Lynne, who knew most of the story, busied herself with the preparing of a breakfast tray for all of them.

Lavina's mind drifted back two years, to that devastating day. She started talking slowly, narrating the devastating drama.

"…you remember after Peter, I completely went off African men, especially Kenyans? I was still hurting and smarting after what he'd put me through, but I now realise in hindsight that it was the wrong path to take. But then, I've never done the conventional thing, have I? Well, I was still working at the hospital and one day I went to this rave with my colleagues, hosted by some insurance firms, and the rest as they say is history. You know that I met Rawal there. We linked up the following week for a couple of coffee dates. After a few months he started insisting on placing our relationship on a different footing. In the subsequent months he completely swept me off my feet, I mean in total sincerity I was sold over! Before I knew what was happening, he'd changed me. For one, I started drinking alcohol heavily and I never used to drink. The next thing I knew was that I'd moved from my brother's place and Rawal had rented a furnished apartment for me. I was not completely green you know, I worked in the medical fraternity and I knew about the dangers of HIV and AIDS. I was a head lab technician, dammit! So I was careful and for one full year we used condoms."

She paused for breath.

"I remember when you used to come down to Mombasa for hols and the occasional weekend. You used to blow your top off about my relationship with Rawal. You warned me time and time again to be careful about him. You kept wondering why a man of Asian origin, of his age, was not married. He was about forty by then, and why he was not staying at the family residence as most Asians do. He lived alone in his apartment. I would spend the occasional weekend or week at his digs and vice versa. You guys know that he gave me everything. I used to have this sneaking suspicion that he was more than just a millionaire. He seemed to have a stake in construction, his fingers were forever in lucrative pies, be it insurance, stocks, entertainment, treasury bonds, you name it and he was there."

Lavina paused to stretch herself. Her friends were staring at her enthralled as if watching those first person narrative movies.

"He provided me with various credit cards and two cars. We had VIP entries into all the exclusive clubs in the country and parties aboard yachts on the entire East African coastline. We pub-crawled on most nights. It was not surprising to bump into the world's richest persons aboard these luxury cruises. Our bank accounts were overflowing with millions and I came to really believe that the Asian community truly controls the Kenyan economy. We would hop into planes and fly to any destination in the world in a moment's notice. He was influential. All he had to say was 'jump' and people would shout 'How high?' He provided insurance and medical cover for me. You name it, I had it. Naturally, you remember my family was very disappointed with the relationship and my dad actually cut me off from his will and said that I was persona-non-grata in any of the family residences and farms. Though he was a teacher, HIV-AIDS was still such a mystery to him then. He forbade the entire family from talking and associating with me. But I still did it anyway, that is, provide for my mum and communicate with my sisters in secret. My mother encouraged me to invest in the property market and I bought several farms in Kitale. She normally checks up on the workers and the wheat grown there. Lately, my dad has come around in his own small way because he knows they benefit financially from the wheat farms. I'm sorry girls, I've jumped the gun and digressed a bit there, let me go back a bit. Rumours started circulating to the effect that Rawal had another girlfriend. I heard that he had built an apartment block for a Somali model in Mtwapa, in Mombasa's north coast. I asked him about it in a gentle way and he denied. I decided to give him the benefit of doubt. Little did I know that I was courting death, and that soon I was going to be issued with a death sentence and that my death certificate was in the offing…"

Lavina's voice became a tiny painful whisper as it trailed away.

"By then we had been together for one year and a half and we were still using condoms. So when he suggested that we stop using condoms, I did not hesitate and agreed. I was in my proper state of mind, but I sometimes think it was a prolonged infatuation of sorts! That is why when people say that AIDS just sneaked up on them and zap! They have it, I believe them. I mean, it happened to me! The man had my knickers twisted up into a terrible muddle! And I let him hand me my death certificate in a neat package like one of his closed deals!"

Lavina paused to look at Anne-Marie and Lynne bitterly.

"And then to my shock, I discovered through the grapevine that he had opened up this supermarket complex at Diani in the South Coast for another lady, a Nubian refugee from Sudan. The man had insatiable appetite! Little did we know that each one of us was one of several and that he was on a destructive trail. I confronted him and he denied it again, by now I was too far gone and madly, as I thought, in love with him. Then came the weekend when he totally disappeared without even a word and was gone for several days. I finally tracked him to Mtwapa at his Somali lover's residence. I heard about it from friends and colleagues and drove over there to put my fears to rest. When I saw his wheels in the parking lot, I flipped my lid! Something in me just gave in, like a pricked and deflated balloon and I knew that my family and friends, like you, had been right to have misgivings all along. I reversed and drove home. When he turned up four days later, I gave vent to my anger. I hurled abuses at him. I hit him. I let my frustrations flow. I cried. I smashed expensive electronics in my so-called apartment. He was not moved by my silly tantrums, as he called them. He said that I'd turned bothersome and he wanted me out. He suggested that we part coz he needed some space! Some space, my foot! Unbelievably, he moved his things out and told me that I could have the apartment for good! I mean just like that!"

Lavina demonstrated with a snap of her fingers.

"After our break-up, I started having this constant, nagging sensation that something was not right. A sort of sixth sense. An inner voice that I couldn't put my finger on. How could he just suggest a break-up without even an effort at putting the record straight or a reconciliation? He didn't even bother to cancel my many credit cards. The apartment was a birthday present that was bought in my name. He had even transferred a few choice ventures we held together into my name! No. Something was definitely not right! No wonder he'd never even suggested putting our relationship into a more permanent footing through marriage. Though, when I once suggested it, he said that his Asian family would never consent to his marriage to an African! I soon shelved all my misgivings and life went on. I plunged headlong into my lab at the hospital and even started recording the most overtime. Any spare time I had, I would spend in my workroom churning out carvings for my own use and for friends on request. I put behind me days of ordering the latest designer labels from catalogues, or even before they hit the catwalk at showcasings of haute-couture of Christian Dior, Elle and Yves Saint Laurent at spring and summer collections! I dropped out of social circles because people kept asking me about what had gone wrong, except for the occasional appearance at the book club meetings. And then came the bombshell."

Lavina paused for effect.

"Yearly at the hospital where I worked we were screened for various ailments before we filled out our medical insurance forms, and a HIV test was mandatory. We all gave our consent, after all, the tests were conducted by ourselves! My job was normally to draw the blood and two of my colleagues would screen the samples. On the morning the results were out, I had just reported on duty as usual and donned my white lab coat and got down to work. It took me a moment to register that the atmosphere crackled with tension. The air flowing in the disinfected lab was practically charged with an overload of emotion! I turned to my two colleagues, you guys you remember Albert and Atika?"

"Yes." whispered Ann-Marie and Lynne simultaneously.

"I asked them why they wore long faces, as if someone had died. If only I'd known, I would not have talked about death, how morbid! It was as if they'd gone deaf and dumb! I mean, they were visibly shaking with an emotion hard to describe, almost akin to fear! I just couldn't understand it! I practically had to shake Atika whom I'd worked with longest to spit it out! I will never forget the tone of his voice that day as long as I live. It was the harbinger of bad tidings… 'La… Lav… Lavina…' Atika had stuttered like a parrot darting despairing glances at Albert. I was surprised because as far as I knew, Atika didn't have the problem of stammering. So, understandably I was flabbergasted, something traumatic must have shaken him. 'Atika…' I threateningly moved closer and then he blurted out 'La…Lavina, we don't know how to tell you this, but your sample is positive!' I remember I stared at him fixedly. 'You mean as in hepatitis A and B or menengitis?' I asked cautiously. I stared at his mouth as he formed the words of his rejoinder. 'No.' He said, 'I mean as in HIV and AIDS!' he said with a bewildered tone of finality.

My friends! I tell you my life came to a complete standstill. What was functioning in my body was only the beating of the heart and flowing of blood! I finally understood what people meant when they said their lives had been shattered. That's what I felt on that day. Atika and Albert were shaken too because they were used to announcing such results to strangers and distant relatives, and after counselling sessions, but not to colleagues and friends! I was shocked beyond belief, I could not work and went home. I was like a zombie. Later on the aftermath of the shock hit me hard. I went cold all over. My blood actually went to below room temperature. In the centre of my very being, despair permeated my whole body. In subsequent days denial set in. It was like a blow to my solar plexus. From then on, every aspect of my life took a downhill turn and I decided to confront Rawal at his office.

When I informed him that he'd infected me with the virus, his coolly impolite and impersonal countenance proved that my accusation was justified. He neither accepted nor denied my allegations. He ordered me out of his office and told the security officers that I should never be allowed to step into the premises again! I was reeling with shock! I knew that there was nothing I could do. I would have said that I was going to sue him and go to court, but still I would need proof. I gave up that line of thought and prayed that our parliamentarians would pass a law making it illegal to knowingly infect another person with HIV. I was worse off a year down the line when I was told that he had died after suffering terribly. I thank God for the Munges because without their support I would have died. Several times I attempted suicide and Lynne and her husband saved me in the nick of time…"

Lavina's voice broke off and she looked at her friends. Lynne just leaned over and gave her friend a tight hug.

"Lavina, I just thank God that we were here for you and the good thing is that you are now leading a positive life and you eat well-balanced meals."

Anne-Marie was contemplative for a long while and then started speaking.

"Lavina, most people who contract HIV in one of the more conventional ways like consensual sex, like your case, accept their zero status easily and live positively. Some people are infected with the virus and their stories are heart rending. A good example is one case study I once handled, this refugee lady was a mother of four. She had fled her country Rwanda during the genocide after losing her entire family, I mean her husband and all her four children! She was scarred for life, because she was raped and brutally mutilated and left to die in this church building with piles of bodies on top of her. Attackers thought everyone was dead, but she wasn't. She fled from Kigali and her native village, Nyamirambo, during the 1994 genocide involving the Hutu tribe and the minority Tutsi. The hundred day genocide, that left close to a million people dead, was triggered by the death of Rwandese President Juvenile Habiryamana of the majority Hutu tribe, whose plane was shot down on sixth April 1994. Once in Kenya, a land this lady called heaven even on her death-bed, this mother lived with nightmares of her family's massacre in front of her very own eyes; a machete strike here and a limb would fall off, a club swing there and a skull cracks open, a spear strike, a bullet through the forehead, a garden hoe across the back and a lifeless body falling down.

She would wake up in the refugee camp at Daadab screaming that she was running from the interahamwe, Hutu militiamen out to terminate all Tutsis and moderate Hutus, seeking solace and refuge in trenches and churches. She even changed her surname from Mukamurenzi to Hachizimana, a local Tutsi name meaning, God will protect. And on to top it all, she was suffering from full blown AIDS and everything that goes with it. I mean the full works of herpes, night sweats, and wasting away of the body and pain. So, Lavina, in short, all I'm saying is that you are indeed not too badly off. You are well and not sick and I would urge you to start taking herbs. I have been introduced to some patients who are not responding well to anti-retrovirals, but are responding extremely well to alternative medicines, so the call is yours."

"I know." Lavina said, "I thank God that I'm actually hardly ever sick. Just an occasional fever, and that I sometimes remember our school read of years back, Elechi Amadi's The Concubine and where it says, ...death is an untimely reaper often choosing the most promising fruit, hitting at the inappropriate time and expecting to be thanked for it..."

Anne-Marie and Lynne hugged Lavina in one bear hug with tears in their eyes, knowing that they would always be there for one another. Ann-Marie was the first to break away laughing and rubbing tears from her eyes.

"Now Lavina, on a lighter note, what is this I hear that your fiance has made you an expert on the Opera and F. Choppin and F. Schubert?"

Lynne joined in, "She will soon be flying off to Italy for recitals by the acclaimed Italian pianist Michelangelo and later on be a collector of Van Beethoven, Lombardi and Solbiati! Not forgetting shopping at Fazal's in Nairobi where a pair of socks goes for three thousand shillings and a Gerry Weber pantsuit thirty thousand!"

Ann-Marie could not resist one last dig.

"I understand that Giorgio has to wear power suits, or so they are called, because of their cut. You know, the cut of these suits sits exceptionally well! In Kenya you can only get them at Italian Men's Wear on Kaunda Street in Nairobi, a must visit whenever he's in Nairobi; a Mario Barruti goes for forty thousand, a Cannali between fifty thousand and eighty thousand and a Karl Kaiser twenty five! The cheapest by far is a Francisco Tolli going for around ten to fifteen thousand or thereabouts..."

Lavina took their ribbing well by responding,

"Don't bet your lives that I'm going to change from being a Yuppie, you know, Young Urban Professional Person! I bet I can combine being an upwardly mobile urban sophisticate and socialite with being an Italian wife!"

Lynne suddenly looked at Anne-Marie with a mischievous glint in her eyes.

"Hey, Anne! You've hardly said anything about your current beau! Who is it this time?"

Ann-Marie cast them a mock woebegone expression.

"I can't seem to get a man who will stick around long enough to contemplate marriage. My career seems to be a challenge to them. My six-figure salary too daunting for them to face! They think I will soon end up as a CEO of the corporation!"

"Welcome to the club. I quit years back when I married Tim!" Lynne quipped after listening to Ann-Marie's complaints for a while.

"Which club?" A puzzled Ann-Marie asked.

"www-dot-can'tkeepamancozofmydemandingcareer-dot-com." Lynne replied matter-of- factly. All three burst out laughing and collapsed in giggles, but immediately sobered up.

Lavina stared at her friends.

"You know, when I'm alone and I think about you guys I realize how much we've shared. It's like stepping into a time machine... and Anne-

Marie, we will miss you once you leave tomorrow, but please be coming down here as frequently as possible and we will also visit you regularly. And the phone line is always open for you!"

They soon started discussing ways to contribute to make Lavina's latest project a success. The name of the art gallery she wanted to open was 'Lavina's Alfresco'. Lavina went on to explain that Alfresco was Italian for outdoors... Soon she was teaching them the basics in Italian dialogue.They collapsed in giggles when Lavina insisted on them speaking in staccato to attain the right accent.

"*Mi chiamo* means My name is…"

"No! Anne-Marie! No! You are pronouncing it all wrong… Lynne is doing better!"

Chapter 22

London.

The bustle of activity at London's Heathrow airport had drained them yesterday! No wonder it was said to be the world's busiest airport with a live flight information system. The four terminals with four foreign exchange bureaus had confused Lavina and though they had come in through terminal three, when Giorgio had gone to change some money, she had gone looking for him at the two exchange bureaus in the public area instead of the two in the passenger area!

So today Giorgio had decided that he should give Lavina the complete tourist circuit of London city before they went to the gallery. Since two days ago when they had alighted at the busy Heathrow airport, they had not had a chance to sight-see.

The chime of Big Ben traveled through the cool London afternoon, its sound reaching Lavina's ears before she could see the world's most famous clock. The chime was a familiar sound since the BBC took it as its signature tune on December thirty-first of 1923.

Giorgio insisted that no trip to England is ever complete without a stroll through Central London. They saw the London Eye from afar and hurried to buy tickets at the old quarters of the Greater London Council. Lavina learnt that the imposing building overlooking the Eye was officially opened in 1922 by King George the fifth. It houses Dali's

Universe Exhibition and the London Aquarium.

They didn't need the services of a tour guide as Giorgio had been to London many times. They climbed into the capsules stringed along the gigantic wheel which seems stationery until you were in it and realized that it moves at a snail's pace reaching around a hundred and forty feet high above the skyline of London.

They were with about twenty other tourists in the spacious capsule. The higher they climbed the more of the city's landmarks came into view. The Houses of Parliament, the Thames river coursing its way below, Tower of London, Saint Paul's Cathedral, Buckhingham Palace, Canary Wharf with its Gherking shape, Jubilee Gardens and a host of other land marks.

They decided to go for a stroll on the South Bank of the Thames where kings and queens walked centuries before including and one of the world's literary icons Charles Dickens. They finally reached the gallery with the Africa shows in the gallery at the renovated OXO towers. Lavina was dismayed at the face of Africa with its usual war-torn misery and longed for her visit later on to Bjorn's gallery for a taste of positive African art.

Next was the Tower Bridge opened by Prince Albert in 1894 and a new addition, the Millenium Bridge down by the Tate Art Gallery. Further on was St. Paul's Cathedral opened by Queen Anne in 1707 awesome with its spectacular dome. Lavina remembered how as a small girl she had watched on television the live broadcast of Prince Charles and Princess Diana's fairytale wedding in this church.

They later stopped at a Starbucks for coffee by the Victoria Embankment.

In the evening they left the five star London Sheraton where they were staying and which they had chosen because of its location in

Mayfair of Central London and proximity to most tourist sites and went for the showcasing of Zimbabwean art at Bjorn's gallery. He had invited Lavina specially so that she could see for herself what he was doing for African art before they arranged for her own special show.

Lavina was stunned beyond belief when she met her icons Dominic Benhura and Agnes Nyanhongo in the flesh! Giorgio knew she was in her element and soon left her discussing with her fellow artistes how art is all about balance, scale and proportion.

The gallery was already full. Many other tourists and art lovers were buying and placing orders. At first Lavina was awed in the presence of the two greats, *especially Nyanhongo, a reknowned Second Generation female sculptor in Zimbabwe*, but soon started discussing how international fake artists were targeting them and imitating their famous sculptures and how it takes a practiced eye to notice the difference.

Agnes Nyanhongo was saying:

"…I want to be judged as a sculptor, not as a woman sculptor."

The motherly dark-skinned older woman's wise sayings held Lavina captive for the entire evening.

"…You don't drown a stone in texture, put it in the bath like a baby and scrub it clean."

Lavina was much more interested in Nyanhongo today than Benhura because she had studied his works in more depth than Nyanhongo's. They went around the gallery dissecting her works.

Her First Child – in Opal Stone
Advising Aunt – in Opal Stone
Spiritual woman – in Springstone
Mbuya Nehanda – (Meaning Spirit Medium)
Woman Fetching Water – in Opal Stone
Responsibility – in Opal Stone (A woman with a toddler
and a babe in her arms)
Discussing – (3 women sitting and talking)
Rainmaker – in Opal Stone
Foetus – in Springstone
Grandmother Fetching Water
Beer for the Bira – After harvest, a ceremony of Thanksgiving
Divided Family – A group sculpture of a family with broken
noses and faces, some backs turned on others.
Woman Sowing Seeds

Proud of my wedding dress
Secrets – In Springstone
Muroora (Daughter-In-Law) in Springstone

Later the discussion turned to the sensational Kenyan family of carvers from Tabaka in Kenya, Lavina's paternal ancestral home, who had landed a contract with a US filmmaker to carve the dysfunctional cartoon family of The Simpsons set in the fictional town of Springfiled in the US.—the whole works from Old man Homer, Marge, Bart, Maggie and Lisa, for the new season premiering soon.

They had to mass-produce three hundred statues a week! Including their Monopoly game, The Homer Drinking Hat that feeds you beer through a drip secured above your ears. The even more complicated to carve – the long crooked nose of Montgomery Burns the evil owner of the nuclear plant and Chief Wiggum the fat lazy police chief.

The discussion went on to how perfect in likeness the sculptures produced so far were and what dedication and talent it takes to produce such world class works.

Chapter 23

Lavina was startled out of her sleep by the fierce barking of the watchdogs. She was not worried, knowing that they had only heard Giorgio's car driving up to the electronic gates of their residence. The watchman would be there as the Dobermans and Alsatians ran over to welcome him.

Giorgio bounced up the few steps leading to the verandah and strolled to the pool area with his favourite close to his heels. The twin Dobermans, Rosy and Lucy, were inseparable. They were licking his hands as he patted them, their tails wagging happily. Lucy ran over and plopped herself at Lavina's feet, she reached out and patted the dog on her head, as she lay down contented. Giorgio came over and dropped a kiss on Lavina's head.

"Hello lovely."

She slipped off her Calvin Klein shades and put down the book of Italian phrases she had been holding.

"Hi sweetheart." She replied as he dropped onto a deck chair and Rosy immediately plopped down at his feet. Giorgio absentmindedly tickled the dog's tummy, she growled happily at the petting.

Lavina noticed that he looked more tired than usual. The local engineers had been antagonistic towards him of late. He seemed to be getting stressed by the animosity they showed day in day out. Lavina tentatively asked,

"How did it go today honey?"

Giorgio started explaining to her what he had accomplished. He had spent the whole day at the Regional Planning Board office with Tony, poring over maps and discussing a bridge. After conducting a feasibility study, Giorgio was against the idea of building the bridge. He did not understand why the government was favouring a bridge and not a tunnel, which he had recommended. A bridge was going to wreak havoc to the local community on the south coast side. The majority of the Digo who inhabited the area would have to be relocated. His argument was that the bridge was going to take up a huge tract of land and compensation of owners would run into a colossal amount of money.

The government claimed it did not have the money, yet it didn't want to heed his advice. Smacks of politics, if you were to ask him.

He was thoughtful once more. On the Mombasa mainland side, several hospitals were going to be affected, like the Aga Khan, Pandya Memorial and Mombasa hospitals. Several well-run, established schools would also be on the receiving end; like Loreto Convent, Star of the Sea, Mama Ngina and Aga Khan schools, just to name a few. Several firms would suffer economically, including several hotels. The government's insistence on going ahead with the bridge building project seemed unwise to him. His voice went on and on.

Lavina listened indulgently, and then interrupted.

"There is a lot of tension in the south coast. A simmering pot that turned into a time bomb that was the genesis of the 1997 Likoni[47] land clashes. I've always believed that there should be honest investigations so that the bitterness about land alienation can be assuaged, because prominent families from upcountry have been blamed for grabbing land from indigenous owners aided by the first government of this nation."

"I like it that you are so passionate about the land issue. I've also been concerned about it and we have had occasion to discuss all that. So I was rather surprised today to find that Tony has undergone a certain metamorphosis, I'll call it a change of heart, and dropped his misgivings about constructing the tunnel."

Lavina was silent as she digested the news about Tony's about-turn, she knew the guy from her past, and he wasn't a very likeable chap. He must have a sinister motive, or an unpleasant surprise up his sleeve. She thought of the way he'd treated her during the mayor's Christmas ball.

Giorgio stood up.

"Let me have a quick swim before we go in for dinner."

He went to the changing rooms, and soon he was in the pool, taking some energetic laps. Lavina was watching him, but she was subconsciously thinking of what Anne-Marie's reaction deep down her heart had been to her revelation on her HIV status…

She knew of people who had taunted her, Tony being one of them. But she had already explained about Tony to Giorgio, when he brought him over for dinner just the other day, and Giorgio had sensed the tension in the room…

She could forgive people for being condescending, but she could not understand why, when HIV/AIDS came up in any discussion, you discover how shallow and callous the people closest to you can turn out to be. She would never forget her first moment of stunned horror and disbelief, but she knew that Anne-Marie had feelings that ran deep, she wondered how it was going to be for her to judge a loved one, to weigh a loved one on scales and find her wanting, not to be dealing with one of her case files or statistics…

Giorgio dragged himself out of the pool, and stood over Lavina, stunned by the look of unhappiness in her eyes. He loved her so much that it hurt He wanted so desperately to make her happy, make her forget, yet she was making it difficult with her disbelief.

"Lavy, up you get and into the shower, it will soon be time for dinner, and I know you've cooked my favourite, and you know how fussy old Karisa gets about the dinner going cold…"

He chuckled as he held out his hand for her. She didn't need a second invitation. She obligingly grabbed his large hand in her small one, and they ran inside, and up the stairs laughing like a couple of kids, their feet making damp foot outlines on the wooden treads.

She shut herself in their master bedroom's bathroom, stripped out of her bikini suit and put on a shower cap and stepped into the shower, she adjusted the water to steamy hot and reached for the soap.

She had just started soaping herself, when she heard the sound she had subconsciously been waiting for. The shower door opened and Giorgio stepped in, naked and gorgeously male. Her stomach fluttered. That's why she preferred the shower to the bath, so that he could join her. He slammed the door shut behind him and stood very still for a moment, his eyes travelling slowly down her slim, petite and slick wet body.

He never seemed to tire at marvelling how beautiful and delicate she was. Then he said huskily,

"Hand me the soap."

Unable to do anything else, she handed it to him. He began at her shoulders, moving his soap-slicked hands in slow circles over her rounded bones. His fingers slid down a path to the valley between her breasts. She felt a heavy warmth in her veins, and an almost intolerable suspense as she waited for him to reach her nipples, the peaks already taut and quivering with anticipation.

When at last he cupped her taut upright breasts, she shuddered with pleasure. He let his hands slide lower to her navel, her abdomen and her thighs. Then he bent, went down on his knees and gave his special loving attention to her ankles and toes. When she thought sensual pleasure would overwhelm her, he rose and pulled her into his arms. He was completely, totally, utterly and irrevocably in love, and this was just one of his ways of showing it. His soapy hands went around her to lather her back and hips.

Tingling sensations of need began deep within and radiated through her. The hard leanness of his water-slick body was imprinted on her. He was playing the part of her personal servant, performing the most intimate of tasks, but she was the one who was enslaved and enthralled by his caressing and possessive hands.

He released her from his embrace and said, "Here. Take the soap," placing the tablet in her hands. He rinsed his hands and then cupped his palms, gently redirecting the spray of water towards her, bombarding her body, to rinse away the soap suds. She rotated slowly and when she faced him again, his cupped hands tossed water at her breasts and shoulders, drenching her in sensual pleasure.

Then it was her turn. She was positively salivating at the thought. She revelled in the freedom to massage his body with her soapy hands, loving the feel of the hair-crisp skin of his muscular chest against her soft palms. His back was satiny and smooth with hard musculature and bone underneath. Her hands wandered over him, down further, tracing his thigh muscles, just as he'd done with her, and into his inner thighs. His sharp intake of breath said it all.

When she had rinsed him with splashes of water, she raised her face to him. He stood staring at her. He seemed to do that a lot lately, as if memorizing her, letting his eyes feast on her good figure, committing and imprinting her to memory. Then with a soft groan, he pulled her into his arms and kissed her.

She was on fire with sensation, the water running warm and silky over their skins, his hands sliding possessively over her wet hips and back, his tongue probing her mouth. With dreamlike slowness, he released her and turned off the flow of water.

He drew her with him out of the shower cubicle and slowly patted her dry as you would a baby, with a fluffy bath towel and infinite gentleness. When she had done the same to him, he lifted her naked body in his arms and carried her out of the bathroom. His eyes flashed down at her, taking in the ebony length of her lying in his arms.

A teasing smile lifted her lips.

"Are you going to stare at me the whole evening my dear?"

"No my love. I'm simply overwhelmed and completely bowled over by how much I love you."

He lowered her from the cradle of his arms onto the waterbed and followed her to stretch down beside her. How much I love you. He said those words with such reverence, and they meant so much to her. They sent a charged depth of feeling coursing through her.

She propped herself on one elbow and trailed a questing fingernail through the dark hair on his chest, lightly pinching his tiny taut nipples, she knew he loved her doing that.

"And I love you too dear… so very much…"

Her words seemed to have a deep impact on him. He draped a hand around her neck, and pulled her to him.

"Kiss me," he muttered, his warm breath caressing her mouth.

An impish urge to tease him made her lower her mouth very slowly to his and then, with the lightness of a butterfly's wings, touch the top of his lip with hers. She explored the contours of his mouth slowly, nibbling gently at the upper curve, her tongue deftly flicking out and touching his fuller lower one. He tolerated the exquisite torture until she thought he must be immune to her light toying with his lips. Then a shudder racked his body, and he twisted upward violently and rolled over to trap her under him.

Slowly, huskily, with a thread of laughter in his throat, he said,

"You vixen! For that, you'll pay, lady…. and pay dearly."

"I already have," she breathlessly replied, knowing deep down she had fallen so deeply and irrevocably in love with him. She would never be the same again.

Something came and went in his face, it was so swift, she didn't get time to analyze the emotion, but it was something moving. Maybe the sincerity in her voice had moved him.

"No," he countered in a seductive murmur, moving his hands to the sensitive skin of her throat, he knew she loved him touching her there. "You haven't even begun yet."

He eased his weight away and stretched his hand to the bedside drawer. Whenever that moment came, she knew what he was reaching for. But today something just sort of gave way in her, a thread seemed to snap, is that what people call the last straw?

She just couldn't stand it. Lately she'd had this feeling that she was failing him in some way. He deserved more. So much more. She just wasn't enough for him. He deserved someone he could make love to without hindrance.

Giorgio knew what was coming. They had been going through this tenseness almost every other night lately.

He had fallen in love with Lavina, and they had gone through counselling, because she had come clean with him before they got involved, and they had agreed to the use of condoms every time they made love. But recently she seemed to resent this, because according to her reasoning, she felt that she was letting him down in a way, denying him an essential part of intimacy. She felt that he should get someone else.

She didn't seem to get it, did she? He loved her dearly, he didn't want someone else. He wanted her and her alone. Now to have to deal with hysterics... Something inside her head exploded. She whirled away,

"I know I'm not satisfying you—"

She tensed her muscles as if to get out of the bed, but felt Giorgio's hard hands on her shoulders. She twisted herself and wildly attempted to get away.

"*Dos Santos*! For God's sake! Stop it Lavy!"

He grasped her shoulders and pulled her back against him.

"Damn you, woman, that's what's wrong. You keep focusing on me every night instead of us." He turned her around to face him. "You know I love you, I'm here for you sweetheart, please don't do this. Just because we use protection, it doesn't mean that I get less of your love, it's what comes from the heart that matters…"

"Oh God, no." She buried her face against the cords of muscle on his neck, fighting to maintain her sanity while inside her the dam burst its banks. The tears just started flowing.

"The pain," she sobbed, "years and years… I'm going to waste…." She lifted her head. "You don't know the pain that courses through me everyday as I think of my life, ebbing away, you don't know half of it, I know I'm going to die…"

She couldn't stop crying. She sobbed against his chest and he held her in the warm circle of his arms and said nothing. When her sobbing abated, he said,

"Lavy," the word was husky and possessive. "Tell me. Don't shut me out now. Please talk to me. You know you can tell me anything, that's why I'm here, to help you go through this, baby."

She shook her head silently and his grip tightened.

"We can't have peace of mind if you don't talk to me, you're not supposed to bottle it all up inside, or think about dying. Yes, you're bound to have lapses into self pity or isolated bouts of depression, but I don't want you to think of death, because I won't let you die, so come on, talk to me…"

She did then, in a low, halting voice, filled with pain, spilling it all out; how shut out she was feeling, how scared, the insecurity, the fear of death stalking her… When she was finished she looked up into his eyes, hoping she might see a flicker of understanding and affection, but instead she thought she saw compassion.

Anguish filled her very being, tearing at her soul. He feels sorry for you. She wrenched away, grabbed her negligee from the night-stand, threw it on inside out, ran to the door that led out to their bedroom verandah and tugged at it viciously. It flew open and she propelled herself like a zombie or rather like an automaton. A robot.

She stood in the moonlight's reflection, thinking of that night here when she first told him she was HIV positive. She stared out at the shimmering beach down below. The stars were shining down on the water. What a beautiful sight.

"Lavy! Get back in here for crying out loud!"

His voice was sharp, commanding. He strolled out and joined her, in his night gown.

"It's damn cold out here." His face loomed over her. "Lets get back to bed."

"No."

"Why?" His breathing was fast and raspy.

"I don't feel like it."

"Well I certainly feel like it." He said matter-of-factly.

She stared at him, her black eyes cold, her full breasts heaving.

"I don't want your pity."

His lips twisted, his voice low, savagely harsh.

"What I'm feeling right now, isn't pity," he said, and glanced pointedly at the lower front of his gown as if the protruding imprint of his aroused manhood was proof enough of what he was feeling...

She met his eyes, her courage burning in the bright moonlit night.

"But it isn't love."

The misty smell of the sea at high tide drifted up and down from the beach, teasing their nostrils.

"Well, what do you think it is?"

His words were harsh and insistent, edged with a curious ring. She recoiled, she didn't want to answer him, but his arms on her chest nudged her to speak.

"Desire. Lust. I don't know. Why do you insist on labelling it?"

He replied hoarsely,

"Because that's the way you like things, all neatly labelled in boxes. This much love for Giorgio, this depth of reaction from Anne-Marie, these many calls from Lynne in as many days. All wrapped up in neat packages. Why for heaven's sake can't you just forget everything else, and just love me? I keep expressing and acknowledging my love for you."

He stopped for a moment, his eyes locked on hers. "And do you know what frightens you most of all?"

The gleam in his eyes stole her breath away. The hard pounding of her heart must have been evident to him through his knuckles that were embedded, and seemed almost welded to her chest.

"You are afraid that your love for me is going to be hopeless, and that I'm going to leave you, but I won't. I keep promising you that."

Writhing under his hands, she cried.

"No! I'm not afraid!" Whatever composure she had was dwindling rapidly.

He replied.

"Yes! You are still so scared, even right now you're lying through your clenched teeth!"

His eyes impaled her. She twisted her head to avoid his enigmatic stare. Impatiently, he gripped her hands tighter and shook her.

"Admit the truth, damn you! Sometimes I can even feel it when you can't sleep soundly Lavina, it's developed into some sort of

214

chronic insomnia. And if you're not careful it will metamorphose into schizophrenia or some sort of borderline personality disorder!"

His calm demeanor was a maddening counterpoint to her own unwarranted rage. She turned back, wanting desperately to know what was going on behind that lean face, her temper warming every cell in her body.

"Why should I admit anything? You care nothing for me!"

The silence stretched. She held her breath, she knew she had thrown an angry challenge to him, hoping against hope that he'd deny it. His next words were strangely distant, sort of disembodied as if in disbelief…

"I've given up my freedom, dreams of having many children like any typical Italian family, so that I can be with you, and you want me to prove my love? My family back in Italy are still in shock, they still don't believe that I've finally made up my mind to marry and settle down here… they call me a *lunatico*, that the tropical winds of this *paradiso* have gone to my heado..."

Italian accent slipped into his speech as he was wont to do when emotionally charged.

"…that I'll soon get over it. They thought I would marry Gabriella, her *aristocratico* Donatonni family is old money, vineyards, real estate, but I've disappointed them. And you still question my love…?"

His words trailed off as he shrugged and rubbed his hands over his eyes wearily, sliding his hands in an upward motion to run his fingers through his curly hair. He went back into the bedroom, and tiredly sunk onto the bed, his face held in his hands.

Looking at him, she suddenly realized that he had given her so much room. So much private space. Yet all she needed to do was share just a little bit of that space with him. Hope fluttered and then blazed up in her, and every feminine nerve in her was screaming for her to go to him. And she did. She followed her basic instincts and went and sat beside him on the bed.

"Giorgio. Dear God. Honey, I'm so very sorry. Please forgive me. Yes, I admit I'm scared of where this relationship is headed. I've turned into a commitment phobic and I'm afraid to love again."

He locked up. The love was blazing from his eyes. The room seemed to reel with the powerful emotion. Then he said softly,

"Don't apologize, you'll realize how very much I care for you and love you one of these fine days. You can be sure of that. And please don't worry about the condoms. It's ok with me. I keep reassuring you of that."

"Oh Giorgio! It seems like an obstacle of gigantic proportions, almost insurmountable."

"Don't worry." He said softly as he lifted his weight and rolled to one side of the big bouncy waterbed.

He leaned on one elbow and looked down at her with a dark, unreadable expression.

"Giorgio…."

"What is it my dear?" His tone was tender.

"G, plea - please… touch me—"

"But I am touching you." His hand trailed mockingly down the silken length of her thigh. A moan escaped her throat.

"Giorgio – *il mio amore* –"

As she provocatively moved her hips, she felt him grow and tense. A low sound like the satisfied purr of a lion escaped from his throat. He slipped her negligee from her shoulders.

He bent to her, and where his hands caressed, his lips trailed, setting her on fire with want and need. She raked his shoulders and back with her fingernails, her body in a frenzied state of waiting and wanting. His lips took a leisurely path to her breasts, and then he moved, covering her nipple with his mouth. She gasped aloud and clung to him. He lifted his head and eased her torment, only to take her other breast in his mouth and tease its taut crest into an aching peak with his tongue.

Inside she felt like a volcano ready to erupt. Her body arched involuntarily, almost making him lose control.

"Giorgio! Please… Please! No more…"

He laughed softly.

"Patience, *mia cara*, patience. Let us dispense of the necessary first."

He handed her the silver packet, and this time she didn't freak out.

He watched her as she peeled off the silver foil covering and helped him put on the latex. He lifted his hands and they discovered each other all over again. Lovingly, lingering in the secret feminine and masculine places, bringing each other a devastating delight. He was taking her to heaven and beyond.

She kept whispering his name in an aching sound of longing and yearning, as he kept whispering how much he loved and needed her. His erotic pleasuring lengthened into tortured rapture, until at long last he heeded her whispered pleadings and made them as one. And she felt as she always did when he slipped his penis into her—safe and secure.

If she thought she had seen heaven before, she now knew she had only glimpsed a far horizon, because with him, for the first time in her life, she felt a complete woman as he plunged his member into her moist, warm tight sheath time and time again.

With him, each time was like their first time together. Rediscovering over and over again. She had never been this way with any man before. When she experienced as much pleasure as she had never believed possible, he took her on a new soaring flight which peaked in an explosion of passion and ecstasy.

How she yearned to feel his seed spilling in her, but the condom prevented that. How she wanted a baby of their own. But how was that going to happen, short of an adoption agency? She pushed the traitorous thoughts aside.

When it was all over he held her gently, letting her float slowly back to earth with him.

A moment later, her even breathing signified that she was fast asleep, purring contentedly with a smile on her face like that proverbial cat with nine lives that got away with the cream. Giorgio possessively held her in the circle of his arms as she subconsciously snuggled and fitted into the curve of his body. He never felt such peace before. She had a strange power over him. Soon he also drifted off.

Dinner could wait, old mama Karisa was going to hit the roof if the dinner went cold!

Otherwise, what was the microwave oven for?

Chapter 24

Giorgio stared around the clinic, he hated the atmosphere here: the usual pin-drop silence in the drab room; the usual quiet silence in the drab room. The mood was always subdued. That was vintage Lavina, her determination admirable. But he always wondered why she insisted on coming for testing at the public VCT[48] centre instead of the private hospitals in Mombasa.

He chided himself for not answering that one! After all he'd been the one to cajole her into coming for her test month after month. It was her fear manifesting itself again, the fear of bumping into people she knew. Most of the empty gazes cast around by those in the room, revealed a deep emptiness that human empathy alone cannot fill and heal.

Effortlessly he had by now crammed the familiar words that the receptionist always told her mostly youthful audience. He could chant them off-head,

"…We do HIV counselling and testing, the results will be given to you verbally, but no certificate is issued…"

Every other month, the ten-minute wait had become the longest ten minutes of their lives. It had become a sort of suspense ritual. The lancet would pierce Lavina's middle finger. Short, sharp and quick. Then the pipette would guide the oozing drops of blood into apertures on both kits. The medics called it parallel testing. In ten minutes, the drops aided by a buffer solution would show where Lavina stood this month. They both knew the routine well by now; like clockwork. A line of any intensity forming in the test region, plus a line forming in the control region, indicated that she was still positive. A line appearing in the control region only would indicate that she has turned negative.

Lavina smiled to herself wryly, thinking… if wishes were horses! In my wildest dreams!

If no line appears in the control region, the test was declared inconclusive and had to be repeated.

Giorgio and Lavina were not overly concerned about the result, for they knew that they adhered to the strict routine only to establish her CD4 count, which determined her immunity level, and indicated if her viral load had gone down.

As they walked out of the clinic, they discussed how simple HIV/AIDS testing had become, and this even brought a rueful smile to Lavina's lips as Giorgio said,

"Two red marks, bold in their declaration on a straight line in the control region only, a crimson mark of health."

"Pity you still can't do it yourself at home, like with a pregnancy kit, unless you are a doctor." Lavina quipped, tongue in cheek.

They now had personal jokes most times concerning her erratic CD4 counts, but they knew that in most instances drastic drops in CD4 counts heralded death knells.

Suddenly Lavina blurted out.

"G, I don't think we should get married!"

"And why not my love, if I may ask?"

Lavina sighed listlessly and drew in a long breath before replying.

"It's months now and you know that my CD4 has dropped drastically from around 800 to 300. It's scary and alarming. I'd worked myself to the bone to get it to such a high level."

"Sweetheart, it's coz you are stressing yourself too much. At least the doc discovered what has been suppressing your immunity. You just have to keep taking the treatment regime he prescribed. It's not such a bad cocktail of drugs! Your CD4 will improve once more."

Giorgio had seen first-hand what nightmares Lavina had been going through lately! She was constantly nauseous and threw up all the time, diarrhoea was a call away and the doctor said that it was neuropathy, also caused by abnormalities of the nervous system.

Giorgio had committed himself to her and was in this for keeps, so he just hugged her tighter and dropped a kiss on her forehead.

Chapter 25

Three months later in Mombasa.

The dark man had positioned himself two feet or so from the bank entrance to their right. He wore a casual, nondescript gray shirt. Nothing about him was unusual. He looked utterly like the common businessman out to deposit the day's takings.

So why was her attention drawn to him? Because she realized that he was a parody of too much normality. She had always had this extra sensory knack of foreboding. A sort of forewarning when something was wrong; a strong intuition that a strange scenario was about to unfold.

To their left she noticed another man, this one not too dark, but an aura of wildness clung to him, surrounded him, permeated from him and set him apart from the rest of the clients thronging into the bank. Strangely, she started thinking of the recent bank heist in Nairobi where robbers led bank workers in singing hymns before proceeding to a nearby hotel for tea and getting away with their loot.

Her eyes strayed again to the man with the wildness aura emanating from him, his muscles were flexed taut, as if in expectancy of something. His eyes protruded a bit, as if being crowded from his head, yet seeming dilated at the same time. She was familiar with that dazed look. He was stoned to high heaven! He was too spaced out. She shifted her gaze to the other man, his eyes were still fixed to the bank's doors, but the pupils had contracted to wary pinpoints.

Were the two men pickpockets? Nevertheless, she felt reassured when she noticed the GSU (General Service Unit, a paramilitary wing of the armed forces) in their jungle, brown-green coloured camouflage khaki uniform stationed at strategic points, their AK47's at the ready. For what? Maybe they were escorts for a businessman withdrawing his employees' salary?

After all, it was the end of the month. Or maybe additional security for the bank? All this registered in Lavina's mind in the few minutes it took her and Giorgio to approach the bank's entrance. She gripped Giorgio's arm tighter than she had been holding it, feeling the lean muscles, wanting to draw him away from the dark man's piercing gaze, yet unable to speak.

Did I have time to warn him? This fine point in time would haunt her every waking moment and every sleeping moment in the weeks to come. She blamed herself because she was quite streetwise and should have trusted her instincts.

She saw the dark man's hand reach into his pant pocket. At the same time the bank's revolving doors burst open, two men rushed out, toting what looked like sub-machine guns in one hand while their other hands held the cream coloured bags used by banks to hold coins.

She was not surprised when, with a movement so swift, yet also incredibly predictable, the dark man pulled a small pistol from his pant pocket and brandished it in the air to clear the way for his accomplices so that they could make it to their get-away car.

She was dazed. It was like a reenactment of scenes from countless action-packed movies she had watched. She had never been witness to an actual robbery before. So much for GSU soldiers and also other bank security, she thought, as the gangsters shoved her out of the way. She turned, instinctively looking for Giorgio, whose hand had slipped from hers. She heard a harsh voice barking at her:

"*Wewe mama wazimu! Unataka kifo? Songa kando!*"

She stared around and realized that almost everyone, in typical Kenyan style with survival instincts in overdrive, had hit the pavements and sidewalks prostrate, covering their heads with their hands.

She was still too dazed. When the brown man pointed his pistol at her because she had not moved as commanded by his dark brown accomplice, what he wanted to do at point-blank range was all too clear. That was the moment when Giorgio chose to hurl himself between the pistol and Lavina.

Simultaneously, a cracking sound filled the air. Acrid smoke. Giorgio's mouth opened in a silent scream, he toppled over, hands reaching out to break his fall. She held him upright, instinctively knowing he had been shot instead of her. He had tried to protect her, taking a bullet for her! Her screaming filled the air in a long, drawn-out, desperate soprano!

"G-I-O-R-G-I-O-O-O-O-O-O-O…"

She heard other crackling shots, glanced around and saw that the GSU men had intercepted two of the gangsters before reaching their car, thus the ensuing exchange of fire. One of the gangsters was already down, writhing in pain, a bag of coins and scattered bank notes beside him. The other robber ran off limping down Nkrumah Road towards the Makadara grounds. Maybe the driver of their get-away car had panicked and driven off without them!

Giorgio's fingers gripped her shoulder, digging through her blouse and into the flesh in the briefest fraction of time. He swayed in an uneven circle, his face bewildered, his feet not moving. Then his body sagged.

Adrenalin blazed through Lavina, filling her muscles with strength. She grasped his waist, not realizing that she was sobbing with fright, and with effort lowered his limp body gently to the asphalt.

Hot as it was, she knelt over him. Still uncertain and praying that he had not been shot, she saw the neatly indented hole just to the left of his top shirt button. She stared at his Sergio Ferno shirt, as bright redness oozed onto the white Italian silk serge. She pressed the base of her thumb against slippery fabric, a primitive, instinctive attempt to stop the flow of her love's life blood.

Why? Oh why? She couldn't remember her first aid, or anything she had learnt as a Girl Guide. Why did all such basics disappear at such critical times?

"Lavina…" the struggle of Giorgio's laboured whisper, heaved, slippery below her hand.

She looked at his face and shivered. How come his colour had darkened so quickly?

"*Mia… cara…?*" He was staring at her. Never before had she been so aware of his eyes… so very blue… and then a thin, s-shaped squiggle of redness moved in the left sclera… moisture clumped his thick, straight lashes.

In this infinitely stretched moment, she was possessed with a metaphysical certainty, a true religious fanaticism. She thought that only through her gaze, could she infuse Giorgio with a redemptive life force. The totality of her visual concentration regaled her other senses. She started praying to the Jesus that Ann-Marie believed in, she thought of the Resurrection Garden in Karen, Nairobi, that her friend was always talking about. A few choice favourite Bible verses came to mind.

She didn't hear the cries and thundering footsteps of the traumatized crowd, who by now had gotten to their feet. She was oblivious to the pushing. She smelled neither acrid gunfire smoke, nor the sour pungency of panic, nor that of sickening blood.

She scarcely felt the brutal unintentional kick land squarely between her shoulder blades, aimed unknowingly by someone in the stampeding crowd. She just wanted to protect Giorgio's recumbent body from being trampled underfoot in the pandemonium.

Everyone was in a state of panic. At the back of her mind she subconsciously equated the hellish scene to the one witnessed during the 1997 terrorist bomb attack in Nairobi. She had been in the thick of it. Kenya's own Bloody Friday. Though aimed at the US Embassy, many innocent lives were snuffed out in just a few minutes of fanaticism and terrorist outrage that knew no rhyme nor reason.

She stared at Giorgio's eyes as if guiding him through the depth of some dark, primordial forest. She had always viewed death as a frightening topic. Now this… She couldn't believe that he was going to die before her, with her being HIV positive and all.

She started whimpering in pain and asking for help.

"…please… please help me…"

Nobody seemed to hear her.

After a while, she noticed that the bank's managers had come out and taken over. Soon the police were there as well as an ambulance. She recognized the bank manager squatting beside her.

The paramedics and emergency crew rushed over, carrying a stretcher and oxygen equipment. The oxygen mask was put over Giorgio's face… Lavina absentmindedly noted 'THE MOMBASA MEMORIAL HOSPITAL' emblazoned on the ambulance's side. At least Giorgio would get the best medical attention. Anyway, it was the nearest hospital.

❦❦❦❦

Later.

Lavina and Anne-Marie were in a large private room at the Mombasa Hospital. She looked at Ann-Marie gratefully. She really needed someone close to her to help her go through this. The minute Anne-Marie had received the call from Lynne she hopped onto the next flight from Nairobi to Mombasa, which had taken approximately forty five minutes.

The Munges had come and gone. They were so devastated. They promised to be back the following day. Gabriella had just arrived from Malindi, but kept going on and on about how Lavina kept landing Giorgio in trouble ever since they met. They had had an altercation on the basis of the accusations. Anne-Marie and hospital staff had separated them, otherwise it would have degenerated into a cat fight!

Earlier on, the hospital authorities had inquired if Lavina and the others could be tested, and if their blood groups were compatible with Giorgio's, then they would donate blood. Lavina said that she couldn't because she was HIV positive, and some of the nurses and interns exchanged wondering looks. Maybe it was rare for them to hear first person confessions.

Now just the two of them, Lavina and Ann-Marie kicked off their shoes to unwind from Gabriella's dramatics. Lavina had changed into clean clothes courtesy of Lynne Munge who had the insight to grab a change of clothes for her before starting the forty-five minute drive from Malindi to Mombasa with her husband.

On a small table near a large window overlooking the Indian ocean were cups with tea bags oozing brownly onto saucers. Lavina sighed dispiritedly, glancing at her watch. She stared at the tea bags and suddenly out of the blue said,

"No wonder Nancy Reagan, or was it Eleanor Roosevelt, said that a woman is like a tea bag and that you never know how strong she is until you put her into hot water."

They had been here approximately three hours, and Giorgio was still in the operating theatre. Ann-Marie had asked for privacy, because they were swamped by visitors and well-wishers. Lavina had requested her to ask the hospital switchboard to screen the calls to their room, as they didn't want to answer any calls from the press, who by now had found out that the reknowned engineer Giorgio Santini had been rushed to hospital after a near fatal shooting by robbers in a bank robbery.

Lavina discussed the incident with Ann-Marie, but at the same time avoided discussing what was going on in the OP. In a little while. She glanced at her watch again. Trust this to happen in Mombasa and not Nairoberry as our capital city has been nicknamed!

"It's been more than four hours." she whispered to Ann-Marie. But it was Gabriella, who strolled nonchalantly into the room and answered her.

"Thoracic surgery takes a long time, and getting a bullet out is very complicated and can turn tricky." This sniggered in a condescending retort.

"We know that Gabriella. Lavina sweetheart, it will be ok." Ann-Marie said, patting Lavina's hand, knowing she hungered for reassurance.

They went outside to sit in the OP waiting room.

Ten minutes later a pair of surgeons came out and headed for the scrubbing room, but Lavina jumped to her feet and blocked them. The shorter of the two, who was African, looked at Lavina, his shoulders slumped wearily. To her anxious query about Giorgio's condition, he replied in a low sympathetic voice, explaining to them that they had managed to remove the bullet, repairing as much damage to the heart as they possibly could.

Lavina's eyes closed in a silent prayer of relief.

"Doc, how is he— really?" Demanded Gabriella, ever the pessimist and trouble maker.

"His condition is critical." The short doctor's Asian counterpart volunteered, "The prognosis is what we call guarded."

"It can go either way?" Lavina's tremulous voice interjected.

"Yes." He hesitated, looking sheepish, and then, "Before the anaesthesia took over, he was asking for his African mermaid and African princess, I don't know if it's one of you, or a material possession he treasures, you know, an object of great value. It will be therapeutic if he sees the mermaid. He went on deliriously about it for quite a while expressing his wish, but he's under sedation right now."

Gabriella could not disguise the shocked, disbelieving look creeping into her eyes. Lavina gave a little discreet cough.

"Umm… I think he was referring to me, it's a personal joke. My name is Lavina. When can I see him?"

"They'll let you know upstairs in the intensive care unit Lavina." The doctor replied.

The trio trooped to the third floor. On the right of the lifts was the ICU reception area.

Gabriella and Ann-Marie had to sit in the waiting room, as only one visitor was allowed in at a time.

Lavina accompanied the nurse on duty. What Lavina saw chilled her to the bone. All sorts of contraptions were sticking into and out of Giorgio. His bandaged chest rose and fell rhythmically, and a tube strapped to his face disappeared into his nose. A multitude of machines with graphic lines flashing a luminous red and green at intervals beeped like robots.

"He's heavily sedated, but he's going to be ok. It will wear off soon.

In an hour or so." Said the robust nurse as she went out.

Lavina sat in the room holding Giorgio's hand for approximately one hour and prayed like she'd never done before. Soon the nurse came and tapped Giorgio's bare shoulder.

"Mr. Santini. Santini."

With no flicker of response from her patient, the nurse delivered a much more audible slap.

"Please don't do that." Lavina whispered. The nurse ignored her. Another audible tap.

"Santini, your wife is here."

"I'm not his…" Lavina began, but stopped on realizing that the African princess and mermaid joke and the fact that she'd admitted to being HIV positive must have done the rounds by now. After seeing how Gabriella and Ann-Marie had let her come in first to see Giorgio, Lavina knew the nurses had already jumped to their own conclusions.

Giorgio looked up, his eyes filmy and dazed. Lavina leaned over him, kissing his cool forehead.

"Sweetheart…" she murmured.

His eyes flickered, and became less dazed. She gripped his hand which, lax and passive, didn't feel like his hand at all.

The nurse looked at one of the clear fluid plastic bottles that dangled from the metal IV stand and increased the flow of the liquid through the syringe attached to his hand.

"If he wakes up completely and asks for water, feed him some with the teaspoon." She paused to glance at her watch. "Only ten more minutes with him Mrs. Santini. He needs to rest." She said, moving silently towards the door at the farther end.

"I'm not Mrs. Santini..." It was hopeless. The nurse had already closed the door softly behind her. Giorgio's dry lips moved.

"Operation…..?"

"It's ok. You were shot, but the doctors have removed the bullet." Lavina answered him.

True to the nurses prediction, he licked his lower lip and tried again.

"...*Aqua...*"

She lifted his head a bit by fluffing out his pillow, dipped the teaspoon into his glass of water by the bedside table and touched it gently to his parched lips... and again he sipped several teaspoonfuls before resting his head.

He was muttering something.

"...princess... stay with... me... Lavina..." His eyes closed momentarily only to flicker open again. Lavina held his hand gently.

"Shhhh. Don't talk sweetheart, just try and get some rest." He struggled to open his eyes again.

"...got... got to tell you something... the nurse... jarred... my memory... got to tell you... so... so... sleepy..."

His hand tightened on hers. He had gained some strength.

"Is... is it truu-ee that in – in the Af- African context... when one gets married.... they not only... marry... each other... but thhh-e... entire clan?"

He gasped to a laborious halt, but his eyes were smiling and fixed on hers determinedly.

She simply held his hand, the tears falling silently down her love-filled and tear-washed face.

"Honey, is that another proposal?" She asked gently.

"Yyy-es..." he whispered tiredly.

"Then I accept, *il mio amore con tutto il cuore (*'my love, with all my heart'), but go to sleep now darling."

As if that was the million shilling answer he'd been waiting for, he incoherently muttered something about all being fair in love and war as he slipped into a delirious sleep.

Chapter 26

Kericho (**Highland tea-growing zone**).

L avina's mother was the quintessential African mother. She was not going to give up her hope of restoring sanity and reconciliation among her family.

"Mama!" Lavina had screamed moments earlier as she threw herself into her mother's arms.

She noted that her mother was aging, maybe due to the worries in the family about Lavina's well-being, but her mother seemed pleasantly surprised that Lavina was looking healthy.

"Well! So this is the man who has swept you off your feet." The elderly Mrs. Kante remarked as she looked Giorgio up and down.

"Mama!" Lavina exclaimed again. "You're making him uncomfortable."

Giorgio squirmed under the old woman's scrutiny, but was glad Tim had agreed to come with them.

Lavina's mother welcomed them all warmly into the house and served them tea. Green tea, she insisted, was the best, made the Kenyan way, and good for the heart! Lavina followed her mother into the kitchen as Tim made Giorgio comfortable.

Giorgio was awed at the beauty of this highland paradise. The cool, almost mountain top cold air and plantations upon plantations of tea that looked like unending carpets laid across the ridges. The dairy cows in the farm that brushed against you as you walked. The streams you had to skip over. And even more attractive was the architecture. Tiny bungalows built using red bricks that Lavina said were made by the locals using the kiln firing method.

Meanwhile in the kitchen, mother was sort of interrogating daughter.

"So, when is the wedding?"

"Oh mama! I don't think I'm ready for marriage. I keep thinking of my HIV status and I freak out! Giorgio is also recovering from the shooting I told you about."

"Honestly girl! I'll let you know that marriage is not an easy step to take. But once you take the plunge the two of you soon get to understand each other even more. And to be sincere with you, I know you are HIV positive, but you deserve a good life with someone to love you and be there for you. And God has given him to you on a silver platter. So what else do you want?"

"Mama, I'm just wondering. I know that you've accepted him, but what about baba? I mean will he not mind that he's not a Kenyan? Much worse not an African, but an Italian to boot?"

"He knows. I told him everything and he seems to accept all. The man took a bullet for his daughter, and if it weren't for him, we would be in mourning right now for heaven's sake! Why don't you go and talk to him before he goes out to see them? He's in the study. Let me tell him that you want to talk to him."

❧⋙⋘❧

Her mother was gone for slightly over ten minutes when the study door opened, but not before Lavina heard a snippet of her mum's closing comment to their conversation...

"...I think we should be able to rise above our differences and have our daughter married in peace. You need to apologise Baba Vincent." She said, referring to the old man by using their eldest son's name.

Lavina suddenly wished with all her heart that Vincent could have been here, but she knew that it was virtually impossible at such short notice with him away at a university in the UK studying medicine.

Her father strolled out and stared at her for a long while. They had not talked for over a year now, let alone meet face to face! Lavina took the first diffident step forward and stretched her hands towards him.

"Baba."

"My baby! I'm sorry for being such an idiot." The distinguished grey-haired, bespectacled, former headmaster mumbled something else about growing senile, but Lavina hugged him even harder with tears falling from her eyes.

Lavina could not believe that her father had just apologized to her for shunning her and ostracising her from the family when he learnt that she was HIV positive. Though he had couched it in his own way saying that senility was getting the better of him, she was very happy because she knew how much it must have cost him in pride to look her in the eye and apologise.

Lavina hugged him again.

"Papa, don't call yourself senile. People say only the poor grow insane and senile, the rich grow eccentric, and you are on the richer side of the divide!"

৯৩৫৩৯৬

They found that Tim and Giorgio had moved outside into the yard with their stools. Mr. Kante was familiar with Tim Munge and so he naturally greeted him first before turning to Giorgio. Giorgio stood up respectfully and tried to look impassive, but failed miserably. His nervousness betrayed him. Who wouldn't be nervous when a distinguished piercing gaze sizes him up?

The lady he loved and his future mother-in-law left him to his fate and went back into the house. Suddenly the old man's baritone voice boomed out.

"So you're the man who took a bullet for my baby girl! And now, this marriage business! So you are the liberal mzungu who wants to save my girl's life two-fold, taking it that she's HIV positive, and marry her? Don't you think it's too soon son? Shouldn't you take time to know her better?"

Giorgio took a deep breath before answering the old man, searching his brain for the right words.

"Not to me. It's not too soon. It's enough that I know your daughter is not moved by riches or by how many cars I have, and also knowing that even if I didn't have them she wouldn't mind."

Tim's body language relaxed visibly and it seemed that Giorgio had given an acceptable answer as the old man's tension also seemed to loosen up a little bit.

"Well," the old man continued, "we can now move over to the next homestead. It's my elder brother's, Lavina's uncle. Everything is set up there. As you had indicated through Lavina yesterday that you only have today, we better get over this then."

❧❦❧

While in the living room, Lavina heard voices coming from the backyard and went to have a look. Her mother told her that there was a surprise for her.

She rushed through the kitchen and into the backyard. She almost bowled her younger sister over, who still managed to effortlessly shift the precariously balanced water pot from her head to her knee, steadying it there for a few seconds, and then placing it onto the earthen floor in one sweeping and graceful motion. Just the way they had been taught to do it by grandmother.

"Tecla! When did you come from Nairobi?" Lavina demanded of her sister who was twenty eight, just two years younger than herself.

"Yesterday. But I'm from the river right now. Oops! Sorry, not the river, the old folks now have piped water in the backyard!"

"And who is this little angel?" Lavina asked, stooping to pick up a two year old adorable girl pulling at her sister's skirt.

"That's the youngest of your nieces, I know you last saw her when she was two months old!"

"Alright! Alright! I believe I have a hefty fine to pay for neglecting my nieces!" The sisters hugged again, then sombrely stared at each other and thought they had gotten stuck in a time warp.

Lavina's mind slipped into an endless time-jump. As she stared at her mother's traditional kitchen with the string storage bags hanging from the rafters of the ceiling storage place, she remembered how as small girls her sister and herself would furiously milk the cows, trying to outdo one another before rushing to get their winnowing trays. They would try to outdo one another again to see who would hold her the traditional hyacinth reed tablets correctly as she swirled it round and round to separate the chaff from the grains, of beans or pigeon peas, and also ensure that it was only the arms that swayed, and not the entire body. They twirled the hyacinth trays 'oroteru' towards the direction of the wind.

They had changed so much once they were dispatched to boarding schools. Lavina had subsequently hooked up and become best friends to Lynne and Ann-Marie.

Tecla on the other hand was also musing silently… Where was the girl with whom she would expertly place her milk gourd on her thighs and extract ghee out of curd to get cholesterol-rich cooking fat and home-made lotions for our bodies? Just like the village girls….

Lavina suddenly made a vow not to turn out like most Kenyans, a citizenry and country that divides everything into affordable, sellable sizes, including memories. She came down to earth and they started examining the baby's features.

"Isn't she pretty? Wow!"

"Kwani, what did you expect you idiot? She takes after her mum!" Tecla playfully teased.

"*Kwenda huko wewe*! Can't you see my snub nose right there?" Lavina tweaked the baby's tiny button-like nose.

The baby suddenly smiled. The toothy smile tugged at Lavina's heartstrings.

"Anyway, where is my husband?" Lavina asked of her brother-in-law in the African way.

"He stayed behind with the other two children as they are writing their mid-term exams. He regrets the absence, but he asked me to pass his regards to you."

Tecla got around to discussing her sister's love matters, albeit in a round about manner.

"So you've finally made up your mind about him?"

"Actually, he made up his mind about me!"

"Do you think it will work, especially in view of your different sero status?"

"I believe it will. We practise safe sex."

"Lavina, you are so lucky that you've found a man who loves you. Miracles do happen and I believe that a cure for HIV and AIDS won't elude our doctors for too long."

Their mother suddenly entered the room and interrupted their animated conversation midstream.

"Girls! We need to go over to your uncle's haraka sana and help your aunts and cousins with the food preparation. They have slaughtered a goat."

Chapter 27

Giorgio and Tim, together with Lavina's father, joined a group of elders sitting on traditional stools at a grass-thatched enclosure. A centrally placed pot of traditional brew dominated the middle space.

After the elders offered libation to the ancestors by pouring beer on the ground, Giorgio followed Tim's lead and sipped through the reed offered to him by one of Lavina's uncles. Giorgio thanked God for Tim's presence, as the brew flowed.

A lot of talking and sort of behind-the-scenes haggling seemed to be taking place. To Giorgio it only looked as if most of the guests present, and even small children, had just come to put to rest the rumour doing rounds that Mwalimu (Teacher) Kante's eldest daughter, who had AIDS, had done the abominable by bringing a 'mzungu' home to marry her! Some had come to listen in awe to snippets of conversation in Italian between the engaged couple.

Lavina's paternal uncle, introduced to Giorgio as Mr. Kante's eldest brother, was the chair during the talks.

"…Fifty head of cattle. That's the standard these days." He finally announced loudly, coughing discreetly as if uncomfortable at the high bride price they were asking for.

It was as if they were only testing Giorgio's resolve in marrying their daughter. So much so that when Giorgio agreed to their final demand of fifty head. There were sighs of disbelief in the crowd of men gathered in the homestead.

Tim knew it was a bit on the higher side, but also knew that it was because Lavina's cousins and uncles myopically viewed white men as monied individuals. After consultations with Tim and cost calculations, Giorgio paid the cattle equivalent in cash, not so much as paying dowry, but as a way of respecting his hosts' traditions and also appreciating the parents for bringing up and taking care of the bride to be.

"At least we now know that our daughter will be well taken care of, even if she goes to a foreign country."

One old man, sneezing as he sniffed his snuff, suddenly shuffled forward.

"My son," he addressed Giorgio in the tribal dialect, "What do you intend to do about this AIDS thing troubling our daughter here?"

Giorgio did not understand the mother tongue, so Tim translated for him. Giorgio asked Tim to tell them that he loved their daughter dearly and that she was his priority now and would ensure that she got the best care and medicine that money could buy if ever the need arose.

The old men seemed satisfied with the answer, but a second old man stood up and told Tim to advise Giorgio and Lavina to go and see one Lemayan for some herbs that cure AIDS. Tim passed the message to Giorgio, who nodded that they would discuss it later.

Lavina and her mother were summoned by the council elders. Her mother came out carrying 'mursik', the traditional sour milk, in a gourd. The elders mixed it with the traditional beer and sprinkled drops of the mixture on Lavina and Giorgio, as a sign of the blessing of the intended union of marriage. Next, all the elders spat globs of spittum on their forehead. Giorgio did not even squirm, as he had come to respect all Kenyan tribes and how they have tried to uphold their traditional values and rites.

Lavina counted her blessings mentally after she suddenly remembered a female acquaintance who was HIV positive and had died of opportunistic infections. When she was sickly her extended clan members, mostly the men, had kept telling her, *muka gati kwao...* (a woman has no permanent abode) and *muka gati mwiriga...* (a woman has no clan) and some had even added unashamedly, especially if she has AIDS. Another HIV positive lady from a different tribe had been told, *mokungu tabwati sobo...* (a woman has no home.)

Lavina shuddered as she wondered why even in the twenty first century patriarchal African societies still tended to deny women their rightful status in society, relegating them to the peripheral of development, even though they contributed immensely to economic development. An example is right here in my home. The women are the ones tilling the tea and coffee plantations and tending the wheat fields.

She looked over at Giorgio and realised again how lucky she was...

Chapter 28

Later in the evening Lavina, Giorgio and Tim were calling on Lemayan before they left.

Lemayan was Lavina's first cousin. Her cousin had been many things before he decided to become a herbalist. He had been a mitumba (second-hand clothes) seller, a brick maker, a mason, and a teacher at the local primary school, among other professions. It was not the money that had made him quit teaching to join other herbalists, he always insisted, but rather his seeing fellow teachers die en masse from AIDS and other related and opportunistic infections, while all along there were alternatives to conventional drugs that seemed to work wonders.

The local district government hospital was overwhelmed by the number of the sick and dying. The government was not able to provide enough ARVs to the poor who, even with the cost sharing, could not afford the drugs and even if they could afford them, meant they would go hungry or make do with unbalanced meals, which was a disaster. The mounds of fresh soil on graves in several homesteads was testimony to that fact.

Suddenly, in the still of the night, from across the ridges and the two rivers fording at their base they heard the throbbing sound of drums. The wind blowing in the highlands brought the sounds nearer.

"What is that sound?" Giorgio asked Lavina.

"Drums. They signify a death. I wonder who has died."

Then they heard the singing voices of women.

"I'm not very sure, but I think it's Lepokot's mother. She was very sick this morning and was rushed to the hospital." Lemayan added.

Lavina proceeded to tell Lemayan how she had followed his advice given the previous year and was still boiling the leaves of the 'muarubaini', which means 'forty' in Kiswahili, that is, the neem tree. It heals forty different ailments like malaria, herpes, dysentery, diarrhoea and various opportunistic diseases which attacked her recently with a ferocity.

Lemayan told them that currently in the highlands they were using herbs, barks, shoots, roots and leaves from the various trees and shrubs in forests like the Karura forest in Kiambu and even as far away as the Mau escarpment. Most of the shoots and roots were used by Doctor Davy Koech and his team at KEMRI (Kenya Medical Research Institute) in the late nineties to produce the drug KEMRON that had showed good results in patients using it.

Lemayan had by now shifted gear into his lecture mode that he had carried over from his days as a teacher. He went on to explain that the lack of follow-up by the government had led to the drug being manufactured and patented abroad. The other drug combination that Lemayan introduced to them was Professor Arthur Obel's concoction. Patients to whom the good professor had administered the drug had gained weight. Local herbalists, and even midwives whose patients had delivered HIV positive babies, had gone on to experiment with the two cocktails. With the two cocktails, most of the older patients' CD4 counts soared, and the babies with a well balanced diet had gone on to test negative later on in their formative years.

They discussed how Lavina had stopped using AZT and a host of other anti-retrovirals prescribed to her by her doctor and instead shifted to the herbs and she had marked improvement to her immunity.

Lemayan introduced them to several herbs, which he said Lavina was to mix with asparagus which had proved competent in helping his patients gain weight and prolong their lives. Lemayan gave them bundles of *sutherlandia frutescens* plant, introduced to him by a South African friend, which he said combats AIDS-related wasting, and really helped in clinical management of HIV-AIDS.

Giorgio learnt that such herbs are affordable and Lemayan charged around three hundred shillings a week for a concoction for HIV patients that he said boosted their immunity levels, while pharmacies charged at least a thousand and seven hundred shillings for an equivalent dose of antiretroviral drugs.

"…Lavina, you should not stop, but continue using the neem leaves as they have both pesticidal and medicinal properties. You can see how they have helped with their immuno-stimulating properties for both lymphocytic and cell-mediated systems." Lemayan cautioned. Continue ingesting small quantities of neem leaf or bark powder every other day and also start drinking neem tea as an alternative to your normal herbal tea. The neem tea will enhance antibody production and the body's cell-mediated immune response, thus helping to prevent opportunistic infections."

Giorgio was very attentive because he knew that he would have to keep Lavina on her toes to make sure that she followed her herbalist cousin's prescriptions.

"…I would also like you to use the neem cream and a combination of the aloe vera pulp. They help and forestall bacterial and fungal skin ailments. The application of the combination of aloe vera sap and neem cream reduces inflammation of the skin. In fact, aloe vera is credited for rejuvenating weary nerves and cells and buttressing the immune system against a wide array of diseases…"

By now Tim was also engrossed in Lemayan's lecture.

"…Aloe products are used in the treatment of various skin conditions like insect bites, sunburn, acne, boils and fungal attacks. It stimulates the renewal and growth of new tissues at the cellular level and accelerates the healing process. It cleanses and detoxifies the digestive system, boosting the body's immune system and healing abilities. As an anti-inflammatory, it is actually a natural treatment for swellings and tissue injuries. Lastly, but arguably the most important, is that it has nutritional value, it contains a wide variety of vitamins and minerals that are vital for various functions of the body…"

At the end of the day Lavina had a duffel bag full of dried and crushed herbs and promised to call her mum to send her more by courier when they got finished. Cunningly, she looked at Giorgio and Tim.

"Boy! Am I glad. No more lamivudine, abacavir and zidovudine tablets for me. I'm sure the old doctor will freak out!"

Giorgio laughed, knowing she was referring to her Italian doctor in Malindi, Doctor Crivelli Piatto.

"But you do have lots of work for your pestle and mortar now, other than crushing garlic when cooking! Crushing all those herbs and roots! You will now have to go a bit modern and get a food processor!'

They all burst out laughing, knowing Lavina and her antiquated ways. Lavina nevertheless was happy that she was not going to swallow any more tablets, she was so sick and tired of them!

Chapter 29

Lavina felt like she was in heaven. Her ivory colored strapless wedding gown made of raw silk complemented her complexion. The gown, with a corset style pinched in at the waist, made the most of her tiny waist with a trailing train.

She stared at the twinkling lights of houses across the vast ocean, at cliffs and the old town in the far distance. They glided past the old Fort Jesus and the Kilindini harbour.

She was holding Giorgio's hand and they were not even talking, just taking the scenery in. It was breathtaking. This was what the tourist circuit called 'Mombasa by night'. The Kenya Ports Authority imposingly beckoned at seafarers.

It was her wedding day, night, evening. They had just been married aboard the world-famous dhow.

The Tamarind Dhow circled the harbour again and detoured back through the English point, cut across the Tudor creek and back towards the Mtwapa creek and onto the five-star Severin Sea Lodge where it was usually anchored.

She rubbed at her wedding band to make sure that this was all real and still intact. She was so happy that Giorgio's mother and vivacious sisters had taken to her like fish to water.

The enchanting evening with a blend of exotic seafood was romantic above the 23 metre Arab dhow Nawalikher, which was built in 1977 for trading purposes. It was the largest dhow on the coast. It was purchased in 1986 by the then four star Severin Sea Lodge and converted into a restaurant. The original builder Fundi Bini from Lamu island was an expert at building dhows and the Captain to-date was Mohammed Shalle. It now consisted of two dhows joined by Babidkheri measuring 16 metres. The two dhows together accommodated over 100 guests comfortably.

The magical evening had begun as they were picked up from the pier. As soon as the bride and bridegroom stepped off the gangplank and into the dhow, a traditionally dressed waiter showed them to the high table and served them a deliciously wicked house cocktail made from vodka, lime, honey, sugar and crushed ice.

As the dhow slipped gently away from the jetty the resident band had started to play and everyone fell instantly under the spell of the magical Tamarind ambience. Canvas awning shielded guests from excess wind. The romantic candle-lit dinner beckoned and as the dhow departed from the jetty the beautiful rhythms of classics Malaika and Jambo Kenya made the guests start swaying to the beat on the main deck.

The cruise went around Tudor creek with a fine view of Mombasa's old town and Fort Jesus, the T4 D4, then moored in a sheltered bay at the head of the creek. And then the fairytale wedding ceremony had began.

The aroma of grilled lobster and steak filled the air as the chefs pulled out the charcoal grills and prepared the five-course gourmet meal. They served aromatic Arabica kahawa (coffee) from the traditional Arabian brass pot.

The ceremony with Giorgio and Lavina exchanging their personalized vows made the romantic-at-heart present shed tears of joy. They were soon interrupted by the chef and maitre'd inviting them to open the magnificent buffet laid out for the guests.

There was seafood to beat the very best—King prawns, calamari, lobsters, caviar, the finest champagne and of course the traditional coastal dishes like chicken pilaf and mutton biriyani, shish kebabs, samosas and samaki wa kupakwa, not forgetting the coastal coconut wine mnazi. The highland folks were not forgotten either and their culinary favorites like mukimo, mursik, roast goat, various greens and vegetables graced the buffet. Obviously, Italian cuisine was included to accommodate all present—spaghetti bolognaise and noodles with meatballs.

Later Katrina, Giorgio's youngest sister, joined Lavina, her sister Tecla, Anne-Marie and Lynne. Katrina could not hide her envy at how good Lavina's body looked.

"You look so good. A perfect thirty-six twenty-four thirty-six figure! An actual hourglass and such flawless skin! How do you manage to keep in such shape in this hot and humid atmosphere?"

Before Lavina could answer her Ann-Marie interjected,

"Ask her please! I for one will have to take a visit to cosmetic surgery doctor Crescenzo D'onofrio, in Nairobi, for a liposuction that's going to cost me three hundred thousand shillings!"

Tecla laughed, saying that Lavina had always looked spectacular with no exercise regime. Lynne laughed and said,

"One of my friends just came back from a breast lift and rhinoplasty, that is nose surgery, and it cost her the world! But I prefer my natural look. Another went in for elective genito plasty, you know, a designer vagina? Plastic surgery just exploits women's insecurities. I don't for the life of me understand why one should want to shorten or change the shape of the outer lips of the vagina! Lavina is a natural beauty!"

Katrina twirled around and curtsied mockingly.

"Me? I don't think I want to look stupido! You need to introduce me to this doctor! I need a tummy tuck and breast augmentation pronto!"

They all burst out laughing and Lavina said:

"Girls! You don't need any plastic surgery, but lots of neem herbal tea, balanced meals, lots of pure drinking water, some exercises and no junk food! My personal trainer at the gym I frequent also says that fitness is broken down into five categories, namely, body composition, cardiovascular fitness, muscular strength, flexibility, and muscular endurance! And all you need to do is train three times a week for only one hour and you'll be fit within one month. You will need to maintain that schedule. So stop being lazy!"

Katrina pouted and puckered her small mouth as she threw back her long curly hair.

"Not for me then! I love my fries, lasagna and bolognaise!"

This made the ladies burst out laughing.

"I actually support you Katrina. Did you ladies read yesterday's daily and what Doctor Omondi-Ogutu, the Chairman of the Kenya Obstetrical and Gynaecological Society said? He's also a senior lecturer at the university of Nairobi. Some ladies are into such surgeries for cosmetic purposes only and not because it's a matter of life and death! Some are paying up to half a million Kenyan shillings just to tighten the vagina from its opening through to the top of the birth canal for better sex. Why don't we just let nature alone? Capisce?"

After exchanging their vows, the Pastor introduced them officially as Signora and Signorina Santini and the cake was cut. The five-tiered, cream, gold and chocolate wedding cake was another heavenly creation!

Later, Lavina noticed her brother Vincent engrossed in a serious talk with Giorgio and hoped that he was not giving Giorgio the big-brother lecture of: 'Take care of my sis.'

Anne-Marie insisted on the age-old tradition of throwing the bouquet. She had reason to, the three musketeers had recently all turned thirty. Anne-Marie really wanted to be the next bride-in-waiting, for she pushed and shoved and actually fell to the floor of the dhow clutching the coveted flowers triumphantly, to the chagrin of the other guests!

Lavina's mum and dad were quiet, but happy, knowing that their daughter was in good hands at long last....

The following morning.

Lavina and Giorgio were apprehensive as they waited for Gabriella to land so that they could proceed on their honeymoon to the Cayman Islands, which was Lavina's preferred destination. She had always wanted to visit the islands. The jet Gabriella was using had to be serviced in readiness for their trip the following day. Gabriella, her blond bob jumping up and down in agitation, got off the plane and came towards them in a huff.

"Giorgio! I always tell you I prefer the Fairchild SW4!"

Lavina looked quizzically at Giorgio.

"She means the 17-seater plane, the one with the twin-engine turbo prop."

Gabriella continued with her tirade.

"This pilot is inept. He doesn't know how to handle this new plane. Anyway, even the food was atrocious and I'm completely dehydrated!"

Lavina stared at her open-mouthed. Such a tantrum after stepping off a new private jet!

She should know the vintage Gabriella by now; always full of drama even for a simple task or errand like a pick-up from the airport. Gabriella turned to Giorgio.

"So! Mr. Congeniality! Apart from your stray cat of the other day making sculptures for you, she now seems to have developed the deepest hots for you! I can see she accompanies you everywhere like a puppy!"

Giorgio decided to drop the bombshell, as they had kept the ceremony private with only their close family members and friends present. Not even Gabriella had been informed, and Giorgio had even sent her on a cooked-up business trip to attend to matters he knew he still had to follow up himself once he was back from their honeymoon.

"Not the hots Gabriella. She's now officially Mrs. Santini."

"What?!"

"You heard me right, we are even ready to proceed on our honeymoon in a few days time. We were just waiting for the jet. As always, Malindi *l'esperienza ottima sulla spiaggia!*" ('That's how life is... full of fun!')

Giorgio left instructions to the pilot and mechanics to service the jet, telling them that he and his wife would be flying to the Cayman Islands in a couple of days. Once outside the airport and in the car, Giorgio tried to engage Gabriella in business talk concerning the Safaricom tender.

"…I have managed to outsource the BTS equipment shelters, cables and accessories and tower mounted aviation warning lights from elsewhere at a fair price because the Olkaria Geothermal Hydro Power Station needs almost the same makes. Do you have the costing of diesel generators, RF antennas and auto phase selectors from Vienna?"

Gabriella did not answer back.

"…Gabriella, Safaricom have just posted a pre-tax profit of twenty billion and they are out to improve their call network, so we need to work on this pronto! Or don't you want to participate in their soon to be launched IPO?"

Gabriella still kept silent and Giorgio and Lavina knew she was seething inwardly at the announcement that they had just wedded. Giorgio shrugged his shoulders and looked at Lavina as their special bond of telepathic connection arched between them, and they decided to ignore Gabriella's outburst. Soon they were both laughing in common camaraderie as Gabriella sulked in the backseat.

In twenty minutes time Lavina was typing on her laptop the advert they had decided to place in the following day's newspaper to engage a manager to run the cottages while they were away. Giorgio looked over her shoulder and read out loudly,

"*Gestori servisi Bungalows privati in villaggio Italiano in Mambrui, prossimita Malindi Kenya esaminerebbero offerte residenti Keniani per un posto local Manager a Tempo pieno, 90 re Giornaliere richedonsi esperieenza direzione analoghe strutture conoscenza Italiano et referenze Inviare curriculum dettagliati e richieste economiche, contacto senza alloggio - L_Kante2008@gmail.com.*"

"Bravo! Your Italian improves by the day! I can assure you now that only the best who know how to run our holiday cottages are going to apply."

After pausing thoughtfully for a couple of minutes he continued.

"By the way, where is the exercise I gave you the other day to translate into Italian from the English version of the Visitor's Guide I was working on? You need to work real hard if you are to seek employment as a part time translator when we come back from our honeymoon."

Lavina printed out one page and sheepishly handed it to him. Giorgio started reading aloud…

"*Benevenutti, nella coloratissima città di Mombasa. Siamo lieti di presentarvi la prima delle Visitor's Guide. L' edizione del '06-07 da informazioni importanti, se vi trovate qui in vacanze, per affari o per una conferenza. In questa guida, un indice anatilitico simile a quello della Pagine Gialle che gia conoscete, facilita la ricerca di qualunque servizio o società stiate cercando. Troverete anche utili informazioni sulla vita a Mombasa.*

Vi auguriamo un piacevole soggiorno e speriamo che la Visitor's Guide '06-07 renda ancora più gradita la vostra visita nella nostra bella capitale."

Giorgio picked up the English version and went through halfway.

"Hamjambo, Karibuni, welcome to our city Mombasa. We are happy to present you with this first edition of the Visitor's Guide. This Visitor's Guide '06-07 contains relevant information whether you are on holiday, business or to hold conferences…"

"Wow! Abbastanza buono! ('Good Enough!') No need to check through word by word! You've improved, and it seems I am a good teacher…."

Chapter 30

Cayman Islands.

Their honeymoon was almost over and so far Lavina could say that she was having the best time. They stayed at the Cayman Ritz Carlton in an ocean front condo. The Cayman Islands were indeed magical. She had gorged herself on Caribbean gourmet food with no inhibition. The candlelit ambience over seafire steaks had made her fall in love with perfect cuisine all over again!

And best of all, she loved her husband and she knew she was indeed lucky to have such a man to love her.

This morning he was still sleeping in and was yet to join her on the beach. When away from Malindi and home she always packed her current read and this time it was Somali-born model Waris Dirie's 'Letter to my Mother.' She had fallen in love with the UNICEF goodwill ambassador's real life narrations in 'Desert Dawn' and 'Desert Flower' and had made it a point to purchase any book she penned.

Recently she had been remembering Unoka's words (Okonkwo's father in Chinua Achebe's 'Things Fall Apart') "…Whenever I see the mouth of a dead man, it reminds me of the folly of not eating well while one is alive…"

Later she had this incorrigible nightmare that, like Sophie Mol in Arundhati Roy's Booker Prize winner 'The God of Small Things', she would be lying on her byre at the funeral home and suddenly she would turn into a coffin cart-wheeler and would think that death was stalking her and like Aesops' famous fable of the boy who falsely cried 'wolf!'. Her death would do the same.

Lavina and her friends, as children, had learnt fast that in Africa, coming from the wrong side of the tracks meant literally that. She had seen many fair weather friends and foes. But sometimes she thought 'fiend' would be a more appropriate word than 'friend'. It seemed that sometimes the maxim was obsolete.

She thought of Gabriella and the last conversation she held with her. The Italian lady had really tried to apologise in her own way for the way she had been treating Lavina.

"Please forgive me Lavina."

Lavina had simply looked at her and answered:

"Well, I wish I could Gabriella, but I'm not a priest to offer you penitence and only God can really, really forgive. If I say I forgive you of which I truly do, it will only be lip service if you don't go before God to ask of the same..."

Lavina suddenly came down to earth and reminded herself that the herbs, shoots, roots and leaves regime were better than the anti-retrovirals she had been taking. She thought to herself. '...I'm sitting here on the beach and this strange nostalgia overwhelms me. A melancholic nostalgia I call it. How strange, when I know that G is just a few steps away, yet I miss him already. I am so tired of using condoms. Should I suggest that we use the female condom? Do I want him to be HIV positive too so that we can die together? I do not want to die alone, but with him. I will be so lonely in death. How should I suffer for the absence of a loved one who is present?"

She thought of how not so long ago Giorgio would burst into a tirade in Italian when she refused to marry him, at first saying that she would not marry anybody else unless it was 'si deve passare sul mio cadavere! (Over his dead body!)' While she would shout back 'mai in vita mia! (Never in my life!)'

What an epiphany they had shared along the way and a serendipity of making fortunate discoveries by accident. What did it all mean? That my demise beckons or he's going to die first… If God were to call me first, I wonder what epitaph he would want to engrave on my tombstone. Perhaps in Italian: '*HA BATTERSI PER UNA CAUSA LEGITTIMA.*' ('SHE FOUGHT THE GOOD FIGHT.')

She was totally unaware that Giorgio was now awake and staring at her from the balcony of the honeymoon suite. These past few days they had been ecstatic with happiness. He caught on to her melancholic mood and decided to watch her every step to protect her from her nefarious mood-swings…

Chapter 31

Doctor Crivelli Piatto was astounded. He had never seen such a case, neither in Italy where he was born and had been practising medicine for many years, nor in the United States of America where he had studied various case files. He had checked and re-checked the blood samples himself. He had studied her files over ten times.

"...Doctor, we're really serious! For the past two years or so I've not been using any of the ARVs you prescribed. Not lamivudine, zidovudine or any of the other cocktails! And we are just from Mombasa for an ultra-scan. We're having twins!"

Doctor Piatto still continued to stare bemused at the papers he was holding.

"Lavina! You have a dramatic CD4-T cell count increase. If I were God, I would conclude and say that you have no strain of HIV. This dramatic increase seems to have been effective in restoring your immunity to opportunistic infections."

He turned to Giorgio. "Are you still using condoms?"

"Yes we are." Giorgio replied calmly.

"I'm simply amazed! And you say you're pregnant. How do you explain that?"

"We heard of Doctor Noreh's breakthrough in Nairobi with in-vitro fertilization. We decided to try him, and here we are! We're six months along... I was also encouraged by Asunta Wagura's case. She's the Executive Director of KENWA (Kenya Network of Women with AIDS). She's been HIV positive for twenty years and recently delivered her baby Joshua, who turned out to be HIV negative."

"Which herbs did you say Lavina is using?"

"Neem, aloe vera, and several others from Karura forest and the Mau escarpment, her cousin is a herbalist. You'll need to talk to him on that score! One from South Africa called *sutherlandia frutescens,* and I've forgotten the name of the other one from Tanzania!"

"Congratulations on the babies to come and this wonder concoction, because at this rate soon there will be no need for condoms my friends!"

"That's why we are here. The doctors in Mombasa told us that we should consult you and our gynaecologist for proper administration and dosages of neveripine to protect the babies."

They sat down for the complicated prescriptions. The doctor wrote the prescriptions as he talked.

"Lavina, I know you are in love with your herbs and shoots! But for the babies' sake you'll be on lamivudine 150 mg plus stavudine 30 mg plus nevirapine 200 mg tabs, and later on lamivudine 150 mg plus zidovudine 300 mg plus nevirapine 200 mg tabs, and finally on abacavir 300 mg plus lamivudine 150 mg plus zidovudine 300 mg tabs. Once the babies are born, we will put them on lamivudine 150 mg plus stavudine 5 mg plus nevirapine 35 mg tablets as an oral suspension and then lamivudine 150 mg plus stavudine 10 mg plus nevirapine 70 mg tablets as an oral suspension. That's it."

The doctor put his pen down, clapped his hands and then shook their hands. Lavina clutched the prescription possessively, as if her life depended on it, but rolled her eyes mockingly at Giorgio as if to say: 'tablets again!' But she knew in her heart that she would do anything for their babies!

❦❦❦❦

It was the third time in as many months that doctor Crivelli Piatto was looking astounded! He was the bearer of good tidings and was thrilled. He could not wait to place the long distance call to his friend Bruno.

"Merry Christmas Giorgio and Lavina! Congratulations for becoming parents!"

"I have amazing news for you. First of all Lavina, you are HIV Negative, we have done the tests five times just to be sure! And the babies are HIV negative too! And Giorgio, since you said that you stopped using condoms for the past two months, we've also carried out the test on your sample. You are also still negative!"

The ten minutes old babies were still in the nursery, so Lavina simply closed her eyes and held Giorgio's hand as she looked heavenward and sighed softly.

"Thank You Jesus!"

It was not so simple for Giorgio, who looked stunned for a few seconds and let out a deafening 'Whoopiie!' like a battle cry!

"Hurray! No more worries Lavina! And now we can arrange your art show at the Ritz in London. Bjorn is really on my case! And once we are back and you and the babies have rested for a month or so we can climb Mount Kenya as we've wanted for a long time! I mean all the three peaks, Batian, Lenana and Nelion. Wow! To finally climb those peaks named after the three pre-colonial Masai legendary Chiefs, the Laibons!"

Lavina chuckled fondly at Giorgio's display of boyish pleasure.

The minute he returned to his offices, Doctor Piatto placed a long distance call to the United States of America and the John Hopkins School of Medicine based in Baltimore, Maryland.

"Doctor Bruno Enrica, please."

"Bruno! How are you? I'm good. You need to get down here to Africa pronto! Actually to Kenya, and Malindi near Mombasa to be precise! I think we have a breakthrough and might have a cure for HIV-AIDS! This patient I've been handling has actually turned negative! She's been on some herbs."

There were some interjections from his friend. Then after a while he continued:

"Yes! Yes! I know. Some are neem and aloe vera, but there are some from the Karura Forest, Mau escarpment and the Menengai crater, a place the locals refer to as '*Kirima kia ngoma*' meaning the devil's place. That's where my interest lies and is the link to the sero status change in this lady. She even stopped using condoms with her husband and he is also still negative!"

He listened a while to some more interjections from the other end.

"Yes! Yes! They just had healthy twins though they were on neverapine. The herbalists up there are combining it together with a Tanzanian root and the South African *sutherlandia frutescens*, but I tell you the secret lies in the crater and the escarpment! You get down here. We might just win the Nobel prize for medicine. It is too bad that last year one of the trigger-happy teenage gangsters shot and killed top AIDS researcher Professor Job Bwayo, the leading the researcher on HIV and AIDS at KAVI." (Kenya AIDS Vaccine Initiative).

He was on the brink of a breakthrough. He would have loved this. No wonder Professor Wangari Maathai won the Nobel Peace Prize for protecting these same forests… this lady who has been cured has beautiful long healthy *bei capelli* ('nice hair') and enjoys incredibly *godere di buona salute* ('good health'). The cure is right under our very own noses…"

❧❦❧❦

Later on the babies were brought from the nursery and Lavina had just been taught how to breast feed. They were moved to tears as they watched the little babies search for their mother's breasts and suckle. They still could not see with their eyes and the nurse told them that they depended on their mother's smell. Giorgio and Lavina had to direct the nipples into the tiny mouths!

The babies seemed to recognize Giorgio's voice and he knew it was because he talked to them a lot while they were still in their mother's womb for nine months, just like the Munges had told him to. They had even played music to them, as they had read in some self-help books and on the internet. They could not wait to take them back home to the nursery which Giorgio had designed himself and Lavina had painted with playgroup murals, and to the family and friends waiting there to welcome the coveted babies.

Giorgio and Lavina, still stunned speechless but nevertheless contented, stared at their infant son and daughter with their blue eyes, black curly hair and their delicate tiny finger, toes, ears and nose and skin a colored mixture of Lavina's deep chocolate brown and Giorgio's ivory white.

The new parents looked deep into each other's eyes, for they knew that they had come a long way and were now bound by cords of love that could not be broken… All Lavina wanted to do was set in the pipeline the HIV-AIDS Foundation she had talked about with Giorgio to cater for the orphans left behind by the catastrophe. She had seen over-burdened grandmothers in their twilight years recalled from retirement to care for the orphans. The funds could also speed up the search for a cure. She might just have set the tide rolling with her healing using alternative medicine via herbs instead of conventional drugs.

Lavina knew that sometimes she acted like the Pope of Fools in Victor Hugo's 'Hunchback of Notre Dame', yet like the imitable Melchizedek in

Paulo Coelho's 'The Alchemist', Giorgio always seemed to know, with his subtle innuendos, how to nudge her gently in the direction of her dreams. And like the shepherd boy Santiago she had listened to all sorts of voices where her dream of setting up the foundation was concerned. She and Giorgio had indeed been put on the crucible and become refined silver and through the raging furnace to become as fine gold…

"No one knows what's going to happen in the next few minutes, yet people still go forward because they have trust, because they have faith."

Paulo Coelho (Brazilian novelist) in Brida.

ENDNOTES

1. One of the few remaining Tropical Rain Forests (2nd largest only to the Congo) found along the Kenya Coast in Malindi and Kilifi districts. It is unique with birds, animal and butterfly species that are threatened with extinction.
2. Formerly Duke Of Edinburg in the colonial era—an adventurous project for High School students with various themes for the youth on how to endure in tough situations—environmental and otherwise.
3. A traditional colourful cotton wrapper for women, that is tied at the waist and drapes over the hips to the ankles, or in a sarong style. Much liked by the locals and especially coastal women, sometimes also referred to as "khanga". (Has a Swahili proverb printed on the edge near the hem.)
4. Sacred groves (as shrines) deep in the forest, revered as ancestral communication mediums.
5. The nine sub-divisions of Kenya's coastal tribes.
6. Flat, rectangular box-like, Mijikenda traditional, percussion instrument, made out of dried bamboo reeds and filled with dried seeds. Sewn at the edges with dried mangrove strings. Held with both hands & shaken to the song's rhythm.
7. Traditional drums.
8. Traditional dancing inner attire for women made out of sisal. Worn around the hips to enhance them and tied at the waist before the leso is draped over the hips. Worn even when not dancing.
9. Traditional cotton wrap-around for men, sometimes referred to as 'Shuka'.
10. Strong species of oak wood from the interior of Kenya used for wood carving.
11. Area of lion savannah plains; famous because of glass works by Ms. Nani Croze.
12. Famous Maasai Mara triangle, a game reserve. One of the world's richest wildlife sanctuaries. Spectacular annual migration of wildebeest, zebra, and gazelle pass through here on their way to the Serengeti, in Tanzania crossing the Mara River.
13. Game reserve found in the vast savannah plains of Kenya, famous for the movie 'The Man Eaters of Tsavo', depicting the terror Indian workers were put through by marauding lions during colonial era laying of the Kenya-Uganda railway line.
14. Swahili proverb which means 'What has already happened is of no consequence, look to the future.'
15. LSK – Law Society of Kenya, umbrella organisation for countrywide membership of lawyers: that governs, and checks ethics, and conduct of its members.
16. Swahili for red soil. Dongo Kundu is a project still in the pipeline, with suggestions of either building a tunnel, or a bridge to link the island of Mombasa with the south coast mainland of Kenya, instead of using passenger and vehicle ferries.
17. Acronym for Export Processing Zone – Designated and demarcated tracts of land set aside by the Government for Foreign Investors to build and start factories to produce goods for export. The Government offers subsidies to attract the investors in utilities and amenities, e.g. electricity, water. Goods produced are tax free.
18. Coastal port town and second largest city of Kenya.
19. Soapstone mining location in Kisii district, in the tea growing highlands of Kenya. The only region in the world with soapstone quarries.

20. 13th Century Palatial ruins (Arab settlement) 18km south of Malindi. Gede forest is a sacred site for traditional rituals and sacrifices for the surrounding community. Gazetted as a historical monument.
21. Translated into English as 'House of Slaves', gazetted as a national monument by the National Museums of Kenya. The 14th century ruins are situated in the North Coast of Mombasa in Shanzu-Mtwapa.
22. Giriama is one of the nine sub-tribes of the Mijikenda (nine clans) of the Kenyan Coast. The other eight are Digo, Chonyi, Rabai, Duruma, Kauma, Ribe, Jibana, and Kambe.
23. Dried coconut leaves weaved into roof thatches.
24. Local mats weaved using dried mangrove reeds.
25. Kuku is the Kiswahili word for Hen.
26. Kiswahili word for chick.
27. Kiswahili for French plait.
28. Deep fried wheat cinnamon buns much liked by the Coastals.
29. Garlic.
30. Traditional charcoal stove.
31. Central Business District.
32. gods.
33. Drum, drums or drumming.
34. Traditional Giriama dance accompanied with percussion instruments.
35. Flat plates made of intertwined dry mangrove strips.
36. Traditional wooden grater made of wood, with metal teeth at one end; traditionally it refers to goats.
37. Long narrow pouch made of intertwined mangrove strips—a local sieve.
38. Initial heavy milk squeezed first from coconut.
39. Nazi is the Kiswahili word for coconut.
40. Wooden cooking stick/spoon.
41. Ginger.
42. Wooden mortar and pestle.
43. A large, flat aluminum plate also used for a lid.
44. Popular reference in Tourist circles to Lion, Leopard, Elephant, Buffalo and Rhino.
45. Kiswahili proverb, loosely translated means 'What goes around comes round'.
46. Swahili title meaning 'There is a way'.
47. Politically instigated tribal clashes of 1997, in Likoni area of the South coast of Kenya during the run-up to the general elections, contentious land issues being the cause.
48. Voluntary Counselling and Testing Centres.